Praise for
Lucinda Rosenfeld's
The Pretty One

An Elle Lettres Readers' Prize 2013 Pick

"Lucinda Rosenfeld perfectly captures the intricacies of sister-hood in this hilarious and perceptive tale of one family's quest to 'get along'.... I absolutely loved this novel!"
— Emily Giffin, author of *Something Borrowed*
and *Where We Belong*

"With a light touch, Rosenfeld portrays the 'conspiratorial, even magical' relationship among sisters that makes failure to com-municate all the more painful."
— *The New Yorker*

"In this impish new novel from the author of *I'm So Happy for You,* three sisters who have grown up cranky and competitive are itching to shed the stereotypes they've always represented to one another and their parents.... By the time everything's resolved, you'll have come to love them in all their hilarious imperfection."
— Helen Rogan, *People*

"Appealingly dark."
— Emily Cooke, *New York Times Book Review*

"Although the novel's twists and turns are entertaining, it's the sisters' realistic swings from jealousy to unity that make it compelling. Once again, the author of *I'm So Happy for You* portrays women with insight."
— *Booklist*

"Here is why I loved *The Pretty One,* and Rosenfeld's other novels: her characters are mean.... The lack of female as victim here is, frankly, thrilling.... These are the sorts of books you wince at while reading, and maybe even put down for a moment, then pick up again, needing more of the black stuff. You don't read a Lucinda Rosenfeld book with tea; you pour yourself a scotch and retreat to a dark room while your kids scream for you outside the door.... In other words, she's very, very good at sculpting her fiction."

—Katie Crouch, *The Rumpus*

"A witty character study of that contentious organism: sister-hood."

—*Kirkus Reviews*

"Although accomplished adults, the Hellinger sisters remain quick to judge each other and sometimes grapple with jealousy and resentment. Their relationships are tested when their mother winds up in the hospital, but Rosenfeld shows, with humor and charm, that these familial bonds are strong enough to withstand even the most trying circumstances."

—Samantha Samel, *Brooklyn Daily Eagle*

"Funny, biting, and unsentimental."

—Judith Greenberg, PhD, *Huffington Post*

The Pretty One

Also by Lucinda Rosenfeld

The Pretty One

a novel about sisters

Lucinda Rosenfeld

Back Bay Books
Little, Brown and Company
NEW YORK BOSTON LONDON

Back Bay Books / Little, Brown and Company
Hachette Book Group
237 Park Avenue, New York, NY 10017
littlebrown.com

Originally published in hardcover by Little, Brown and Company,
February 2013
First Back Bay paperback edition, January 2014

Back Bay Books is an imprint of Little, Brown and Company. The Back Bay Books name and logo are trademarks of Hachette Book Group, Inc.

The publisher is not responsible for websites (or their content) that are not owned by the publisher.

The Hachette Speakers Bureau provides a wide range of authors for speaking events. To find out more, go to hachettespeakersbureau.com or call (866) 376-6591.

Library of Congress Cataloging-in-Publication Data

Rosenfeld, Lucinda.
    The pretty one: a novel about sisters / Lucinda Rosenfeld. — 1st ed.
    p. cm.
    ISBN 978-0-316-21355-4 (hc) / 978-0-316-21358-5 (pb)
    1. Sisters — Fiction. 2. Domestic fiction I. Title.
    PS3568.O814P83 2013
    813'.54 — dc23
                                                    2012019559

10 9 8 7 6 5 4 3 2 1

RRD-C

Printed in the United States of America

For my father, Peter Rosenfeld (1936–2012)

"*But it is very foolish to ask questions about any young ladies — about any three sisters just grown up; for one knows, without being told, exactly what they are: all very accomplished and pleasing, and* one *very pretty. There is a beauty in every family; it is a regular thing. Two play on the pianoforte, and one on the harp; and all sing, or would sing if they were taught, or sing all the better for not being taught; or something like it.*"

— JANE AUSTEN, *Mansfield Park*

The Pretty One

O LYMPIA LOUISE HELLINGER HAD always been the "Beautiful One" in her family. Among her sisters, she was also understood to be the Artistic One, the Flaky One, the Chronically Late One, the Mellow One, the Selfish One, and the Unambitious One. Whether reality reflected reputation was a matter of opinion. But at thirty-eight she was the events coordinator of a small museum of contemporary Austrian art, located on the Upper East Side. She was also a single mother. Little wonder that, as much as she loved spending time with her three-and-a-half-year-old daughter, Lola, she also longed for more hours to herself.

For years, Olympia had been painting watercolors of little girls and furry animals. This had been true even before she'd given birth to Lola — or brought home Clive, a borderline-obese New Zealand white rabbit with pink eyes, from a local pet store. In her spare time, Olympia also enjoyed shopping for clothes; listening to music; setting up other single friends on blind dates; perusing symptoms lists on WebMD and fearing that she'd contracted a fatal disease (and feeling, somehow, that she deserved it); and then, as a distraction from her worries, drinking too much and reading the mystery and espionage novels she'd loved since she was a child, beginning with *Harriet the Spy*.

A week before Christmas, however, a more serious form of sleuthing beckoned. Impatient to begin, Olympia started "bath time" fifteen minutes earlier than usual. "Story time" followed. For the sixth night in a row, Lola wanted Olympia to read her *Madeline's Rescue*. Miss Clavel having turned off the light for the last time, Lola demanded that her mother "ask her a silly question."

Olympia complied with this request as well. "Excuse me," she began. "But there's something I've been meaning to ask you. Can you explain to me why there's a slice of pizza coming out of your elbow?"

"Ask me another silly question," Lola replied with a giggle.

"I was also wondering why there's a piece of celery sticking out of your ear?"

That was apparently an even funnier image to behold. Lola laughed so hard she burped.

"Also," said Olympia, "could someone tell me why there's a cheese sandwich attached to your behind?"

Now in stitches, Lola collapsed onto her mother's lap, then the rug. Enchanted by the sound of her daughter's laughter, Olympia momentarily forgot what a rush she was in, bent over Lola's tiny body, and, in an attempt to prolong her hysterics, tickled her exposed tummy. (Lola's beloved Disney Princess nightgown, a hot-pink firetrap given to her by her babysitter and featuring the entire royal assemblage clustered like newscasters on a billboard, had ridden up to her armpits.)

Shortly thereafter, Olympia's internal clock resumed ticking.

"And now it's sleepy time for Sleeping Beauty," she announced, lifting Lola into the air with her as she stood up.

"I'm *Belle* — not Sleeping Beauty," declared Lola, her laughter abruptly ceasing.

"Well, Queen Mommy has decreed that all princesses must be asleep by eight thirty."

"One more silly question."

"No. You have school tomorrow."

"It's not real school. It's daycare."

Olympia released a heavy sigh of exasperation before attempting to regain the upper hand. "Okay, here's my *last* silly question: can you please tell me why you're not in bed already?"

"That's not silly."

"Nighty-night."

"But you didn't sing 'Favorite Things' or do 'This Little Piggy' yet!"

Olympia had a new tack. "If I do both things, do you promise to go to sleep?"

"Okay," Lola agreed.

"But do you *promise?*"

"Promise."

And so Olympia assigned neighborhood destinations to all ten of Lola's toes. Then she did her best Julie Andrews impression. *Girls in white dresses with blue satin sashes!,* she sang in a high register, secretly impressed with her own vocal skills and, for a split second, wondering if she could have made it a career. *Silver white winters that meld into spring*, she went on. Or was it *melt* into spring? And did it matter? Finally, Olympia arrived at the last of the *feel so bad*s. "Okay, that's it. It's eight thirty," she said. It was actually eight twenty-seven; luckily, Lola hadn't yet learned to tell time.

Olympia deposited Lola in her toddler bed, then switched off the butterfly lamp on her dresser. The room went dark but for the fluorescent glow of a night-light.

"Noooooo!" moaned Lola. "No sleep. Not tired."

"Lola, you promised!!" said Olympia, her temperature rising.

"I'm scared."

"What are you scared of? I'm going to be in the next room."

"I'm scared of the dark."

"Don't be silly. It's not even that dark in here."

"Is *so*."

"Is *not*."

"Is too," said Lola, throwing her legs over the side of the bed as if preparing to stand up again...

Blood rushed to Olympia's cheeks and forehead. "ENOUGH!" she cried. "YOU'RE DRIVING ME FUCKING INSANE!!" With that, she pushed her daughter back onto the mattress — harder than she'd meant to.

Lola burst into hysterical tears. Guilt and fear consumed Olympia. How soon before Children's Services arrived? "I'm sorry I yelled at you," she said, taking Lola back into her arms. "Mommy's had a long day." As Olympia held her close, she lamented the wet spot forming on her new blouse, but felt unable to justify altering the position of her daughter's drooling mouth.

"You pushed me, too." The child wept. "You're a bad mommy!"

"All right, all right," said Olympia, who, despite feeling bad, thought Lola was laying it on a little thick. "Sometimes grown-ups get mad just like kids get mad."

"What does 'fugging' mean?"

"It means 'very.' But only grown-ups can use it."

"Like, *I'm fugging hungry?*"

"Something like that," said Olympia, cringing.

Lola's bedroom was really just an alcove of her mother's, separated by a curtain. "Will you lay on your bed until I'm asleep?" she asked.

Every night, Olympia told herself she wasn't going to do so anymore. And every night she did. How could she say no now? "Okay, but only for two minutes," she said.

Two minutes, of course, turned into twenty-five, during which time Lola issued a stream of unanswerable questions ("Why can't people fly?" "Why does cheese smell?" "Why don't cows and dogs wear underpants?"). Finally assured of her daughter's slowed breathing and splayed limbs, Olympia tiptoed out of her bedroom and, half closing the door behind her, felt as if she'd just posted bail from a developing-world prison.

Her interests never strayed far from her captor, however. After downing the remainder of a half-filled glass of Côtes du Rhône, Olympia walked over to her black file cabinet—once a floor model; hence the dent—and pulled out a manila folder marked "Lola-Birth." She opened the folder and removed several sheets of rumpled copy paper, the first page of which was headed "Anonymous Donor Profile #6103." It had been several years since she'd looked at the printout. Earlier that evening, gazing in fascination at Lola's hazel eyes, abundant freckles, and flaming red curls, Olympia—who had straight brown hair, light olive skin, and green eyes—had wondered if she'd missed some salient detail that the profile contained.

To both her relief and her disappointment, as she read through the document, she found nothing new in it:

Ethnicity: Anglo-Saxon
Height: 6' 1"
Weight: 185 lbs
Hair: brown
Eyes: blue
Education: B.A., Ivy League college
Occupation: medical school student
Describes himself as: motivated, thoughtful
Athletic skills: rowing, lacrosse, and cross-country
    skiing
Education/occupation of father: businessman
Education/occupation of mother: homemaker
Favorite movies: *Shawshank Redemption, Wedding
    Crashers*
Favorite sports team: Boston Red Sox
Favorite author: Ralph Waldo Emerson
Chromosome analysis: normal male 46...

Clearly the hunky scion of a grand old WASP family, down on its luck, Olympia had thought at the time she'd purchased his genetic material — back when that assumption had been enough. Back then, she'd liked the idea of having a child with no identifiable paternity. Wounded by a tumultuous love affair with a married man that left her in doubt about the self-sufficiency on which she prided herself (and deeply ashamed as well), she'd seen the arrangement as refreshingly uncompli-cated. Plus, the married man had had a vasectomy, so there had been no question of becoming pregnant by him.

It was only recently that Olympia had begun to question her decision to have a family on her own. Increasingly, she felt as if there was no one to share her daughter's small but, to Olympia's mind, miraculous milestones — from Lola's first steps without holding on, to the first time she'd drawn a figure with arms and legs, to her sudden ability to write her own name in crooked caps. Olympia's friends, even those who were parents, couldn't be expected to care. Her own parents seemed distracted. And when Olympia tried to tell her older sister, Imperia (known as "Perri"), her sister invariably pointed out that *her* daughter, Sadie, had done whatever it was six months earlier than Lola had.

Olympia also dreaded the inevitable day when Lola would ask who her father was. What would Olympia say? *He was a doctor who moved to remote Bangladesh to aid cholera victims?*

Little wonder that she'd begun to fantasize about finding the man behind the number. On one level, she knew it was a terrible idea and that she was better off idealizing a set of disembodied statistics than going through the inevitable heartbreak of locating someone — if it was even possible — who didn't want to be a father except maybe in the most abstract sense. According to his listed birth date, #6103 was nearly ten years younger than Olympia; in all likelihood, he'd donated for the beer money. But curiosity and longing had proven stronger than reason. And so Olympia had taken to picturing the three of them — herself, Lola, and Lola's virile young father — engaged in wholesome outdoorsy activities of the kind she imagined he must like (e.g., rowing across an algae-infested lake in New Hampshire). Not that Olympia had ever enjoyed sports or the outdoors, but maybe she could learn to do so.

She'd also taken to imagining #6103, a reluctant father at first, being won over by Lola's undeniable adorableness. These visions fixed in her head, Olympia had already started to make inquiries. She'd combed various message boards and donor registries — so far to no avail. But maybe there was another way...

Olympia woke the next morning to find that it was flurrying outside. Considering that she could locate only a single pink polka-dotted mitten, she bundled Lola up as best as she could — and instructed her to keep one hand in her pocket. ("Bad mommy," Lola told her for the second time in twelve hours.) Then, just as she'd done countless times before, Olympia wheeled her daughter the six blocks necessary to reach the Happy Kids Daycare Center, where she turned her over to two sexpots from Brighton Beach who appeared to be barely out of high school; wore low-cut glittery tops and sweatpants with words like "Player" and "Foxy" spelled out in script across the ass; and seemed utterly indifferent to children. Then again, Happy Kids charged only ten bucks per hour, which made Olympia a Happy Grown-up.

After dropping off Lola, Olympia caught the 4 train to the Upper East Side. Exiting the 86th Street station, she walked east to the modern town house that contained the museum. The director and chief curator was Viveka Pichler, a barely thirty possible android with a Cleopatra haircut who wore four-inch-high gladiator sandals all seasons of the year. Viveka had never been seen eating anything except eel sushi. She was also legally blind, a point of fact that, for obvious reasons, she kept a secret. Rumor had it that the money for Kunsthaus New York had been provided by Viveka's father, who'd made his fortune inventing a high-performance tire rubber for Formula One racing cars and other speed machines. Three years earlier, despite limited familiarity with the region and only rudimentary knowledge of the native language, Olympia had been delighted to accept a job at the museum. *How bad could it be?* she'd thought. Maybe she'd even score free airfare to Europe. And weren't Gustav Klimt and his protégé, Egon Schiele, two of her favorite painters? What's more, she'd left her previous position to spend time with Lola, then an infant. And her checking account had been hovering dangerously close to zero.

The museum's curatorial offices were to the right of the galleries. Viveka worked in one of them. The other three employees—Olympia and Viveka's assistants, two unsmiling twenty-something Austrians named Annmarie and Maximilian—worked in the other. The walls, chairs, desks, and computers were all white. For any measure of privacy, one had to leave the museum entirely or barricade oneself in the bathroom or supply closet, which, naturally, was filled with white paper clips and white pencils.

Later that morning, unable to forestall her curiosity until lunchtime, Olympia found herself crouched in the closet and calling the Cryobank of Park Avenue in search of Dawn Calico (now Cronin), her old high school classmate turned head nurse.

Four-plus years earlier, Olympia had been prostrate and in stirrups—and about to be inseminated—when she'd discovered the connection. "Wait, don't tell me you're *the* Pia Hellinger I used to know at Hastings High?!" Dawn had crowed excitedly from between Olympia's legs.

Olympia had wanted to disappear under the examining table. How soon before her entire high school graduating class knew it had come to this? "That's me," she'd said in a tiny voice.

"So, if you don't mind me asking," Dawn had gone on as she

parted Olympia's thighs and inserted a catheter. "How does 'Miss Most Likely to Become a French Movie Star' end up in need of sperm?"

"I wasn't 'Most Likely to Become a French Movie Star,'" Olympia had protested meekly. "I was 'Most Likely to Live in France.'" A founding member of the high school improv troupe, Dawn herself had been voted "Most Likely to Have Her Own TV Talk Show by Age Twenty-five." Though, if Olympia had had any say in the matter, Dawn's crowning superlative would have been "Most Annoying Person in All of Westchester County."

"All I know is that Brad Gadzak was hot for you," Dawn had continued. "And he was the hottest guy in high school."

"Brad Gadzak. Wow. I haven't thought about him in years. Do you know what happened to him?" asked Olympia, flinching on all fronts.

"Last I heard, he was an Outward Bound instructor in Alaska with a harem of Inuit supermodels. Anyway, that's it!" She withdrew the catheter.

"Great!" Olympia had said, while fighting the urge to flee to the frozen north herself.

"Does Dawn still work here?" she now asked the receptionist, her back pressed to the supply closet door.

Within seconds, Dawn came on the line, and said, "Hello?"

"It's Pia...Hellinger!" she said, trying to sound upbeat.

"Hey, Baby Mama," said Dawn. "How the heck are you?"

"We're all great. How are you and your brood?"

"Haven't pulled an Andrea Yates yet."

"Well, that's good." Olympia laughed lightly as she ran through the accumulated tabloid stories in her head and tried to recall to which one Andrea Yates owed her notoriety. Was she the woman who drove off a bridge with her kids? Or was that Susan Something? "So listen," she began again in a faux-casual voice. "I'm sure you don't remember this, but I used six-one-oh-three."

"Ah, the ever-popular six-one-oh-three." Dawn sighed, alarming Olympia. Exactly how many of his "motivated, thoughtful" progeny were toddling around Brownstone Brooklyn and the Upper West Side?

"Right, him," said Olympia. "Anyway, this is kind of embarrassing, but I've sort of been obsessing about the guy. And I was wondering if there was anything you could tell me about him that isn't on the profile, even if it's just a first name." She held her breath.

"Listen, sweets: nothing would make me happier than dishing dirt," said Dawn. "But I can't. Bank policy."

"I totally understand," said Olympia, already wishing she'd never asked.

Before she hung up, Dawn made Olympia promise to stop by "the bank" some time with Lola to say hello.

Olympia would rather have run naked through Times Square.

Exiting the supply room, she was further distressed to find Viveka standing there, hands on her nonexistent hips. Had she overheard Olympia's conversation? "We promote the fine art of Austria here," was all she said before stomping away in her gladiators.

"Too bad you can't see it," Olympia muttered to herself on her way back to her desk.

And then, two weeks later, the Inevitable Day arrived. It happened to be January 1. Olympia was getting herself and Lola ready for the Hellinger family's annual New Year's Day brunch. (Olympia looked forward to and dreaded the event in equal parts. She fitted Lola's arms into her favorite pink polyester-velour jumper dress with the rubberized heart decal. Lola's closet was filled with beautiful European fashions by Jacadi, Catimini, and Bon Nuit, most of them purchased secondhand on eBay. But the child's most cherished dresses were from Target and the Disney store. Olympia was wearing skintight dark-wash cigarette jeans, a black wool turtleneck, gray suede booties, a short fake-fur jacket, and oversized square sunglasses. Which is to say that she still cared about keeping up appearances in front of her two sisters — namely, the appearance that she led such a busy and sophisticated existence that she lacked both the time and energy to care what they thought of her, even though, in truth, she obsessed about them constantly. "Mommy, who's my daddy?" Lola asked.

"You don't have a daddy, cookie," Olympia replied in the most lighthearted voice she could summon.

"Why not?" she asked.

"Because not everyone has a mommy and a daddy. Some kids have just a mommy. A few have just a daddy... There, you're all zipped!" How could she lie? If she made up someone, Olympia had decided, Lola would just ask to meet him. In preparation for this moment, Olympia had bought her daughter picture books about "modern families." But the child seemed completely uninterested. Apart from *Madeline,* her favorite titles were *Olivia* and *The Story of Babar,* both of which featured mommies *and* daddies, all of the four-legged variety, but still.

"And a few kids just have gymnastics teachers," Lola said.

Olympia had no clue what her daughter was talking about. But not wanting to disappoint any more of her expectations, she said, "That's right. A few just have gymnastics teachers." Then she lifted up Lola's dress and yanked her bunching turtleneck down over her Tiana underpants. Tiana was Lola's favorite Disney Princess, a fact that Olympia advertised widely, believing it reflected well on her own parenting since Tiana was the only African American in the stable.

Seemingly unfazed, Lola soon moved on to a new line of questioning: "Mommy, what day comes after Friday, again?"

But the earlier inquiry haunted Olympia the whole way from Brooklyn to Larchmont. That was where Olympia's sister, Perri, almost forty, lived with her husband, Mike, forty-one, and their three *naturally* conceived children: Aiden, nine; Sadie, six; and Noah, just two.

To pass the time it took to get there, Olympia suggested that Lola try to count the number of people in their Metro-North car. "One...twoooo...threeeee," the child began in a high-pitched cheep, standing up in her seat as she pointed at the various domes in her line of vision. "Foooour...fiiiive...six...seven...eight...nine...ten...eleven...twelve...thirteen...fifteen...sixteen."

Olympia sighed and tutted with undisguised frustration. "After thirteen comes *fourteen. Then* fifteen." How many times did she have to go over it? She knew you weren't supposed to judge children at this age. And yet Lola's inability to count to twenty had left Olympia secretly dubious about the child's intelligence, and, by association, the mental faculties of #6103. What if he'd lied about his Ivy League degree and was actually a high school dropout who worked in a supermarket parking lot, corralling shopping carts? Or maybe he didn't even have a job, not on account of the recession but because he'd never even tried to get one, preferring to spend his days on street corners making lewd remarks at passing women — when he wasn't busy relieving himself at sperm banks. Or maybe it was all the infant formula that Olympia had fed Lola when she was a newborn. Olympia had managed to breastfeed for only four weeks, and even then she'd supplemented. No doubt that was ten points erased from Lola's IQ right there. Olympia fretted, then scolded herself for obsessing.

Mount Vernon East was the next stop, followed by Pelham and New Rochelle. Finally, the train pulled into lily-white Larchmont. The doors slid open. Olympia grabbed Lola's hand, and the two stepped down and out. BMW's 5 Series ruled the station parking lot. Olympia flagged an idling taxi. Five minutes later, she and Lola were turning up North Chatsworth Avenue, past a fake stone well, into a woodsy development with big old homes. Perri and Mike's circa-1930 "stockbroker Tudor," as they were locally known, sat up high on a hillock. Pristine snow blanketed the sloping front lawn. A silver late-model Lexus SUV was parked at the end of a neatly shoveled, S-shaped driveway. Another well-defined path led to an oak front door with miniature yellow square windows and a giant brass knocker. "Here we are," chimed Olympia in as enthusiastic a voice as she could muster.

"I want to ring the bell," said Lola.

"Hold on," said Olympia, lifting her into the air.

With difficulty, Lola pressed her tiny thumb into the opalescent button.

Moments later, Perri appeared in the doorway. "Well, look who's *shockingly* on time!" she declared.

"Happy New Year to you, too," said Olympia, leaning in to greet her big sister.

"Same to you, Anna Wintour," said Perri, returning the air kiss.

"Try to be nice," said Olympia, sighing as she lifted her sunglasses to the top of her head. Did her sister ever stop?

"It might kill me," conceded Perri as she closed the door behind them.

"Try anyway," said Olympia.

"And how's my favorite niece?" asked Perri, squatting to embrace Lola. "You know, your aunt Perri has missed you."

Lola dutifully clutched Perri around the knees before she announced, "I want apple juice."

"Lola, say 'please' before you ask for something," said Olympia.

"Please I want apple juice," said Lola.

"I'm sorry, sweetie," said Perri, making a clown face. "We don't keep juice in the house for kids." She glanced up and over at Olympia. "You know, juice is terrible for their teeth."

"She doesn't drink very much of it," said Olympia, irked again. "Besides, it's mostly bourbon for this girl." She patted Lola's head.

"Excuse me!" said Perri, eyes bugging.

"That was a joke."

"Oh. Funny!" Perri flashed an exaggeratedly bright smile as she stood up.

While Olympia removed her jacket, she glanced around her. To the left of the entrance, a silver-framed botanical print hung over a mahogany console topped with an alabaster lamp fitted with a silk shade. She thought of the many guided tours through the Great Homes of the Hudson Valley to which their mother had subjected them while they were growing up. *The writing desk to the left is a Chippendale original, purchased by Josiah Archibald Stanhope III, Franklin Roosevelt's great-uncle once removed, in 1761.* Olympia still remembered getting chewed out by a guard for trying to swing on a velvet rope...

"Sorry," said Perri, teeth gritted apologetically, "but would you guys mind taking off your shoes, too? We just got our rugs cleaned."

"Not a problem," said Olympia, unfazed as she bent down to unzip Lola's boots. Her sister's hang-up about dirt and germs had a long history. What's more, Perri's neurotic worldview wasn't entirely alien to Olympia herself. The two shared a deep loathing of stray hairs, especially those found blanketing drains and curling around bars of soap. Unlike Olympia, however, Perri had found a way to monetize her madness: she was the cofounder and CEO of a home organization company called In the Closet. After starting out as an in-home consultation service, it had since expanded to encompass an online store, a magazine, a catalogue, a smart phone app, and numerous accessories lines. When the economy improved, Perri was hoping to take the company public.

"I appreciate it," said Perri who, Olympia noticed upon closer viewing, was wearing an ivory silk blouse with a wedding present–sized bow, a long brown cardigan the color of dog doo, boot-legged camel-colored wool trousers with a crease down the front of each leg, and matching patent leather flats with hieroglyphic-like gold hardware on each toe.

Olympia had never understood where her sister got her fashion sense. Insofar as it made for a sharp contrast with what Olympia considered to be her own impeccable eye, it both alarmed and tickled her. "New pants?" she found herself asking.

Perri suddenly froze in place, her expression stricken. "What? You think they're ugly?" she asked.

"I just asked if they were new!" cried Olympia, not entirely genuinely.

"I could tell what you were thinking."

"You have ESP?"

"I'm not stupid. You think I look fat in them, too. Just admit it."

"Ohmygod, can you *please* stop being so insecure about your appearance?" said Olympia, sighing and rolling her eyes again (and secretly enjoying herself).

"But you don't like them," said Perri.

"They're a little—I don't know—*mustard* for my taste," said Olympia, wrinkling her nose. "To be honest, I think your whole look could use some updating. It's kind of stuck in the nineties." A thought struck her: Was she being a horrible bitch? Did Perri deserve it?

"Well, I'm sorry we can't all be fashion plates!" cried Perri, neck elevated.

"You asked!"

"Anyway." Apparently done with the topic, Perri cleared her throat. Then she turned to Lola, and said, "You know, Sadie is very excited to play with you."

"I want to see her. Where she is?" said Lola, who worshiped her not-quite-three-years-older cousin as if she were a small god. Olympia found the attachment both endearing and disturbing.

"I think she's up in her room," said Perri, raising her eyes to the stairs, over which dozens upon dozens of family photos in identical, pristine white wood frames blanketed the wall. "Oh, Saaaadiieee!" Perri called up to her. "Lola and Aunt Pia are here!"

"NO KIDS WHO AREN'T IN HOGWARTS SCHOOL OF WITCHCRAFT AND WIZARDRY ARE ALLOWED IN MY ROOM!" came the reply.

"Sadie, Lola has come all the way from Brooklyn to see you," Perri barked with a noticeably tense jaw. "Please be nice."

"I don't feel like being nice," Sadie called back.

Turning back to Olympia, Perri shook her head, and, her lids heavy over her eyes, sighed. "Apparently, this is what you get when you birth a frigging *genius,*" she said, making quote marks in the air. "You know, Sadie has an IQ of two-ten and is reading at a fourth-grade level already."

"I didn't know that," said Olympia, flinching internally. "Cookie, why don't we go say hi to Grandma instead."

"But I want to see Sadie!" cried Lola.

At that very moment, Carol Hellinger, Perri and Olympia's mother, appeared in the hallway. She was dressed in a purple cowl-neck sweater, a long peasant skirt made of kente cloth, and a clunky necklace that appeared to have been made of shark teeth and that sat nearly horizontally over her prodigious bosom. A navy blue bandana, tied like a kerchief, half obscured her silver-speckled pageboy. More or less the right age to have been a member of the original hippie movement, she'd somehow managed to absorb the style of the day without any of the tenets (i.e., free love, drug use). And she'd clung to the look long after her more freewheeling peers had moved on to sportswear. For the previous twenty-five years, Carol had been teaching social studies at the local high school, with a special focus on ancient Rome and Greece. At Smith College in the 1960s, she'd been a classics major—hence, the heroic and dynastic names of her three daughters, names to which they could never live up. (Olympia and Imperia's younger sister was named Augusta.) Or, at least, *Olympia* felt as if she could never fulfill the dreams of world domination sacrificed by her mother after she got pregnant and failed to pursue graduate school—and put all her ambition into her kids.

"Pia!" declared Carol, arms outstretched as she walked toward her middle daughter.

"Hi, Mom," said Olympia, bending down to kiss her mother, who, at five foot one, stood nearly eight inches shorter than her.

"Don't you look like your glamorous self."

"Thanks."

"And how's my Little Orphan Annie?" Carol turned to Lola. "Come say hi to your old grandma."

"Mom, I really wish you wouldn't call her an orphan," said Olympia, annoyed already. "She *does* have a mother."

"I was just alluding to the hair!"

"Grandma," came a voice from inside Carol's bosom. "Are you going to die soon?"

"Lola, shush," said Olympia, irritation turning to embarrassment.

"I certainly hope not!" Carol said, laughing caustically as she released her granddaughter.

Lola turned to Olympia, her brow knit. "But you said people die when they get really old."

"Grandma's not that old," Olympia said quickly. Then she turned back to her mother and said, "Sorry, she just learned about death."

"It's fine," said Carol, smiling stiffly.

Lola disappeared up the stairs, yelling, "Saaaaddieeeeeeee!"

Then Olympia turned to Perri. "Is Gus here yet?" she asked.

"She's on her way," said Perri.

"Some kind of political rally," said Carol with a flourish of her hand.

"On New Year's Day?" said Olympia. "It's a national holiday."

"You know my daughter Augusta!" cried Carol. "Every day of the year is Cinco de Mayo."

"Is Debbie coming too?" asked Olympia. A field organizer for the National Gay and Lesbian Task Force, Debbie was Gus's girlfriend of several years' standing.

Carol shrugged and turned down her lower lip, "I assume so. Isn't she always tagging along?"

"I wouldn't mind having a rally with my bed right now." Olympia yawned. In the presence of her immediate family, she often found herself suffering from some variant of narcolepsy.

"I hear you. I've had a completely crazed week," said Perri, who could get competitive about who the busier, more exhausted, and more overworked sister was. Though, since Perri slept only four hours a night, woke at five twenty a.m. each morning to run on a treadmill, and breastfed all three of her children until they turned four, she always took first prize. The only check in Olympia's column was the fact that she was a single mother. Which is possibly why Perri was always downplaying her husband's contribution. "And of course Mike's barely been here," she added.

"Speaking of fathers, where's Dad?" asked Olympia, keen again to change topics.

"In the living room, no doubt staring into space," said Carol, pursing her lips and, in doing so, revealing deep striations in her philtrum, remnants of a long-ago love affair with Virginia Slims. "Between you and me, I wish he'd never retired. You know, he sits in his study all day long playing with Gus's old Rubik's Cube!"

"How do you know if you're at school teaching?" asked Perri.

"Because I know," Carol snapped back.

"I was actually the one who liked the Rubik's Cube," Olympia felt compelled to point out.

"Funny," said Carol. "I don't remember you being good at spatial things."

"Thanks," said Olympia.

"He's not even riding his bike?" asked Perri, looking concerned. Every morning until just recently, Bob Hellinger, now seventy, had ridden his ten-speed along the old aqueduct to the historic Irvington estate on which Nevis Laboratories was housed. Despite being a particle physicist who studied motion, he'd somehow never managed to pass his driver's test.

Carol shook her head and tsked. "He says he's conserving angular momentum where L is the moment of inertia. Some kind of inside physics joke."

"Funny, I'm sure—if you understand it," said Olympia. "What about the banjo?"

"Not interested in playing."

"And what's the latest on the medical front?" asked Perri.

"What medical front?" said Carol, even though, the month before, her husband had experienced pain while urinating and received a borderline-high PSA score. All of which either did or didn't indicate early-stage prostate cancer.

"I thought Dad was going in for a biopsy next week," said Perri.

"Oh, that," said Carol, looking away. "If you ask me, it's all in his head."

This time, Olympia's and Perri's eyes rolled in sync. Their mother's refusal to engage with modern medicine was becoming more and more extreme. Not that she was any more interested in the homeopathic version than the Western variant. For a decade at least, the same peeling jar of ginkgo biloba supplements had been sitting unopened next to the herbal teas.

Mother and daughters proceeded to Perri's huge kitchen. Judging from the smell, several frittatas were baking away in various corners of the room. During her recent kitchen renovation, Perri had had three separate convection ovens installed — in case she decided to become a professional pastry chef on the side? "Anyway, here are the bagels," said Olympia, setting a large paper bag down on Perri's cryptlike island.

"Oh, thanks," said Perri, standing on tiptoe to reach an oversized Deruta majolica serving bowl in one of her double-height cabinets. "I have to say, that's the one thing I miss about living in the city," she declared upon her return to earth. "You just can't get proper bagels out here." For several years in her mid- to late twenties, while working as a junior analyst at McKinsey, Perri had lived with a roommate in a generic postwar high-rise on Broadway in the 80s.

"That's the only thing you miss?" asked Olympia.

"Well, not the *only* thing," said Perri, laughing lightly.

Olympia didn't inquire further.

"Well, we have a wonderful new bagel shop on Main Street in Hastings," said Carol, who seemed truly to believe that the suburbs were Bounty Incarnate.

"Meanwhile, did you hear about Cousin Stacy?" said Perri, bowl in hand as she made her way back to the island.

"What?" said Olympia.

"Apparently, Scott has moved out." Stacy, a massage therapist, was the daughter of Bob's troubled sister, Elaine. Scott was
Stacy's wine-distributor husband.

"According to who?" said Olympia, who, although she pretended otherwise, never tired of family gossip—so long as it
wasn't about herself.

"Gus, of course," said Perri. (Gus had always been the family
big mouth.)

"Well, I say, 'Good riddance!'" declared Carol, a committed
Hillary Democrat. "Wasn't he a follower of that awful Rush
Limbaugh?!"

"Where did you hear that?" snapped Perri, who was married to a man whom all the Hellingers suspected of being a
Republican as well, though he'd never admitted as much. Even
so, Mike Sims's politics were a source of tension between Perri
and her mother. (Perri herself insisted she was "apolitical.")

"I thought you told me," said Carol.

"I never told you anything like that," Perri said quickly. "In
any case, politics are the least of Scott's problems." She overturned the bagel bag into the bowl. Sesame and poppy seeds
sprayed across the white marble countertop, whereupon Perri
quickly secured a spray can of "stone revitalizer" and a roll of
paper towels. "According to Gus, he's an online poker addict,
and he owes massive debts," she continued as she cleaned.

"He's a gambler?!" cried a now flabbergasted Carol, who
was as uninterested in the amassing of money as she was in
modern medicine. "Poor woman."

"Gus said Stacy sounded okay when she talked to her. But
Scott Jr. is apparently taking it *really hard*." Perri turned pointedly to Olympia. Or was Olympia projecting? Maybe Perri was

just glancing at the clock to see how soon the frittatas needed to come out of the ovens. But even if the eyeballing was unintentional, she might have skipped that line about how hard the split was on Scott Jr. Lola didn't have a father at home, either. It wasn't necessarily the end of the world. Her sister could be so insensitive, Olympia thought as she lifted the bagel bowl off the counter and walked out.

She found her own father seated open-legged on a microfiber sectional in Perri and Mike's beam-ceilinged living room, diagonally across from a lackluster fire burning in a stone hearth. The flattened toes of his enormous brown suede Wallabies lent his feet a kangaroo-like appearance, while his silver beard bore a certain resemblance to Santa Claus's. His body type, however, had more in common with Ichabod Crane's. His long hands rested on opposing knees of threadbare brown corduroy pants. Beneath his not-quite-matching blazer he was wearing a paisley shirt with giant swirling patterns and a spread collar that looked as if it had been lifted from Led Zeppelin's dressing room in the late 1960s. "Hello there, Daughter!" he said with a quick wave. Which either did or didn't imply that he couldn't remember which daughter she was.

"Hi, Dad," said Olympia, kissing her father's sunken cheek. "What's happening?"

"Oh, nothing much. Just hurtling through space at sixty-seven thousand miles per hour!" he replied.

She'd heard that one before — several times. "Whatever you say, Pops," she said.

Then she turned to greet Aiden, Perri and Mike's blubbery elder son, who lay tummy down and elbows up on a geometric

area rug, his butt crack visible over the waistband of his Spider-
Man underpants. A pack of baseball cards spread out before
him, he appeared to be in the process of composing a fantasy
all-star team. He was also surreptitiously nibbling on a pack of
Twizzlers that he'd hidden in the pocket of his gray hoodie.
The only candy Perri allowed in the house were Yummy Earth
Organic Vitamin C Pops. Also, the kids were required to brush
their teeth immediately after eating one. "Aiden," said Olympia, "what's up?"

"Hey," he mumbled back without looking up.

Finally, Olympia turned to Perri's husband, Mike, who
stood fifteen feet away through the archway to the dining room,
thin-slicing a giant slab of smoked salmon with the crouched
posture of the high school defensive tackle he once was. Now a
salesman on the trading floor at Credit Suisse, where he sold
stocks to pension funds and other institutions, he was wearing a
pink button-down oxford and pressed jeans with a belt. "Mike,"
she said — and found herself blinking into the glare, courtesy
of a brilliant midwinter sun blasting through a newly installed
picture window. (Perri was constantly "upgrading" their already
flawless home.) "Happy two thousand whatever this is," Olympia went on, her head aching. The pain may have had something to do with the mystery punch she'd helped herself to the
night before at a loft party in Dumbo thrown by friends of
friends. She hadn't been all that keen on going — what if her
friends didn't show up and she didn't know a soul there? — but
the New Year's invitations had been scarce this year, possibly
owing to the fact that nearly all of her old friends were now
married with small children and seemingly happy to "stay in."
This was partly thanks to Olympia, who, not long before, had
successfully introduced the last two single people in her address

book, figuring that, if she couldn't manage to be happy in love, she might as well bring joy to others and live vicariously.

Not that Olympia lacked for male attention. In fact, just the previous night, a handsome young Web entrepreneur had approached her by the drinks table and asked her in an ironic way if she believed in astrology and, if so, would it bother her when she found out he was a Scorpio. But after two minutes of flirting, Olympia had shied away, claiming she needed to use the bathroom. She couldn't precisely say why — the Web guy was charming in his way — but she'd been struck by a familiar sense that there was no point in pursuing things since she was sure to mess them up eventually. Or maybe it was that she was never quite interested enough; or didn't feel she had the time for a relationship; or thought whoever it was would flee once he found out she was the mother of a young child; or felt uncomfortable bringing strange men back to her apartment, especially since Lola didn't have her own bedroom. "Rough New Year's Eve?" said Mike, who never seemed to miss a single expression on her face.

"Could have been rougher. What about yours?" said Olympia who, after ten-plus years, had grown almost but not quite fond of her brother-in-law's frat boy banter. She'd also grown fond of trying to outdo him. He and Perri had hooked up her junior and his senior year at Wharton, where both had been in the undergraduate business program. Save for one nine-month breakup during which time Perri either had or hadn't slept with someone else — Olympia had never gotten a definitive answer — they'd been together ever since. "Rumor has it that there was some serious brewski pounding in the 'burbs last night," she went on in a dry tone.

"You could say that." Mike smiled congenially before he went back to his salmon slicing.

Fifteen minutes later, the doorbell rang. "It must be Auggie," said Carol, popping out of the kitchen, followed by Perri. Carol was the only one who still called Augusta by her childhood nickname, the rest of them having shifted to the high school–era moniker Gus.

"I'll get it," said Perri, practically elbowing their mother in the face as she made for the front door, spatula in hand.

There were footsteps, muffled voices, the gentle thud of a knapsack hitting the floor. "Where's Debbie?" Olympia heard Carol ask her.

"She couldn't make it."

"She didn't get arrested again, did she?"

"No, she didn't get arrested again."

"So, where is she?"

"Jesus. Can I have five minutes before being subjected to the Spanish Inquisition?!"

"I was just asking!"

"You're always just asking…"

Carol and Gus bickered endlessly. Olympia, in turn, grew tired of listening to her mother complain during their own once- or twice-weekly phone calls about how mean Gus had been to her. (Suggestions that Carol mind her own business and, what's more, that she and Gus didn't have to talk on the phone *every day* fell on deaf ears.) Finally, Gus came into view—in jeans and a filthy oversized anorak with fake fur detailing. Her skunk-dyed pixie-cut hair was in dire need of a wash, or maybe just a brush. Olympia found her younger sister's personal style to be nearly as baffling as her older one's was. (Why look homeless if you weren't?) That said, Olympia knew better than to tease her younger sister, whose ability to laugh at herself was basically nonexistent. "What's up?" she said.

"Hey," grumbled Gus. She took off her jacket and tossed it over the back of a leather club chair, revealing a completely shredded lining. But when she turned back to Olympia, an incandescent smile had overtaken her face. "We have a winner," she announced.

"And it's Aaron Krickstein!" The words seemed to come out of Olympia's mouth of their own accord.

"Or is it Shlomo Glickstein?"

For Olympia, the exchange—an ancient greeting ritual whose origins lay in the 1980 U.S. Open, in Forest Hills— encapsulated everything that had once been conspiratorial, even magical, about her relationship with Gus. Seeking further con- nection, she reached out to embrace her. As was usual in recent years, however, her younger sister recoiled at the gesture. "Ow, you're hurting me," she said, slithering out of Olympia's arms even before they'd made it around her squirrel-like back.

"Oh—sorry," said Olympia.

"It's fine," said Gus. "You just fractured my rib cage, that's all."

"I got you a birthday present," said Olympia, producing a small box wrapped in tissue.

"Oh, thanks, that was nice of you," said Gus, who'd turned thirty-six the day after Christmas. She removed the box from Olympia's hands, then set it down in the corner next to Perri and Mike's giant potted bird-of-paradise, in no apparent hurry to find out what was inside.

"Aren't you going to open it?" asked Olympia, feeling hurt, even though, truth be told, it was a "regift" — skull earrings given to Olympia for her own birthday, a few months before.

"I will, I will!" said Gus. "Just give me a minute."

"*Someone's* feeling crabby today," said Olympia, suddenly crabby herself. She'd accepted the fact that her younger sister hadn't given her a real Christmas or birthday present in ten years. (Once a decade, Gus, for whom "consumerism" was apparently a dirty word, would be moved to wrap up some cookbook on her shelf regardless of the peanut butter stains on the cover and knowing full well that Olympia only boiled pasta and microwaved.) But Olympia still expected her younger sister to show a modicum of enthusiasm and appreciation when accepting a gift for herself.

"I'm not crabby," Gus replied. "I'm just freezing." She crossed her arms and rubbed her shoulders.

"Come sit near the fire," said Carol, patting the empty seat next to her.

"Ohmygod, can everyone *please* stop fussing over me?!"

"You were the one who said you were cold," Olympia dared to point out, as much in defense of reason as in defense of their mother who, for once, seemed wholly undeserving of Gus's impertinence.

"Did anyone ask you?" Gus shot back.

Olympia said nothing more. But the question stung. Once, Gus *had* asked her stuff. If not all the time, then sometimes. Olympia could still recall explaining to her thirteen-year-old sister that the cardboard applicator had to be removed after you inserted a tampon (hence, the shooting pains when Gus had tried to walk). In recent years, however, Gus had treated Olympia less like a sage than a village idiot.

"Girls, enough," said Carol.

"Why don't I just turn up the heat," said Perri, ever the peacemaker as she walked over to the thermostat on the wall.

"Thanks," muttered Gus. Then she banged her palm against her forehead, and said, "Oh, shiiit! I completely forgot to buy orange juice. I'm really sorry. I could run out—"

"It's fine," said Perri, inhaling through her nose. As if she were trying not to be mad but not trying all that hard. So everyone would understand the vast burdens shouldered by the Martyrs of This World, such as herself. "All the stores in town are closed. But I might have a few cans of emergency concentrate in the basement freezer. I'll run down there as soon as I finish cooking for all nine of you!"

Olympia was tempted to point out that hosting New Year's brunch had been Perri's idea. (In years past, the event had taken place at their parents' house in Hastings-on-Hudson, with Carol playing hostess and chief dispenser of rancid cold cuts.) Olympia also wished to have it noted that, should *she* have forgotten the requested bagels, Perri would most definitely have gone ballistic. But in the interest of keeping the peace, she kept silent.

"Speaking of beverages, who's game for a Bloody Mary?" said Mike. "What about you, Olympia? Hair of the dog never hurt anyone." He had a can of tomato juice in one hand and a bottle of Absolut in the other.

"So right you are," said Olympia, now seated on a tufted ottoman next to the fireplace, leafing through a coffee table book about the great beach houses of the Connecticut Sound. "Just make it a virgin."

"Virgin Mary it is," he noted with a sidelong glance, followed by a wink. "I always assumed Lola was born by immaculate conception."

"Read between the lines," muttered Olympia, her three middle fingers lifted into the air, her eyes still on a boathouse in Old Lyme.

Just then, a cry came through the baby monitor. "Well, that was the shortest nap in world history," said Perri, sounding aggrieved yet again as she stomped out of the room in her patent leather flats.

No one asked you to have three kids, Olympia thought but didn't say.

Perri reappeared five minutes later with Noah balanced on her hip. His face was the color of rhubarb; his eyes were as narrow as slits; his hair (what there was of it) was yellow gold. He had the vaguely competitive, vaguely intoxicated expression of someone who'd been playing beer pong until all hours. Which is to say, he looked like a clone of his father. With his fat legs and triple chin, he was also ridiculously cute. "Can you say hi to Grandma?" said Perri, putting the two in striking distance of each other.

"Gama," he said, touching Carol's nose.

"Hello, bubala," said Carol, tickling her grandson's chin. She turned to Perri. "You know, he really has that presidential look."

"Except not the current presidential look," Gus cut in, "since that guy is black."

Carol scowled. She and Gus had tension over politics as well, since Gus felt her mother wasn't sufficiently left-wing.

"May I?" said Olympia, extending her arms toward her nephew.

But her older sister had other ideas first. Seemingly out of nowhere, a shot of hand sanitizer appeared on Olympia's palms. "Sorry—if you don't mind," said Perri, smiling meekly. As Olympia dutifully rubbed her palms together, she allowed herself a gentle lift of the eyebrows. Finally, Perri handed him over with a "Here you go!"

Olympia pressed Noah's hot cheek into her own, breathed in his nutmeg scent, and found herself longing for another child—and didn't see how it was possible, financially or otherwise. "Do you know who I am? Can you say 'Aunt Pia'?" she asked.

In response, Noah gazed quizzically at his aunt—before inserting a finger up her nose.

"Hey, buddy, no treasure hunting today," she said, head flung back to expel the digit.

There was laughter all around, pleasing Olympia, who liked to be liked by her family more than she liked to admit to herself. Even Perri, not known for her sense of humor and usually repelled by all mention of bodily orifices, chortled heartily and, apparently resisting the urge to whip out more hand sanitizer, mysteriously declared, "Great. I've birthed another booger lover!"

But the high proved temporary. Suddenly Olympia felt heat on her forearm, then something foul-smelling. "Hey," she said. "Are you pooping on me?"

"I poo-poo," Noah gurgled proudly.

The smell was overwhelming and did nothing for Olympia's hangover. "Sorry, kiddo, the party's over," she said, just as quickly doubting her own desire for a second child. "You're going back to Mommy." Olympia was about to hand Noah to

Perri when she realized she'd be giving her sister yet another reason to lament her Perfect Life. "Or, even better, let's find Daddy," she said, changing course. She walked over to where Mike stood, talking to his mother-in-law.

"In answer to your question, school is excellent, thank you," Carol was telling him. "We've just finished Thucydides's *History of the Peloponnesian War.*"

"Is that so?" said Mike, eyes glassy.

"And next semester we'll be reading excerpts from Sophocles's *Three Plays* — as well as Adler's *Aristotle for Everybody.*"

"Cute title," said Mike.

"Speaking of cute," Olympia cut in. "I've got a present for you." She transferred the child into Mike's arms. "Someone needs changing."

"Dude, have you been adversely affecting the olfactory environment of this house?" asked Mike, seeming both relieved to have an excuse to escape Carol and also genuinely smitten with his younger son.

"I poo-poo," Noah said again, clearly pleased with himself.

"I thought so," said Mike, turning back to his mother-in-law. "Excuse me, Carol. Noah and I have some business to take care of."

With that, the two vacated the room.

Father and son reappeared five minutes later — to Perri's pressing question: "Did you remember powder?"

"Yes, Mommy," Mike said in a dronelike voice that made Olympia shudder. If marriage was calling the person you had sex with the same name you called your parents, she was glad to have bypassed the institution.

Mike put Noah down on the floor to play and poured himself another Bloody Mary. Two slugs in, he turned to the wider group and asked, "So, who's made a New Year's resolution?" He took another sip. "Myself, I'm thinking of mastering the fine art of cha-cha-cha, having recently perfected the samba." In a shocking display of Latin dance acumen, he took a step forward, then backward, while swiveling his hips. Then he grinned broadly, one side of his mouth lifted higher than the other.

"Wow," said Olympia, mystified. "Have you been taking lessons?"

"I have indeed," said Mike. "I'm actually considering a name change to Miguel."

Just then, Gus doubled over and began to sob, her shoulders rising and falling like old-fashioned typewriter keys in the middle of a memo.

Perri rushed to Gus's aid before Olympia or her mother had a chance to do so. Or maybe Olympia hadn't actually wanted the chance. Maybe it was easier letting Perri be the family's anointed caretaker — especially when it came to taking care of Gus. Olympia found her younger sister's emotional swings to be exhausting. She also found them unfair, insofar as it often seemed as if Gus had co-opted the family's entire supply of tears, leaving none for anyone else ever to shed. Gus had co-opted the family's storehouse of anger, too. At least, that was how it had always felt. Indeed, the dominant image of Olympia's childhood was of herself tiptoeing through the living room in the aftermath of one of Gus's explosions, as if in danger of stepping on a land mine.

A nubbly brown arm (Perri's) draped itself around a holey striped shoulder (Gus's). "Sweeeetie," Perri crooned in a saccharine voice. "What's the matter?"

"Debbie left me," wailed Gus.

"Sweeeeeetie!! I'm so sorry," said Perri, tucking an overgrown bang around her youngest sister's multiply pierced ear. "Are you sure you didn't just have a bad fight?"

"There was no fight," Gus choked out. "One day last week, while I was at work, she just moved all her stuff out. When I got home, she was gone." She sobbed again.

"I never thought she was good enough for you, anyway," muttered Carol, now standing rigidly to Gus's left. "What was the name of that college she went to?"

"Mom—shush!" said Perri.

Gus, too, took the opportunity to glare at their mother before she wiped her nose on her sleeve, causing Perri to visibly recoil. "The worst part is, I hate myself for feeling this way," Gus moaned on. "Compared to ninety-nine percent of the world's population, I'm so incredibly privileged—"

"You're not *that* privileged!" Perri said with a quick laugh.

"I *am* privileged!" cried Gus, who had famously (in the Hellinger family) begun to collect spare change for the Sandinistas in Nicaragua at the age of twelve. "There are a lot of people in the world with actual problems, like not having enough food to eat or money to pay the rent—not fake problems like their girlfriends leaving them." Gus let out another sob. "It's just that...I feel like such a loser."

"Please! You are so far from being a loser," said Perri. "For starters, you have a completely heroic job helping people in need—when you're not busy educating the next generation of lawyers."

"I'm also thirty-six and alone!" wept Gus, who split her time between the civil division of the Legal Aid Society of New York, where she worked as a family law attorney out of the

Bronx office, and Fordham Law School, where she was a recently tenured professor specializing in gender and contracts.

"I'm really sorry about Debbie, but you can be single and still have a life," Olympia felt suddenly compelled to interject, her own choices seemingly on trial yet again.

"Well, maybe *you* can," said Gus, with a quick laugh.

Olympia flinched. Was Gus trying to imply that she had no heart? That she thrived on cheap hookups? *You don't think I want someone in my life, too?* Olympia was about to say, wanted to say, but pride stopped her. "Why am I any different from you?" she asked instead.

Gus wiped her eyes with the back of her hand. "Let's just say I'd never have a baby on my own."

"Try *three* babies!" Perri cut in, not to be outdone. "And a husband who's never home."

"I heard that," Mike called from the background.

"I'm nine years old, Mom," came another male voice from yonder. "And *you're* never home, either."

"That's *not* true, Aiden!" said Perri, looking like she, too, might start crying.

"I didn't set out to have a baby on my own," Olympia heard herself telling Gus, and growing defensive too, and feeling unable to stop herself on either count. "I just happened not to have had that kind of relationship with Lola's father. I'm sorry that's so hard for everyone to understand."

Fearing that Gus would deem her an elitist for having used a donor with a clearly privileged background, and that Perri would disapprove of her having used a sperm bank at all, Olympia had kept the entire matter of Lola's paternity a secret from everyone but her college roommate, who lived in Japan.

It was more than that too: What if her sisters saw her as a failure?

"Well, how are we supposed to understand when you've still never told us who Lola's father is?" asked Gus, prosecutorial even when in a crisis.

"*Must* we go there now?" said Olympia.

"I'm sorry for being curious!" cried Gus. "I'm your sister. So shoot me."

"No one you know. How's that?"

"But someone *you* did?"

"It's true, Pia. We're all dying to know who the redhead is," Carol trilled in the background.

"Thank you, Mom," said Olympia, wondering why she bothered to attend these family get-togethers, since they always left her in a foul mood. "Now, if everyone is done harassing me, I'm going to use the bathroom." Olympia walked off.

No one called after her. No one ever did. Despite her myriad professional accomplishments, Gus was still the one whom everyone was always whispering about, wondering if she was happy, worrying about whether she was "okay."

"What the heck is *her* problem?" Olympia heard Gus ask Perri with a sniffle.

Once ensconced in Perri and Mike's guest bathroom with its recurring tulip motif, Olympia splashed cold water on her face. Then she took a long look at herself in the mirror over the sink, just as she'd taken long looks thousands of times before. Although Olympia had never been able to judge her own appearance with anything close to objectivity, having always concentrated her attentions on her few faults (such as her ever so slightly beaked nose), as opposed to her many assets (such as her high cheekbones, Barbie doll body, and luxurious mane), she was also aware that she wouldn't have gotten the attention she'd gotten in life if she hadn't looked the way she had. At the same time, she was increasingly aware that her age was catching up with her face. Every morning, it seemed, there were new little lines around her mouth and eyes. It was as if she went to bed with a draftsman lying under her pillow.

It was also true that, after a lifetime spent placing a premium on beauty, she'd begun to tire of her own vanity and of feeling as if she had to be the most beautiful woman in any room. It was too much work, too much pressure. Standing there staring at herself, Olympia wondered how soon it might be before the "you're so beautiful" chorus went quiet. Already, it had decreased in volume from mezzo forte to mezzo piano. Would she be devastated, relieved, or some combination of the two? At least then, maybe, people would stop asking how a woman "who looks like you do" could "possibly be single." Maybe also she'd stop feeling so much pressure to marry. At the insistence of friends, she'd tried Internet dating. But the question-and-answer sessions that passed for first dates reminded her of job interviews. And all the men seemed desperate. As if any womb would do. And hers was getting old. Dating was also expensive. Every mocha latte at Starbucks required paying a babysitter for a minimum of three hours.

Or was she just looking for excuses because she was still obsessed with Patrick Barrett? Four years later, she could hardly say his name out loud. They'd met at the art opening of his friend, Brian, who made shiny red photographs of tree branches. At the time, Olympia had been a glorified "gallerina" at a big-name 57th Street gallery. Brian, while not the biggest of the big-name artists, had been in the gallery's regular stable. Olympia had gone over to congratulate him on the show — and also to find out who the handsome man with the deep-set eyes standing next to him was. "Meet my do-gooder best friend," Brian had said.

"What exactly do you do that's good?" Olympia had asked.

"I run a community center for disadvantaged youth," Patrick had told her.

"In East New York," Brian had added.

"Not by choice," Patrick had said. "It was the only job I could get straight out of prison."

"Prison?" Olympia had asked.

"He's joking," Brian had said. "I think."

"You guys are hilarious," Olympia had told them.

"Some people find me funny," Patrick had said. "Other people, extremely dull."

"Well, I guess you'll have to find out which people I am," Olympia had said, head cocked coyly. It had all been her fault. She'd started the flirting.

"I guess so," Patrick had said. "And what do you do?"

"I work here."

"Doing what?"

"Well, mostly I stand around helping create a certain ambiance conducive to rich people buying art," she'd told him. "I do some other important stuff, too, like ordering coffee."

"It sounds very important," he'd answered.

It had also been obvious at first glance that Patrick Barrett was married: he was wearing a gold band on the second finger of his left hand. Looking back, Olympia no longer fully understood her motives in pursuing him. Maybe it had something to do with his unavailability and his teasing manner. Until the moment they kissed, Olympia hadn't actually been sure that he'd liked her in a boy-girl way. She and Patrick had spent most of their time discussing her problems—until he became her biggest problem of all.

However it had happened, she'd fallen hard. Before Patrick, there had been a way in which love had felt too easy. How many times in her life had Olympia heard "I love you" uttered by men who didn't seem to know the first thing about her and who only seemed to like her for the way she looked? And yet how she'd toiled to maintain that look, paying meticulous attention not just to her skin, hair, clothes, and weight, but also to her soft voice, sense of "mystery" and "vulnerability," and all the other things that the opposite sex seemed to want from her. What *she* wanted from them was all mixed up in her head. But with Patrick, she'd felt as if she'd had to do the work of wooing herself. For once, she'd been able to say "I love you." And Patrick had seemed to feel the same way.

The day after they'd first slept together, however, Olympia had learned that Patrick's wife, Camille, was a daredevil French heiress who, while on holiday in New Zealand, had broken her back and severed her spinal cord partaking in the extreme sport of hydro-zorbing (i.e., rolling down the side of a mountain in a giant ball filled with water). The result was that she'd be in a wheelchair for the rest of her life. Patrick had told Olympia he'd always hated the risk-taking side of Camille's personality: he'd seen it as a pointless expenditure of energy. And he'd said he'd been leaning toward divorce. Before she'd left for New Zealand, he'd been sleeping on the sofa, he'd insisted. But after the accident occurred, he'd felt obliged to stay. Camille's fortune had had nothing to do with it, he'd sworn over and over again.

42

To Olympia's knowledge, Camille never found out about their affair. Olympia hadn't ever met her, either. Olympia felt that none of these mitigating factors made her own behavior any more excusable. Never mind Patrick's behavior. What kind of guy cheated on his disabled wife? But then again, what kind of woman slept with a man whose wife was disabled?

If Olympia deserved punishment, she'd received it—and then some. After leaving Patrick eighteen months into their affair, she'd felt as if her heart had been ripped from her chest and left to wither on the sidewalk. She'd also felt as if the hole in her chest where her heart had once been would never be filled again. Listless despair had defined the waking portion of her days. But what other choice had she had? She couldn't very well have asked him to leave Camille. At Olympia's insistence, she and Patrick had cut off all contact. But the silence had only made it harder—so hard that, on occasion, one of them (usually Olympia) would break down and call the other. Then there would be more tears, even the occasional reunion that led nowhere.

To salve her guilt, Olympia began volunteering once a week as a "meeter and greeter" in the rehabilitation unit of an East Side Manhattan hospital. The patients ranged from quadriplegics to carpal tunnel sufferers. Maybe not surprisingly, Olympia preferred caring for the former. A secret part of her was probably also hoping to one day meet and greet Camille. So Olympia could prostrate herself before the woman, beg for her forgiveness, and be reassured that she wasn't a horrible person after all.

Or was she simply curious to see if Camille was pretty?

In any case, it was in the aftermath of her breakup with Patrick that Olympia made the startling discovery that taking care of others made her feel confident and at peace. Slowly, the idea of becoming a mother began to take shape in her head. Not only would a baby provide her with someone to love who wasn't Patrick, but it would mark a new chapter in her life. At the time, she was approaching thirty-five. If not now, when? She didn't want to end up childless at forty, still waiting to meet the right person.

At first, she tried to think of casual flings of years past that she might be able to revisit, but no one seemed right. And having a baby with a gay friend sounded too complicated. Eventually, she found herself at Park Avenue Cryo, as it was known, leafing through the listings book...

Olympia blew her nose and reapplied her lip balm. Then she went upstairs to check on Lola.

Tiny rosebud wallpaper decorated the second floor hall with its seascape painting flanked by brass sconces. The door to Sadie's bedroom was ajar. Curious as to how the cousins were getting along free of adult supervision, Olympia peeked her head through the crack.

She found Lola sitting motionless on Sadie's bubble gum pink shag rug in an Ariel the mermaid costume, her legs extended before her, her thumb in her mouth. Next to her on the rug in striped underpants and a hooded black cape was Sadie, a Dallas Cowboy Cheerleader Barbie in her grip. "Welcome to Gryffindor Tower. My name is Sir Nicholas de Mimsy-Porpington," Sadie announced in a bad English accent. "But most of Hogwarts know me as Nearly Headless Nick." With that, she yanked the doll's head off its body.

How was it possible that her older sister had birthed such a perverse and beautiful child? Olympia wondered. Sadie was tall and slim, with dark blond hair, porcelain skin, a swanlike neck, and giant aquamarine eyes. Fascinated, amused, and just the tiniest bit threatened, Olympia tiptoed back down the hall.

Returning to the living room, Olympia found the other members of the extended Hellinger-Sims clan indulging their signature manias. Perri was busy DustBusting corn chip crumbs beneath the coffee table. Mike was also on all fours, doing push-ups and sounding as if he were at high risk for having a coronary. Gus was stretched out on the short end of the sectional, barking at Carol, whose crime had been to insist that Aiden's acumen at the baseball card game Strat-O-Matic was evidence of a young Pythagoras at work. "Can't you ever just let anyone *be* without having to make them into something more?!" Gus berated their mother.

"Whatever I say is wrong," said Carol.

Meanwhile, Noah had climbed into Grandpa Bob's lap and was now picking *his* nose, undeterred by Bob's chuckling cries of "Careful there, sonny."

Surveying the scene, Olympia was overcome by the desire to make nice. Being mad at your family was too exhausting and upsetting, she decided. It was far easier to stick to the surface-level chitchat that defined her and her sisters' current interactions. In fact, the three of them emailed or spoke on the phone nearly every day, even if it was just two lines back and forth, or two minutes of talk. "Hey, Perr. Any chance of hot food in the near future?" Olympia said in a resolutely upbeat voice. "I'm famished." (Olympia knew how her older sister loved to feel necessary.)

"Five minutes," said Perri, still out of view. "But the coffee is hot if you want some."

"Great, thanks," said Olympia, next turning to her younger sister. "Hey, I'm really sorry about Debbie."

"Thanks for saying that," mumbled Gus.

Just then, Lola wandered in.

"Yo, mermaid," said Mike, still on all fours. "Want to go fishing in Uncle Mikey's boat?"

"Yay. Fishing!" cried Lola, boarding her uncle's back and throwing her arms around its captain's sweat-beaded neck. To Olympia's vague horror, her daughter seemed to consider "Uncle Mikey" the source of all excitement in the world.

"All passengers aboard!" bellowed Mike, rising onto his knees.

"I see a shark! I see a shark!" cried Lola, pointing at Noah.

"Hey, Lola," said Gus, half sitting up. "Don't I even get a hello?"

"Lola, go kiss your aunt Gus hello," said Olympia.

Lola dutifully disembarked and performed the requested task. Then she climbed into Olympia's lap and stuck her thumb back in her mouth. Olympia felt a rush of proprietary pride. Paternity questions aside, Lola was still the greatest thing that had ever happened to her, she thought — especially when there were other people around to keep her entertained.

Sadie appeared shortly thereafter, decapitated Barbie still in her grip, but wearing slightly more clothing beneath her cape (a T-shirt and leggings) than she had been in her bedroom.

"Who's my favorite little witchy witch?" asked Mike, lifting his daughter into the air and enveloping her in a bear hug.

"Daaaaaaaaddddy," Sadie said languorously as she rested her cheek on his shoulder.

"Hey, what happened to Barbie's head?" asked Olympia, curious as to how she'd answer.

"She wouldn't do a split, so I had to punish her," explained Sadie.

"Sadie—enough!" yelled Perri.

"Oh, stop, Perri!" said Carol, slapping at the air. "She's just an imaginative little girl trying to make sense of the world." She turned to Sadie, arms open, and said, "Come here, My Beautiful Thing!"

As Sadie climbed into her grandma's lap, Olympia looked away. Carol had once called Olympia by that name. It was clear to everyone—except, maybe, to Carol—that Sadie was her favorite grandchild by a margin of ten. No doubt some of the connection could be attributed to the frequency with which grandmother and granddaughter saw each other—at least twice a week. Sadie's house was just a twenty-five-minute drive from Hastings; Lola lived a subway and train ride away. Even so, it seemed to Olympia that her mother hadn't made as much of an effort to get to know Lola as she might have. She even bought her cheaper presents than she bought her other granddaughter. After Christmas, Olympia had found herself Internet-price-checking the gifts that Carol had given to Sadie and Lola respectively. To her intense annoyance, Sadie's Butterfly Bead-Tastic Kit had come in at $26.99, while Lola's Dress a Doll Magnet Set sold for a mere $13.99.

Five minutes later, just as promised, steam rising from a cobalt blue Le Creuset stoneware baking dish she was carrying, Perri announced, *"Le dîner est servi!"*

"Do I have a dream wife, or what?" asked Mike, walking over to where she stood.

"A dream wife for a dream husband," said Perri, seeming to

lap up the praise as she lifted her chin and puckered her lips to meet his own.

As the two kissed on the lips, albeit gingerly in order to avoid the scalding receptacle between them, Olympia found herself looking away again.

"Well, I can't speak for the rest of you," said Carol, making her way to the table. "But that smells absolutely scrumptious." She tapped her eldest daughter's arm. "I'll never know how you do it, Perri — raising three young children while you run your thing." She waved her hand through the air.

"You mean, *my company?*" asked Perri, lower lip extended and clearly miffed at Carol's failure to have come up with the word and, by extension, to take seriously her entrepreneurial success.

"That's what I meant."

"With difficulty, is the answer."

"And did you hear," said Carol, turning to the others as she pulled out a chair. "Perri's been invited to China to give a talk to a business group?"

For an intelligent woman, Olympia thought, her mother was shockingly dense about the ways in which she fostered rivalry between her daughters. Not that the proclivity was anything new. Olympia saw herself as a teenager, sitting at the dinner table, seeing how many canned peas she could spear on one prong of her fork, while Carol informed Bob that Perri's scale model of the Roman Colosseum had won first prize at the History Day Fair — or Gus's poem about an orphan boy with a cleft lip had won an Honorable Mention in the All Westchester Poetry Runoff for Under Thirteens. "Well, how do you like that," Bob would say.

"Wow, good for you," Olympia now said, turning to Perri

and thinking about how she was never invited anywhere — not even to Austria.

"It's really nothing." Perri smiled faux modestly. "To be honest, the whole thing sounds completely hokey. I can't figure out why I was even asked! The keynote speaker is the founder of Apple, Steve Whatshisname. Apparently, the organizers saw that silly article I was in, in *Fortune* magazine last year, about ten female entrepreneurs to watch —"

Olympia felt her body tensing into a thousand individual knots. "I heard Steve Whatshisname is dying of cancer," she said, then felt bad for saying so in light of her father's medical issues.

"I went to a conference in Beijing once," said Bob. "Back then, they called it Peking, of course, raising the question ... is it now called Beijing Duck?"

"I was asked to speak, too," interjected Gus, suddenly vertical. "In court tomorrow morning on behalf of a battered woman who's about to become homeless unless her baby's deadbeat daddy steps up to the plate." She yanked out a chair at the far end of the table, producing a screeching sound that caused Perri to visibly flinch. (Or was it something Gus had said?) "And then, later in the day, I'm giving a lecture on the fundamentals of contract law to three hundred first-years."

"Such ambitious daughters I have!" declared Carol. She turned to her husband, then her son-in-law. "They certainly didn't get it from me."

"Or me," cut in Olympia, fully aware of the nakedness of her own insecurity, yet in that moment somehow unable to disguise it. At her age, she secretly felt she ought to have been running her own gallery or museum, not ordering cases of Riesling and updating mailing lists for someone else's and especially not someone nearly ten years her junior. That, or she should have been one of the featured artists. But despite having attended Pratt for a year and a half and forging some connections in the downtown art world, Olympia had long ago given up trying to be an artist. She'd had her bunny paintings featured in a few group shows, but the exposure hadn't led anywhere. Maybe it was that she didn't have the energy or the drive, or that she secretly suspected that her artwork was trite, even corny, and possibly not even worthy of a Hallmark card; and that she couldn't compete on that front or really any other; and that the only thing she'd ever been good at was looking a certain way, striking a certain pose. That and arranging blind dates. Her sisters were the Impressive Ones, while Olympia flitted from job to job and failed to complete master's programs (two, so far). She was the only Hellinger sister without an advanced degree. Perri had gotten her MBA from Columbia, and Gus her JD from Berkeley. Olympia had also been the only sister not to break 1400 on the SAT.

"Um, you're hardly flipping burgers at Mickey Dee's," said Gus.

"I didn't say I was," said Olympia, hiding behind her water glass.

An awkward silence ensued. It was Mike who lifted the pall. "Well, here's my public speech for the day: What do you say we all eat?"

"Finally," grumbled Aiden.

"Sadie, Aiden," said Perri. "Please go wash your hands!"

"I washed them an hour ago," murmured Aiden.

"It's only blood," said Sadie, lifting her hands, which were covered with red streaks.

"Blood!" cried Perri.

"Just kidding. It's marker."

"Fine. Be filthy, all of you," said Perri as she doled out perfect squares of her asparagus frittata. "Contact cholera. What do I care?"

Sadie lifted a celery stick off her plate, waved it through the air at her mother, and declared, *"Petrificus Totalus!"*

"Anyone care for an omega-three-rich Nova and bagel?" asked Mike, a platter in each hand.

"I do, thanks," said Olympia, suddenly ravenous.

After Mike served Olympia, he moved on to his father-in-law. "And how about you, Bob? I think this everything bagel has your name on it."

"Suppose it can't hurt," he answered.

"And anything to drink with that, sir? Coffee? Water? Defrosted orange juice that looks a little too yellow for my taste?"

"You know, I was just reading that, in certain ancient cultures, the consumption of one's own urine was considered medicinal," said Bob. "I believe the term is 'urophagia.' Apparently, it's quite harmless, assuming it's taken in small amounts and not highly concentrated or laden with bacteria."

"Bob, please," said Carol, making a face.

"Way to be gross, Grandpa," said Aiden, who, in this case, spoke for the rest of the now snickering Hellinger clan.

"You're very welcome," said Bob, smiling brightly.

"I think you mean '*Urine* welcome,'" said Olympia, who, while in her sisters' company and for unclear reasons, often found her sense of humor reverting to that of her two-year-old self.

Perri and Gus appeared to have contracted a similar condition. The two of them suddenly burst into laughter so raucous that it nearly propelled them off their chairs. Olympia joined in. The three sisters twisted and gyrated, clutched their stomachs and shrieked. Why couldn't it always be like this? Olympia wondered and lamented. Why couldn't they all decide to be little kids again, free of ambition, envy, and anxiety? Or was she rewriting history? Had there never been such a time, not even when they were three, five, and seven and building sand castles on the Delaware coast? No doubt Perri had criticized Olympia for failing to achieve the correct water-to-sand ratio, then gone ahead and constructed a sand-based Versailles. Then the waves had washed the whole thing away. And Gus had found a way to take it personally and burst into tears of indignation — and Olympia had just stood there, wondering what she was supposed to do next.

Lola was so exhausted by the day's events that on the train ride back to Brooklyn she fell asleep. Olympia was able to transfer her from lap to stroller to bed without her waking up. With Lola out of the way, Olympia took the opportunity to lavish attention on Clive and feed him a peanut treat. Sometimes she wondered why, in search of a furry low-maintenance pet, she'd gotten a rabbit, not a cat, since rabbits were far harder to house and had shorter life spans too. But having a cat had seemed cliched, even desperate, in a way that a single woman with a bunny wasn't. Also, she'd recently learned from a magazine that cats were actually vicious predators who endangered the world's rare bird populations. So now she could feel righteous, too, about keeping a pet that essentially did nothing all day long but lie on the bathroom floor, twitching its nose, nibbling on carrots, shitting pellets, and looking cute.

After cracking open a bottle of Pinot Noir, Olympia lit a cigarette (she tried not to smoke, but sometimes she didn't try hard enough) and called up the Huffington Post. As she inhaled and imbibed, she read a blog post about how the country's milk supply was being tainted by the use of the bovine growth hormone rBGH. Outraged, she left a lengthy "comment" on the website of the Monsanto Corporation (creator of rBGH and alleged payer-off of the FDA), accusing the powers that be of purposefully giving kids cancer. When had she become such a strident environmentalist? she wondered. Also, when had she become such a hothead? Also, if she cared about the planet, did she have to stop smoking? Did it matter that her cigarettes were made of organic tobacco and additive free? And what if she smoked only two per week? Also, was it criminal that she didn't always recycle tinfoil and plastic take-out containers — and still loved Phil Collins's *Greatest Hits* album?

After a while, Olympia got out her watercolors and worked on her portrait of her friends Rick and Carli, who were Couple #4 on her list of Matchmaking Triumphs. If there was one setup of which Olympia was most proud, it was them. Two years earlier and in the space of one month, Carli had lost her job as Sylvester Stallone's personal art adviser and been diagnosed with lupus. Meanwhile, Olympia's other friends had given up hope of Rick, a war photographer and famous "wild man," ever settling down. Now Carli was three months pregnant; Rick had switched to sports photography; and the two were buying a three-story Victorian house in Ditmas Park. If the painting came out well, Olympia planned to have it framed and give it to them as their wedding present. Although Olympia struggled to be close to her family, she prided herself on being the Ultimate Friend.

But it was getting late, and she had work in the morning. Before she turned out the lights, Olympia checked her email one final time. To her astonishment, she had a new message from Dawn Calico-Cronin. It read as follows:

Hey, sexy. Hope you had a fab new year's. Just wanted to let you know that I left Park Ave Cryo to pursue a masters in accounting. Also, since I'm no longer bound by bank policy, I thought I'd throw you a bone re #6103. Or, shall I say a boner? (Har, har.) On that note, apparently your man used to model skivvies for Sears. Bottom line: all of us at the bank had HUGE crushes on the guy—with an accent on the huge. ☺ Seriously, we used to have a joke around the office about volunteering to help him deliver his sample. LOL. Also, he had a little tattoo of a skull on his upper arm. I know because I administered his blood tests. Real name was something like Randy. From the west—maybe Vegas? At some point I believe he was enrolled in a continuing ed class in sports management at Columbia— hence, the Ivy League creds. Hope all is well with you and your chickadee. Good luck with your search! XOXO, D

Olympia felt like a beach ball that had rolled over a rusty nail. *Randy the well-endowed underwear model—with the tattoo of a skull?! From Las Vegas???!!!* In one email, Dawn Cronin had effectively destroyed her entire picture, however inflated, of #6103, the earnest, well-mannered Deerfield- and Yale-educated young cardiologist. What's more, the woman had offered just enough information to tantalize Olympia's imagination without actually providing her with any tangible leads. She rued the day she'd ever asked Dawn for help. She blamed herself for not being happy with what she had.

Nonetheless, the next day at work, in between writing and editing a press release, Olympia found herself obsessively Googling various combinations of the words, "Randy," "model," "Sears," and "underwear," and, perhaps not surprisingly, coming up with nothing.

2

To everyone's relief, Bob's biopsy in January had come back negative for malignancy. The test indicated a relatively benign case of prostatitis. Since he continued to have difficulty urinating and his enlarged prostate appeared not to respond to medication, however, his doctors had recommended surgery to shrink the offending gland. An appointment had been made for early March. And now Perri was being asked to take time out of her already impossibly crazed schedule to drive him and Carol to and from the hospital and, on the return trip, help wheel or walk Bob out to the car. At least, that was how it had seemed to Perri when, the night before, she'd spoken on the phone to Gus and Olympia. Neither had point-blank asked Perri to retrieve their father. But both had alerted her to the near impossibility of getting out of the city until midafternoon at the earliest. After much prodding, they'd both agreed to come out after lunch.

Perri didn't necessarily mind doing a favor for her parents. Being the Good Daughter was as important to her as being a good mother. She might even have enjoyed the break from the daily grind. What she objected to was her sisters both assuming that she'd be there whenever it was necessary. Perri felt that, while Olympia and Gus were incredibly different, they had one thing in common: self-absorption on an epic scale. *They take me for granted,* Perri thought for the umpteenth time as she pulled into her parents' driveway to pick up her father.

A three-note text alert interrupted her thoughts. She put the car in park, lifted her phone from her bag, and scanned the screen.

Want to see you—when?, Perri read in the front seat—and found her heart beating louder than it probably should have been.

The text had been sent by Roy Marley, her college boyfriend before Mike. The dreadlocked son of a dentist, he'd been the only African American member of the druggie fraternity, where he'd played the role of both token and totem, especially after someone spread the rumor, later proved false, that he was the son of reggae legend Bob Marley. He and Perri had dated for three months of her sophomore year, at which point he'd dumped her without explanation. Twenty years later, he'd found her on Facebook and sent her a message that said, Yo, Hellinger, what's up? Still think of the GREAT TIMES we had together. Things had escalated from there.

In the past week, they'd texted or emailed at least three times a day. Perri couldn't stop hitting Reply. She couldn't stop checking to see if Roy had replied to her reply, either. She'd be in the middle of a business call to Mexico or China and, instead of concentrating on the manufacture of velveteen hangers, she'd be checking her BlackBerry. Every text of Roy's felt like vindication, proof positive that he'd been crazy about her after all and regretted having split. Was that it? Or was Perri looking for affirmation in some larger sense — affirmation that she was still attractive, still young? Roy was now a doctor, divorced with two kids and living in Bethesda, Maryland.

Maybe not such a good idea, she typed. Then she pressed Send, only to be overcome by a wave of regret and fear that Roy would lose interest and/or give up, followed by guilt and shame that she didn't actually want him to do so.

Here she had all she'd ever dreamed of. Not just a loyal husband but three beautiful and healthy children; her own company; prime real estate; a still bountiful if recently attenuated stock portfolio (thanks to the stock market crash of early '09); and possibly the most organized shoe closets, toy bins, and flatware drawer in all of Westchester County. Never mind the Lexus she was driving, or the side-by-side his-and-her sinks in their renovated master bath. Except, suddenly, things weren't that perfect anymore. Mike had lost his job at the beginning of the year. And while Perri could tell herself he was a victim of the Great Recession, she secretly knew otherwise. The mass layoffs had taken place the year before. In all likelihood, the bank was simply clearing out its least productive rung, just as a gardener clears dead wood in early spring. It humiliated Perri to think of her husband as fitting into that category. Her identity depended on them both being winners in the game of life. She found it especially unsettling to think that *she* might be the more successful one of the two. Perri considered herself to be a feminist — to a point. But for a marriage to work, didn't the husband still need to be the chief breadwinner?

For another thing, it had been nearly three months since she and Mike had had sex. And the scary part was: Perri didn't actually miss it. Vibrators, she'd found, made far more efficient partners than husbands did. They didn't require you to look good; or produce vowel-rich soundtracks; or feel self-conscious about how long it was taking you to climax. Yet she feared the things that her abstinence portended. She'd once read an article in *Vanity Fair* magazine about a Greenwich, Connecticut, society family in which the matriarch had opined that the key to a happy marriage was lots of sex with one's husband. The quote had stuck with her. Because while it had been a long time since Perri and Mike had had *a lot* of sex, until recently they'd at least had *some*. Which is to say, twice a month on Saturday night after their biweekly dinner date. It was a schedule that had seemed to suit both of them. It wasn't as if they'd just met — far from it. And they were always short of sleep: if Noah didn't wake up crying, his pacifier missing, Sadie would appear like a ghost in the doorway of their bedroom at four a.m., claiming to have had a bad dream and determined to climb under their covers, splay her limbs, elbow them in the face — and ruin any hope of a good night's rest. (Aiden, god bless him, slept as if he were in a coma.)

Plus, while Mike had been employed by Credit Suisse, he'd had to be at his desk by eight at the latest. Which meant that he'd had to leave the house by six thirty. But ever since he'd been laid off — ever since he'd been able to sleep in — he'd only wanted to cuddle. And Perri hadn't been able to find the words to ask him why. This was partly because she found talking about sex to be mortifying and partly because she feared the answer was that he no longer found her attractive. Not that she could blame him if he did. After three pregnancies and nursing marathons, she felt like a battered boat, its sail loose and tattered, its ropes frayed. Where her large breasts had once been a source of pride and embarrassment in equal parts, now they were only a source of embarrassment—especially since they'd begun to point south. She'd thought about getting a "lift," but it seemed so desperate. Also, she was petrified of being unconscious. How could she control things if she weren't awake? In her late twenties, when she'd had an ovarian cyst removed, Perri had needed a Valium just to enter the hospital.

In truth, Perri didn't necessarily find Mike any more attractive than he found her. Though it wasn't the early signs of middle-aged spread that failed to put her in the mood; it was the fact that he snored and refused even to discuss it with a doctor. It was also that he'd officially taken over childcare duties on Tuesdays. (The other four days of the week, the family employed a Colombian nanny named Dolores.) Though how Mike *actually* spent the nine hours that Perri was in her midtown Manhattan office was another matter. From what she could tell, he filled the morning by shopping for dumbbells and free weights on the Internet, while Noah sat at his feet, drawing on the carpet with ballpoint pens he'd found lying around the house—until it was time for both their naps. Later, Mike would take Noah to go pick up Sadie and Aiden from school. After that, the TV would go on and wouldn't go off again until Perri came home—only to find a sink full of dishes and no milk in the fridge. And for this, her husband seemed to expect a medal! For this, he called himself Superdad and would tell anyone who'd listen that losing his job had been a "blessing in disguise," allowing him to spend the "quality time" with his family that he'd always wanted to spend.

Not that Mike's domestic failings were anything new. But when he'd worked longer hours than she did, Perri had had no expectations that he could possibly disappoint. He wasn't there, so how could he be expected to have stopped and shopped at the

Stop and Shop? The irony was that when Mike had first announced that he'd been laid off, Perri had been secretly relieved. He'd been gone so much the previous few years—had rarely made it home before the kids' bedtime. Now, though, she couldn't wait for him to go back to work. But he'd insisted that he was in no hurry, and that his severance package had been generous enough to buy them both time. He also said he'd rather get a live-in housekeeper and nanny than listen to Perri bitch and moan at him about babysitting for the next sixteen years. But she didn't want some stranger living in her house!

It was also possible that she didn't want to give up the right to complain about how much she did (that Mike didn't appreciate), from making lunches, to organizing PTA Visiting Artist committee events, to packing and unpacking and repacking backpacks, to removing the plastic wrapping from juice-box six-packs, to applying Band-Aids to semifictional booboos, to spraying and slathering sunscreen, to photocopying birth certificates, to filling out permission slips in which emergency contacts had to be named four separate times and primary phone numbers another three. (As if the repetition alone would prevent anything bad from ever happening.) There were also stroller tires that needed air, and special soccer cleats, and ballet tights, and violin chin rests that were unavailable locally and had to be tracked down online. Laundry too—endless laundry, mountains upon mountains of balled-up socks and sweats. (Perri could press Warm/Large/Start in her sleep.) And while it was true that Perri didn't *have* to make her own mayonnaise, Aiden preferred it to the store-bought kind, especially in his tuna fish salad sandwiches. And, of course, there were toys blanketing the floor space of the house each night—football fields' worth of plastic gizmos that had been made in Chinese

factories for the benefit of American children, who could apparently never have enough of them. Perri occasionally thought of
a photograph she'd seen of Palestinian boys of eight or nine in
the Gaza Strip, playing handball in a dirt lot. The boys hadn't
seemed bored at all. And what if the happiest kids on earth
were the ones who didn't have any toys?

Pulling herself together, Perri got out of the car and set off
up the slate path to her childhood home. Her cell phone pinged
again. She looked down, but it had started to flurry, and the
precipitation made it difficult to read the screen. Hunching
over, she wiped it with her glove, then squinted into the glare:

u know you want me, she finally made out—and nearly
jumped out of her Wellingtons.

u r insane, she typed frantically, her fingers stiffening in the
cold.

But as she rang the bell, she had to wonder if she was talking
not about Roy but about herself.

3

OLYMPIA HAD PROMISED HER SISTERS that she'd arrive in Hastings at three thirty at the latest. But it was close to four thirty when the train she was on pulled into the station. She felt guilty, of course—but maybe not that guilty. It wasn't as if she could just leave work after lunch. Also, their father wasn't having open-heart surgery. As Olympia understood it, it was a routine procedure. In truth, she'd only come out to Westchester to avoid the censure of Perri, who'd given her a guilt trip on the phone the night before about not helping out, even as she'd insisted that she was the only one who could handle Carol and Bob. Though it was probably also true that some escapist or standoffish impulse in Olympia made her particularly unhelpful on days like these. In any case, she was here now. Olympia stepped onto the platform and looked around her.

Between the train tracks and the Hudson lay the scourge of her hometown—namely, the remnants of two possibly toxic factories, both of them now enclosed by a barbed-wire fence. The shell of one, the Anaconda Copper Wire and Cable

Company, had always reminded Olympia of a giant hunk of Parmesan cheese that had been painted black. The other one, reputed to be more noxious, had been flattened and paved over, but nobody who knew anything about Hastings-on-Hudson had been fooled. (It was the newcomers who were pushing for a riverside park.) Zinsser Chemical, producer of dyes, pigments, and photography chemicals, had made a mess of the site. Ironically enough, factory founder Frederick Zinsser's name lingered in the form of an idyllic suburban park off Edgar's Lane which featured a jungle gym, baseball field, and community garden. It was by the lamb's ears that Olympia had had her first kiss back in junior high courtesy of Billy Rudolfo.

The house in which Olympia had been raised, and in which her parents still lived, was a short walk from the station — up steep West Main Street, now home to a chichi hair salon and French restaurant; past the public library, with its sweeping views of the Hudson; then down Maple Avenue, with its elegant and well-preserved Carpenter Gothic houses with their upside-down V embellishments. From there, it was a left onto dead-ended Edmarth Place. The Hellingers lived one house in from the corner. At the end of the block, you could see straight across the river to the Palisades. Rectangular, striated, and a rich shade of brown, the section of rock that faced Hastings always reminded Olympia of the Russell Stover chocolates that her great-aunt Helen, famous for her piano legs and thunderous laugh, used to bring over for the holidays.

The block's other distinguishing feature was that every one of its porch-fronted late Victorians was the mirror image of the one across the street. Or, at least, they had been until people started adding on eat-in kitchens and extra baths. As a child, Olympia had become obsessed with what she imagined to be her "shadow house" across the street and, by extension, "shadow life" — as the deaf daughter of the Lumberts, a children's book illustrator and UN translator, who kept to themselves. Every morning, just before eight, Victoria Lumbert, who had yellow-blond pigtails, would climb aboard a mysterious school bus. Olympia never found out where she went. And then, one day, a moving truck came, and the Lumberts vanished forever.

It was Gus who answered the bell — looking marginally spiffier than usual, in black corduroys, a white oxford, and a men's black suit jacket. Apparently, Carol and Bob were still at the hospital. "Sorry I'm late," said Olympia. "Work was crazy."

"Was it 'impossibly crazed'? Oh, sorry — that's Perri's favorite expression," said Gus.

"No, just crazy," said Olympia, rolling her eyes.

"Fisticuffs broke out over the correct way to fry a wiener schnitzel?"

"Something like that," said Olympia, still deciding whether to laugh along or to be mortally offended by Gus's clear mockery of her professional life. "Oh, and nice to see you too."

"Likewise," said Gus. Olympia hung up her coat, then followed her younger sister into the living room. In the twenty years since Olympia had left home, her parents had made minimal changes to the decor. It was still a light-challenged mix of wobbly antiques that had been passed down through the family and "contemporary" pieces purchased at Bloomingdale's in the Galleria mall in White Plains in the 1980s, upholstery now fraying and veneers beginning to chip. Paperback novels that hadn't been opened in twenty-five years (*Watership Down, The Thorn Birds*) filled every last air pocket of the bookcases. Ethnic tchotchkes cluttered every available surface. As empty nesters, Bob and Carol had taken one trip through the unfashionable countries of Eastern Europe (Bulgaria, Albania), with a stop-over in Athens to see the Parthenon; and another trip through West Africa. The living room walls were deep maroon and decorated with blobby pink monotypes, which were by Carol's sister, Suzy, and reminiscent of Rorschach inkblot tests or mutant udders, depending on your perspective. For as long as Olympia could remember, the house had smelled faintly yet inexplicably of rubber cement.

Perri sat cross-legged in Grandpa Bert's old Morris chair, thumbing through the *Times Magazine*. The cover story appeared to be about kids with peanut allergies. Hadn't they run a similar story only twelve months before? "Hey," said Olympia, taking a seat on the old leather sofa opposite her big sister.

"Hi," Perri said curtly and without looking up. She was clearly in a grumpy mood. Not that Olympia could blame her. "How did it go at the hospital?" she asked.

"Fine, I'm about to head back there to retrieve them."

"Oh — cool. Thanks."

Perri didn't answer.

"So, how was Dad going in?" Olympia tried again.

"Dad was fine. It was Mom who was the problem. She'd been there approximately four minutes before she started complaining that no one had been in to see her husband yet, and what was taking so long?"

"That sounds like Mom."

"Tell me about it."

"Well, I appreciate you taking them," said Olympia, trying to be conciliatory.

"I just had to postpone two meetings and a conference," said Perri. "No big deal."

"Sorry about that," said Olympia, who didn't appreciate being guilted, even when she felt guilty. "I really need to get my license renewed. Though I probably couldn't have gotten out of work any earlier. We have a big concert this evening at the museum, which I'm obviously missing to be here."

"It's the first night of the Falco reunion tour?" suggested Gus. "He was the first punk ever to set foot on this earth," she began to sing. "Amadeus, Amadeus, Amadeus, Amadeus."

"No, it's an experimental chamber music ensemble from Vienna," said Olympia, sighing. "And for the record, the Falco guy died in a car accident."

"I didn't know that," said Gus.

"Well, now you do."

Perri's eyes shifted from her magazine to Olympia's feet. "New shoes?" she asked.

"Sort of. I got them at a consignment store in Brooklyn." She angled her leg so Perri would have a better view. "What do you think? They're Chloé."

"Not bad." Perri wrinkled her nose. "But did you spray them with something before you put them on?"

"Not all of us are germaphobes in need of institutionalizing," said Olympia. She was going to add "or rich" but refrained, money being a far more fraught subject between them than mildew.

"They're *your* feet," said Perri, shrugging.

"Well, in case anyone's curious," began Gus, "I spent the first half of the day trying and failing to convince a notoriously sexist judge to issue a restraining order on behalf of a client of mine who's walking around with a huge black eye." She took a seat on the other end of the sofa. "All the fucker cares about is letting the kids see their father, even though their father is a violent drug dealer who has never done anything for them." Gus tutted with derision.

"You don't think the kids should be able to see their dad?" asked Perri, flipping a page.

"I don't give a flying cojone about their father!" Gus replied with a quick laugh.

Olympia felt an unexpected surge of warmth toward her younger sister. "If the guy was violent with her, can't he be charged in criminal court?" she asked.

"He could," said Gus. "But my client wants to avoid that situation."

"That's so weird," said Perri, her eyes back on her magazine. "Basically, no one in Israel is allergic to peanuts."

"Weird," Olympia deadpanned.

Perri motioned with her chin at a cardboard box on the coffee table. "Speaking of food, Sadie made some cupcakes as a get-well present for Dad. But I don't see him eating a dozen of them just after surgery. So help yourself."

"I wouldn't mind, actually. Thanks," said Olympia, happy both for the change of topic and for something sweet to snack on. She opened the box and discovered a dozen mini cupcakes, each with a perfectly executed red heart drawn atop its chocolate icing. Within each heart outline, tiny alternating silver and pink block letters spelled GET WELL. It was clear that Sadie had had some help (and then some). When did Perri find the time to do stuff like this? Olympia wondered. And why did she bother? "No trans fats, I trust," Olympia went on, somehow reluctant ever to give Perri the full thrust of her respect or appreciation.

"Only homemade buttermilk," said Perri.

Olympia bit into the cake, and said, "Mm."

Perri put down her magazine and stood up. "Well, since I'm the obese sister and have no willpower and it was my daughter who made them, I'm going to have another one!" She jammed her hand into the box.

"Stop," said Olympia.

"Excuse me?!" said Perri, her mouth already crammed full.

"I mean, stop saying you're fat!" said Olympia.

"Why? It's true," said Perri.

"It's not true. You look fine," said Olympia, taking momentary pity.

"Boooorrrrringnoonecares," muttered Gus, who, like Olympia, was slim without much effort.

"Anyway." Perri dusted imaginary cupcake crumbs from her lap and stood up. "I should head back to St. John's. Dad is probably already out of surgery."

"I can come help if you want," said Olympia.

"No need," said Perri. "If I'm gone long, maybe you guys can order something for dinner — if that's not too much to handle."

She had to sneak in that last dig, Olympia thought. (And Round Two goes to Perri!) "Not too much at all," said Olympia.

Perri double-wound her pashmina around her neck. Then she walked out. The click-clack of her low-heeled pumps grew fainter as she neared the front door.

4

As Gus watched the headlights of Perri's SUV fade into tiny suns, then vanish into black holes, a feeling of dread overtook her. How would she and Olympia fill the time while Perri was gone? Gus suspected that she knew more about her middle sister than anybody. Yet she also felt she no longer knew how to talk to her, or even what to talk about. In recent years, Olympia had become so unreachable, so cold ultimately — except maybe with Lola. She was like a house with no doors or windows: it was impossible to get inside to see if it was even heated.

Gus knew she could be bad-tempered and confrontational. But at least she had emotions! At least she admitted to being a member of the human race. These days, she found it far easier getting along with Perri than with Olympia, even though she and Perri had almost nothing in common and much less shared history since, growing up, they'd been nearly four years apart. But that didn't mean Gus was above making fun of Perri to Olympia. "I'm sorry — I love Perri," she began, recalling that

Olympia never tired of critiquing their oldest sister's outfits. "But what the *hell* is she wearing today?"

"Don't ask me. She has terrible taste in clothes," concurred Olympia, a half smile already in evidence.

"Like, who wears a fucking skirt suit to go to the hospital?!" Gus went on. "Unless they're, like, a drug rep or something."

"Perri, apparently." Olympia's half smile had already turned into a full-blown grin.

"Remember that time she was wearing those jodhpurs, or whatever they were, and Dad asked her if she was going to a Halloween party?"

"He thought she was dressed as a pirate, or something."

"Didn't he ask her why she had no eye patch?"

Olympia burst into bosom-vibrating guffaws, gratifying Gus, who remembered that her middle sister had always had a wonderful laugh, deep, hiccupy, and, well, warm. Maybe she was still human after all, Gus thought. Keen to leave their conversation at a high point, she reached for the remote and proceeded to flick through a dozen channels. "So, what do you say?" she said. "*Animal Cops: Houston,* local news, or a mysteriously Tivo'd *The Bachelor?*"

"Whatever you want," said Olympia, who wasn't a big fan of television.

"Well, I vote for *The Bachelor.*"

"Fine with me."

"What? You don't think homosexuals are allowed to watch heterosexual shows?"

"I didn't say anything!" cried Olympia.

"But I could tell you were thinking that," said Gus, aware that she sounded vaguely pathetic. These days, something about Olympia's very presence made Gus defensive. Maybe it was the fact that, even when her sister was physically there, she gave off the impression that her mind was somewhere else, somewhere she'd rather be. "Actually, I can't tell anything about you," Gus went on.

"What?" said Olympia, squinching up her face.

"Never mind," said Gus, embarrassed.

The sisters watched in silence as a young woman with a blond ponytail dabbed at her mascara-caked eyes and declared, "I would have bet my life savings I was getting a rose." Then the camera cut to the bachelor himself, a smug-looking guy in a polo shirt with swooshy side-parted hair. "That last rose ceremony was seriously one of the hardest decisions I've ever made," he said with a weary laugh. "I mean, Kristy is a great girl — fun, warm, superhot. I guess I just didn't feel the connection." After that segment ended, another contestant came on the screen — a horsey brunette with visible gums. The TV identified her as "Debbie from Delray Beach, FL." "Speaking of Debbies," said Olympia. "Heard anything from yours lately?"

"We've texted a few times," said Gus, somehow surprised that her sister even remembered Debbie's name.

"Any chance of getting back together?"

"Zero."

"Sorry to hear it."

"She and the new lady love are adopting a baby from North Korea, or something."

Olympia squinted at her. "Are you serious about North Korea?"

"It might be Myanmar or Thailand. I can't remember. Anyway, I'm over it." And it was true, or mostly true. Gus's ego was still wounded. But reflecting on the relationship, she'd come to the conclusion that all she and Debbie did was bicker, with

Debbie accusing Gus of being needy and demanding, and criticizing everything she did; and with Gus accusing Debbie of not being supportive, not taking Gus's work as seriously as she took her own, and caring only about herself. What's more, Debbie rarely told Gus she loved her. Plus, Gus was always worrying about Debbie getting killed on her Harley-Davidson. And she'd only ever read the introduction to the book that Gus had spent five years slaving over, *On Dykes and Documents: Towards a Lesbian Legal Practice* (Routledge, 2009). Which is maybe why Gus's hurt over the split was conflated with relief. At least, that was what she told herself. A part of Gus felt as if she'd been made to sit through some shrieky, seven-hour-long German opera. And the curtain was finally, thankfully coming down—even as another part of her physically ached at the thought of Debbie's muscular arms wrapped around somebody else's midriff...

"Well, that's good," said Olympia.

"I guess," said Gus, gaining nerve. She glanced quickly at her sister. "What about you? Any handsome young Captain von Trapps on the scene?"

Olympia seemed startled by the question. "Me?" she said.

It was one of Gus's pet peeves—how no one in the family ever dared ask Olympia anything about her personal life. As if it were *that* much more important than everyone else's. At least, that was the way Olympia acted—as if she were sleeping with the president. "Who do you think I'm talking to?" she said. "The wall?!"

"Oh, sorry," said Olympia. "Well, in answer to your question— not really." She paused, looked away. "Though I got an email last week from my ex. Which was kind of strange since things between us didn't exactly end on a good note."

"Which ex?" asked Gus, amazed by the rare admission.

Olympia visibly swallowed before she replied, "Patrick. I don't think I ever told you about him."

"I met him at your housewarming party, like, ten millennia ago," said Gus, who still recalled that Olympia had introduced him as her "good friend" and that he'd been wearing a wedding ring. (Did she think Gus was that stupid?) Why did Olympia not seem to realize that sisters could tell almost everything about each other's feelings simply by observing the tilt of each other's heads, the set of each other's mouths?

"Oh, right," said Olympia, looking confused.

"So why didn't it end on a good note?" said Gus, longing to hear the truth from Olympia's own lips.

Olympia appeared to hold her breath — before she announced, "Because he was married to someone else." She looked into her lap. "A paraplegic."

The honesty of her sister's answer shocked Gus. "Was married and still is?" she asked.

"I assume so."

"Huh — that sounds complicated," Gus said with a nod. As if learning *this* information, too, for the first time. In fact, in the years since Lola's birth, she'd formulated the working hypothesis, shared with friends and family alike, that No Saint Patrick (as Gus liked to call him behind closed doors) was Lola's "mystery father." There was no other good explanation for Olympia's secrecy and defensiveness on the subject. "So, what did the email say?" Gus pressed on.

"That he wanted to talk to me."

"About what?"

"Unclear."

"And what did *you* say?"

"I didn't answer." Olympia shrugged quickly. "There's nothing left to say. It ended years ago."

"Right."

Olympia cleared her throat imperiously. "I'd appreciate it if you kept this all to yourself."

"You barely told me anything! Also, who am I going to talk to?" said Gus, bristling at having been accused of being a gossip before she'd even gossiped.

"Perri," said Olympia.

"I'm sure she already knows," said Gus, squirming. In fact, it was she who had told their older sister about Olympia's illicit affair. "Perri makes it her business to know everything about everyone. Also, if you haven't seen the guy in five years, or whatever, it's not exactly news."

"Well, I'm pretty sure she doesn't know about my relationship with...Patrick."

"Whatever you say," said Gus. The show cut to a commercial, and the two fell silent. As a Gillette razor traced a slow smooth path down a disembodied jaw, Gus felt newly riled by Olympia's obsession with privacy. It struck her as not just ridiculous but presumptuous, even self-aggrandizing. "You were always into married guys," she blurted out. It was unkind, maybe. But wasn't it true?

"Ex*cuse* me?!" said Olympia, clearly offended.

"Remember Mr. Grunholz, the English teacher dude in high school with the leather jackets? Weren't you in love with him, or something?" Gus could no longer remember the specifics, but she knew that something embarrassing had happened between him and Olympia that had led their mother to intervene and the man to be let go.

"In love with him?!" scoffed Olympia. "Hardly. He was a

total lech who was always hitting on all his students!" Olympia, who rarely appeared to be rattled, seemed suddenly undone, her mouth slack, her eyes wild. "I had nothing to do with him."

Gus immediately regretted the gambit. As much as she longed to strip the layers (and ego) from her sister, there was something strangely upsetting about seeing Olympia look so vulnerable. "Oh, maybe that was it," Gus said, even as she strongly doubted the veracity of Olympia's version of events. Per Gus's recollections, at the very least there had been heavy petting against or inside Mr. Grunholz's car.

More to the point, Gus couldn't understand why Olympia wasn't proud to have been a teenage slut. By all accounts, Olympia had lost her virginity at sixteen to a nineteen-year-old lifeguard at the local pool. Gus's teenage love life, on the other hand, had mainly consisted of nursing impossible crushes on straight girls while listening to K. D. Lang's "Constant Craving."

The commercial break was over. The Bachelor and his five remaining girlfriends were boarding a yacht. "Oh, come on," said Gus, now keen to make amends. "That woman is *not* wearing a bathing suit. That's like a clothesline with doilies."

"I've always hated that word — *doily*," said Olympia.

Gus could tell her sister was relieved to find the conversation turning to people they didn't know. (Gus was relieved, too.) "Still not as bad as *ointment*," she offered.

"*Goiter* is up there, too."

"And *tushy*. God, I hate that word so much."

"It's still not as bad as *heiny*," said Olympia.

Somehow, they made it through the hour.

5

A T THE SOUND OF Perri's Lexus grinding up the
gravel in the driveway, Olympia went outside to
help escort their father from the car. Emerging
from the backseat, Bob seemed as wobbly as a
three-legged chair. But Perri reported that the surgery had gone
well. He was also cogent enough to be mumbling, "The plea-
sures of oxycodone — not to be discounted!" Even so, Olympia
found it jarring to see her dad looking so helpless and frail. The
two of them rarely exchanged more than two sentences in a
row. Moreover, in the twenty years since she'd left home, Olympia had no memory of Bob ever calling her. (Though on occasion he'd answer the phone when she called Hastings, and say,
"Hello, sweetheart. I'll pass the phone to Mom.") And yet, she
somehow loved him more than she'd ever loved another man.
These were her thoughts as she helped transport him into the
house, then up the stairs, where he collapsed onto his bed and
dozed off with a light snore.

The four Hellinger women gathered in the kitchen, where
Carol shook her head and declared, "A genius the man may be.

But he's a terrible patient! All he did was complain. You'd think it was something actually serious."

"I didn't hear him complain once," said Perri.

"He *did* have to get surgery," said Olympia.

"Fine. Gang up on me, all of you," snapped Carol, her lower lip suddenly quivery.

"No one's ganging up on you, Mom," said Olympia, sighing. On top of being sharp-tongued, her mother was incredibly sensitive.

"Whatever you say," said Carol. Lips now puckered, she hooked her "pocketbook" over her shoulder. "Now if you all will excuse me, I'm going out for some fresh air. I've been cooped up in that awful hospital all day."

"You're going out for a walk now?" asked Olympia. "It's already getting dark."

"I'm not going to turn into a vampire!" She harrumphed. "This is a new one — having to get permission from my daughters to take a walk."

Olympia rolled her eyes but said nothing more. Had her mother been this petulant while they were growing up? It was hard to remember.

"If you're going out anyway, maybe you can save me a trip and drop Dad's prescription off at the pharmacy," said Perri.

"If I still have it, I'll be happy to drop it off." Carol dug her hand into her bag and pulled out her reading glasses, followed by a crumpled slip of paper, which she proceeded to uncrumple, then squint at, before announcing, "No doubt for some kind of sugar pills. But as you wish." She deposited the slip back into her bag. Then she turned to her eldest daughter, and said, "Why don't you go home, Perri. You've done enough already."

"It's fine. I'll wait with Dad until you come back," she said.

"Gus and I can handle it," said Olympia.

"It's *fine!*" Perri declared a little more aggressively this time. Apparently, the Queen of all Dutiful Daughters wasn't ready to abdicate her title just yet, Olympia thought. Perri glanced at her watch. "I'm going to miss Parent-Teacher Conference Night, anyway. Mike will have to report back."

"I didn't know he got home that early from work," said Olympia.

"He was laid off a few weeks ago," Perri replied matter-of-factly.

"What?!" said Olympia, shocked and also a little bit hurt. She may have hated sharing facts about her own life — having them shared, too — but she still expected to be first in the loop when it came to major events in the lives of her sisters. "Why didn't you tell me earlier?" she asked.

"I guess I forgot," said Perri, shrugging.

"So I'm the last person to know?" Olympia turned from Gus to Carol, neither of whom reacted, suggesting to Olympia that the answer was "yes."

"Well, I'm really sorry for Mike — and for you, too," said Olympia, wondering if oversight was to blame. Or was it possible that Perri was somehow embarrassed to tell Olympia? And, if so, why? It wasn't as if Olympia had never been fired from a job — far from it. Or maybe that was the point: Perri didn't want Olympia to think that she and Mike had anything even remotely in common.

"He was looking to change jobs, anyway," Perri said quickly. "And he got seven months of severance. Anyway!" She turned her back, apparently done with the topic. "I'm going to check on Dad."

"And I'm going to check that the sky still exists," said Carol, lowering her beret over her ears.

"See you soon," said Olympia.

The back door went thwwack as Carol closed it behind her.

Olympia and her sisters sat at the kitchen table, snacking on stale Ritz crackers they'd found in the cupboard and talking about health-care reform (Perri had mixed feelings about the "public option"); whether Lady Gaga was derivative of Madonna (Olympia thought yes; Gus thought they were both "plastic poseurs," although she appreciated Gaga's gay-friendly message; Perri wasn't entirely sure who Lady Gaga was); and old classmates whose lives had taken tragic turns. "Remember that kid, Jimmy Trevor?" said Gus, reaching for the nut cracker. She splintered a walnut. Carol still bought them with the shell on. Pieces flew by Perri's face and into the sink.

"Jesus! Watch it!" said Perri, palm raised in self-protection. "That almost hit me in the eye!"

"Oh, sorry," said Gus.

"Who's *Jimmy Trevor?*" asked Olympia, even though she sort of knew.

"Oh, come on!" cried Gus. "You went to junior prom with his brother, David. Jimmy was two years behind him. Hello?"

"Maybe I remember him."

"Why do you always pretend not to know people from your past?"

Olympia wasn't sure herself. "I don't," she said, attempting to match Perri's superior tone with a disaffected one of her own. "It's just—do we always have to talk about high school?"

"No, we don't always have to talk about high school," said Gus, clearly miffed. "I just thought you'd want to know that

Jimmy Trevor enlisted in the fucking Marine Corps a few years ago and got sent to Iraq, where he recently lost both of his *legs!*"

"Ohmygod, that's *horrible,*" said Olympia, feeling guilty. "Poor guy."

Twenty minutes went by. Then a half hour. Then an hour. Then an hour and twenty minutes. They'd covered nearly everyone in their high school and extended family, along with all the major stories in the current news cycle. Still, there was no sign of Carol. *Miss Clavel turned on the light and said, "Something is not right!"... Miss Clavel ran fast and faster.* The words from Lola's favorite picture book flitted through Olympia's head. "What the heck happened to Mom?" she said.

"I'm sure she'll be back in a few minutes," said Gus.

"I'm going out to look for her," said Perri, rising from her chair.

"I'm coming with you," said Olympia, standing too.

"You guys need to chill out," said Gus. "She's probably looking at the sunset or something."

"The sun went in more than an hour ago," snapped Perri, grabbing her keys off the countertop.

"Then there's a long line at the pharmacy, or something. Friday-night Xanax prescription refills. Everyone's stocking up for the weekend."

"You really think Mom would spend an hour waiting in line at the pharmacy?" said Olympia, chin lowered and one eyebrow raised as she fitted her arms through the sleeves of her coat. "She already told us she thought the prescription was for sugar pills."

"Well, I think you guys are making too big a deal out of it," Gus called after them.

By then, Olympia and Perri were already out the door, Olympia without her coat.

As Olympia waited for Perri to unlock the doors to the Lexus, her shoulders shimmied involuntarily in the cold. It had been awhile since she and Perri had gone anywhere together. The SUV was enormous. Sitting up high in the passenger seat next to her big sister, Olympia recalled distant memories of cruising through the neighborhood with Perri in Carol's then ten-year-old Toyota Corolla, hoping to catch sight of someone's crush playing basketball in his driveway. Even when the crush had been Perri's — which is to say, even when Perri and her on-again, off-again boyfriend-for-all-four-years-of-high-school, Andy Lyons, were off again — her sister had acted as if she were doing Olympia a favor, chauffeuring her around town. (Nineteen months older than Olympia, Perri had gotten her driver's license first.)

Yet Olympia had always suspected that her yearbook-editing, flute-playing, field hockey stick–wielding, student-government president sister had enjoyed their pointless, directionless, résumé-building-less jaunts more than she'd let on — jaunts that frequently concluded with Diet Coke and large fries orders at the McDonald's take-out window on Central Ave. and Perri's beloved George Michael on the tape deck, singing, *You gotta have faith, faith, faith.* Olympia had enjoyed their outings, too. In her official version of her childhood, her older sister had been bossy, patronizing, and hopelessly uncool. In the possibly realer version, Olympia had missed Perri more than she'd ever thought she would after Perri left for Penn. She could still picture her in her "first day of college" outfit — pressed Levi's with carefully torn knees, a white polo shirt with the collar up, and a navy blue blazer with gold nautical buttons draped over one arm. Olympia never understood how her sister kept her rope bracelet so clean.

It had also been Perri who had comforted Olympia after the whole Mr. Grunholz mess, albeit in Perri's characteristically abrasive and peremptory way. "I'm sorry," she'd told Olympia. "But the man smells like liverwurst. Also, he has a weird-shaped head. I don't know how you could have gotten naked with him. Anyway, if I were you, I'd take a long shower and pretend it never happened." To Perri's credit, however, that was also the last time she ever mentioned the man, or the incident. Even Mr. Grunholz's eventual firing went uncommented upon by her older sister.

Meanwhile, Olympia had felt guilty and ashamed. Statutory rape laws aside, the blow job she'd given her thirty-eight-year-old English teacher at the age of seventeen in the back of his Pontiac Sunbird in the parking lot behind Temple Beth Shalom had been strictly voluntary. What's more, she'd enjoyed it—if not the actual deed, then the sensation of limitless power it conferred. She'd also enjoyed the sound of Mr. Grunholz's low groans and the sight of his eyeballs rolling back in his head—until she'd made the mistake of telling a friend, who'd told another friend. Eventually, the story had gotten back to her mother, who'd chosen to interpret the situation as one in which a predator had preyed on her beautiful, unsuspecting young daughter. Olympia had done nothing to dispel the notion. Little wonder that Mr. Grunholz had been so furious at her. She still remembered passing him in the hall while the case had been pending before the school board. He'd said nothing, but the look on his face had been of someone who'd been betrayed. Even two decades later, the thought of that unforgiving face still made Olympia shudder.

Gus's casual invocation of the man's name had been cruel and uncalled for, Olympia thought as Perri pulled out of the driveway. Wasn't there a tacit agreement between sisters that certain traumatic events of the past were never to be alluded to again? Olympia had never dared mention Perri's outpatient treatment for OCD and bulimia while she was in college — or Gus's dalliance with self-cutting and speed during late high school.

Perri turned onto Maple Avenue. As she did so, Olympia stole a glance at her older sister's face, at her clenched yet ever so slightly loosening jaw, a double chin that hadn't quite arrived. The sight both fascinated and frightened her. Middle age was sneaking up on them unawares, it seemed. Olympia recalled a black-and-white photograph from the 1940s of her grand-mother and great-aunt, both of them with dark painted lips and short stiff hair peeking out of bizarre hats that resembled airplane neck rests. Not too many years from now, Olympia thought, she and Perri would likely become those unstylish, pity-inducing "ancestors" in the eyes of their own children, and then grandchildren. Maybe they already were? "Where should we go first?" asked Olympia.

"To the pharmacy, obviously," said Perri.

Olympia didn't answer. *Obviously nothing,* she thought irri-tably. Perri was structurally incapable of conceding that she was as clueless as the rest of them about what they were all doing here on earth. And at the same time, it came as a relief just then to be with someone who was willing to keep up the fiction of certainty. "Sounds like a plan," Olympia murmured impassively.

Perri made a left onto Spring Street, then a right onto War-burton. She got only so far. There was a police car parked diago-nally in front of Hastings Prime Meats, its flashers on. The pharmacy was directly across the street. One cop stood to the left of the car directing southbound traffic around the north side of the street. Another stood near a flashlight beam, writing in a notebook, his stance wide. Yellow tape encircled a wide swath of the adjacent sidewalk. "What the hell is this?" said Olympia.

Without answering, Perri jerked the car over into an empty space in front of a hydrant and got out. Olympia followed, her cheeks lowered against the wind.

Upon closer inspection, there were jagged white objects scattered across the sidewalk behind the tape.

Perri approached the scribbling cop. "Excuse me, Officer," she said. "May I ask what happened here?"

The man took his time looking up from his notepad. Finally, he answered, "A streetlamp bulb struck a pedestrian."

Olympia looked up. Sure enough, one of the old-fashioned wrought-iron streetlamps that lined Warburton was missing its opaque white orb. The lamp itself was also leaning at a precarious angle over the sidewalk. "Well, we're looking for our mother, Carol Hellinger," Perri went on. "She was on her way to the pharmacy about an hour and a half ago on foot. She's five foot one with medium-length silver hair. And she was wearing a bright purple winter coat and matching purple beanie—"

"It's more like a beret," interjected Olympia.

"Beret-beanie-whatever," barked Perri, clearly irritated at having been corrected.

The police officer seemed reluctant to divulge any more information. He scribbled some more in his notebook. Then he said, "The victim hasn't been identified yet. She was taken to the ER at St. John's Riverside, fifteen minutes ago. If your mother is missing, I suggest you go to the station and file a missing persons report."

So it was a she, Olympia thought, her stomach tightening around her belt.

"Thank you for the advice," snapped Perri.

"You can't park there," said the policeman, motioning at Perri's car with his lantern jaw.

"We'll be leaving in five minutes after we search the pharmacy for our missing elderly mother!" declared Perri, officious even in a crisis.

Olympia found the description unfair: Carol was only sixty-five. But this time, she didn't dare object.

It seemed that Olympia wasn't the only one feeling cowed by Perri. "You need to move the car in five minutes," the cop mumbled back at her.

"Of course," said Perri, starting across the street.

Again, Olympia followed. The creeping headlights made her feel blind.

The local pharmacy was another of Hastings's f-you's to chain stores, none of which were allowed in the downtown. The first thing you saw when you walked in was an old-fashioned soda fountain complete with chrome stools with vinyl seats. Behind the fountain were the actual health and beauty products, all of them laid out on wooden shelves so pleasing to the eye that even the maxi-pads looked quaint. At the back of the store, next to the drop-off window, was a fish tank featuring Frisbee-sized anemones that, depending on your perspective, looked like cute monster puppets on *Sesame Street* or like extras in an aliens movie. The pharmacists dispensed their magic from behind a loftlike wooden enclosure. Gus must have been right about the Xanax prescriptions, Olympia thought. There were at least ten people milling beneath the loft, all of them looking restless and, well, anxiety-ridden. Or was Olympia projecting her own mental state? It took five minutes to speak to a human being. Finally, Perri got her chance. "Excuse me," she said to the white-coated man behind the counter. "I'm the daughter of one of your customers, Carol Hellinger —"

"Carol Hellinger! Of course." He laughed. "We all get a kick out of Carol when she comes in. She mocks us to our faces. It's really very amusing. *Snake oil salesman.* That's her preferred term of abuse." He laughed again.

"Funny," said Perri. As if it weren't. "Anyway, we're wondering if she came in here an hour ago to fill a prescription for our father."

"Haven't seen her in months," came the response. "But please send her my regards."

"I will," said Perri.

"Let's go," said Olympia, tugging on her sister's sleeve.

Perri took the opportunity to shoot her sister another censorious look. Then she turned back to the pharmacist, and said, "Thank you for your time."

Closing the door to the pharmacy behind them, Olympia was reminded of why she secretly preferred chain stores and the anonymity they promised, especially when filling her own monthly prescription for Zoloft.

They got back in the car. This time, Olympia didn't bother asking her sister where they were going. Perri drove the rest of the way without speaking, or mostly without speaking. At one point, she mumbled, "Could this frigging light take any frigging longer?"

The emergency room was strangely empty but for a few relatives of the injured mulling about with coffees, looking bored or maybe stunned. "We're wondering if a Carol Hellinger was brought in here tonight," Perri asked the receptionist, a large woman with exquisite purple nails.

The receptionist scanned her notes. Then she said, "Hold on, please." With considerable effort, she lifted her body into a standing position. Then she disappeared into a back office. Five minutes later, a "Dr. Grodberg" emerged. He was wearing a bow tie and horn-rim glasses like some parody of a boarding school teacher circa 1950. Except it was 2010, and there was no way he was older than thirty. "Are you the family of Carol Hellinger?" he asked, mispronouncing her last name. As if the final syllable began with a hard *g*.

Olympia felt as if a lozenge had gotten lodged in her throat. Even so, she couldn't stand to let the error slide. "It's Hellin*ger*," she said, with great emphasis on the soft *g*.

"Can you let the man talk?!" said Perri.

Olympia grimaced but said nothing.

"We're her daughters," Perri went on.

Dr. Grodberg cleared his throat and began to explain.

It turned out that the driver of a Coca-Cola truck had been rushing to make a late-day delivery in order to get home in time to celebrate his twentieth wedding anniversary with his wife. While attempting to park, he'd accidentally backed into one of the streetlamps. The impact had bent the pole and caused such a disturbance that the glass orb had slid off its base and fallen. At that same moment, Carol had been preparing to cross the street to the pharmacy. The orb had hit her smack in the forehead, causing her to lose her balance, careen onto the sidewalk, and briefly become unconscious. She had a concussion, a fractured hip (she'd fallen on her side), multiple lacerations on her face, and a badly broken leg. (Her calf had twisted behind her as she fell.) There had also been some internal bleeding, which had been stanched. The situation was not life-threatening, but it required monitoring. Further surgery might be necessary. She'd be in the hospital for several weeks at least, if not a month or two.

Olympia's first reactions were horror and distress at the thought of her mother's pain, followed by relief that she wasn't about to die — not right now, at least. Those emotions, in turn, were followed by a more selfish thought: her father was going to have to move in with one of his daughters. Or one of his daughters was going to have to move back to Hastings to live with him. Despite his groundbreaking work on the origin of quark and lepton flavors, Bob Hellinger didn't know how to boil an egg. Olympia knew instantly that she didn't want the responsibility to fall to her. As unconditionally as she'd always loved her father, his warmth and wackiness as much as his utter obliviousness to the details of daily life, her self-protective streak was stronger.

Even as a small child, Olympia had sought out her own space and walls, establishing a secret hideaway in a tree behind the garage. It was no coincidence that she'd spent most of her twenties traveling the world, beginning with a junior year abroad in Florence. Later, there had been a waitress gig at an expat hangout in Prague, followed by the obligatory treks through Thailand and India, a photo editor stint for a *Time Out* start-up in Ho Chi Minh City, and a bum-around period in Baja California — anything not to be stuck at home. Yet the claustrophobia of high school in particular had never entirely lifted. Not only had Perri been just a grade ahead of her in school and Gus just a couple below, but her mother had always seemingly been *right down the hall,* her reading glasses attached to a red string and banging against her bosom as she walked. In self-defense, Olympia had learned a way of being—but not really being—there.

Maybe that was why, ten minutes later, standing next to her prostrate, incapacitated, and tubed-up mother, Olympia felt as if it were all happening to someone else's family. She stood motionless, her eyes dry, her mind numb.

Perri apparently had no such inhibitions. She was sobbing loudly. "I never should have asked Mom to pick up Dad's prescription," she said. "I should have just gone out and done it myself. It's all my fault!"

"Don't be ridiculous. It's no one's fault," said Olympia, draping her arm around her older sister's bouncing back. They stood like that for a few seconds, Olympia feeling awkward. Unlike Olympia and Gus, Olympia and Perri had never had a physical relationship, not even as little girls—maybe because Perri had always preferred to imagine herself as the third adult in the house. Olympia couldn't ever remember seeing her cry.

Finally, Olympia felt that enough time had passed that she could remove her arm without calling attention to its absence.

Perri sniffled a few more times. Then she said, "I need to call Mike and tell him to get the guest room ready."

Olympia read into the announcement that Bob would be moving to Larchmont with Perri—and breathed a sigh of guilty relief. "I should call home, too," she said, pulling out her own phone. "If you think someone should stay at the hospital overnight, I could ask my sitter to spend the night. She's never done it before but..." She glanced tentatively at Perri.

"It's okay. Lola needs you," said Perri, just as Olympia had hoped and thought she might say.

Ten minutes later, Olympia planted a quick kiss on Carol's forehead and scurried out of the hospital and into a waiting taxi.

6

M
OM, WE'RE OUT OF SYRUP," said Aiden, driz-
zling the dregs of the jug onto his plate.

"Aiden, that's disgusting," said Perri, glancing
over from where she stood at the counter, slic-
ing open a grapefruit. "Pancakes are not supposed to be *floating*
in syrup." Today was the first day of Perri's new diet, and she
was feeling predictably righteous — even as a part of her knew
she'd give up this one, just as she gave up all of them, and regain
whatever weight she'd lost.

"It looks like diarrhea pancakes!" cried Sadie.

"Sadie, you don't have permission to be disgusting, either,"
snapped Perri. "And what is that thing in your hair?"

"A Mad-Eye Moody eye patch. Want to see?" Sadie secured
the band around her forehead so it covered one eye.

"Very amusing, but you know you're not allowed to wear
costumes to school," said Perri.

"I want pancake," said Noah, attempting to climb out of his
high chair, his arms flailing.

"Noah, sit down!"

"Hey, Mommy, is there any butter?" asked Mike, the Sports section open on his iPad.

"I don't know. Have you looked in the fridge?" Perri shot back.

Mike gave her a wary look and grimaced. "Someone woke up on the wrong side of her chaise longue this morning," he said.

"Excuse me?" said Perri, wondering when she'd started to actively dislike her husband, as opposed to merely tolerate him.

Mike sighed, stood up, and, with what appeared to be Sisyphus-like effort, ambled over to the fridge.

"Lovely pancakes, Perri," Bob said. "Thank you."

"My pleasure," said Perri, who also couldn't help but notice, and lament, the morsel of pancake stuck to her father's beard. It would probably be there for days, she thought despairingly. To Perri's knowledge, Bob hadn't taken a single bath since he'd moved in two weeks ago. The towel she'd put out for him was still folded in a perfect square on the dresser. "Meanwhile, have you taken your pills yet?" she asked him.

Bob waggled his head and sighed. "If it hadn't been for those godforsaken pills, Carol would be on her way to school right now." Perri couldn't begin to fathom what made her parents' marriage tick — and keep ticking. But they were clearly still in love, almost nauseatingly so. "I blame myself entirely," he went on.

"Stop, Dad," said Perri. "It wasn't anyone's fault — except maybe for that moron driver. Here's a glass of water." She walked over to the table and set a glass down next to his plate. "Take your pills."

"Thank you, sweetheart," said Bob. Then he turned to

Mike, and said, "Is there any way I could hitch a ride with you to the hospital today?" It was Mike's "big day" to babysit.

"It's a little tricky because I got the Noah-Man all day," he answered. "But let me see. He's got his Music for Aardvarks class down on Larchmont Avenue at eleven. I guess we could detour to Yonkers on the way over, say around ten thirty?"

"Since when is Noah doing a music class?" asked Perri, pleasantly surprised.

Mike flexed his pectorals and arched his back, a self-contented smile to match. "Since Superdad here signed him up for one."

"I see," said Perri, noting that Mike had been making a little more effort lately with the kids — and that she should probably give him credit for it. (Why did she have such trouble praising the things he did *right?!*)

"Well, it sounds like an excellent plan," declared Bob. "Says an appreciative father-in-law."

In his own way, Bob was trying to be a model father too, Perri thought. A model houseguest, as well. And he was. He always thanked her for meals. He spent most of the day in the den, reading physics journals. He even played the occasional chess game with Aiden. But he rarely took off his old vinyl bedroom slippers. And he seemed incapable of making a sandwich himself, or washing the sink after he brushed his teeth. That wasn't really the issue, of course: Perri's resentment went far deeper. Rationally, she knew that, in raising her and her sisters, her parents had gotten the big things right: they'd been both doting on a personal level and encouraging of education and achievement — Carol perhaps to a fault.

Perri's lingering anger was based on her memory of her parents having been so relaxed about the small stuff — about

97

curfews and clean hands, smoking and sunscreen. In their laxness on these and other counts, they'd been highly negligent, Perri thought. How could Bob in particular, a scientist who studied radiation, not have devoted more of his energies to protecting his children from UVA (and B) rays?! Every morning, Perri looked at the indelible sun spots on her cheeks and forehead—she refused to call them "freckles," a misleading euphemism if there ever was one—and felt simmering rage at him and Carol for having failed to preserve what little beauty she could claim. Never mind the melanoma risk.

Perri also suspected that her parents, who had never really disciplined any of them, preferring to look the other way when faced with their antisocial behavior, were responsible both for Gus's emotional instability and for Olympia's inability to sustain a romantic relationship. Bob and Carol had never set limits. So her sisters had never learned that they couldn't do exactly what they pleased at the moment that it pleased them. That Perri hadn't fallen prey to the same impulses was, to her mind, the result of a strong personality that, even as a child, had allowed her to monitor and even police her own behavior. She also firmly believed that she'd grown up amid a disgraceful level of dirt and sloth, her parents having placed history and science before personal hygiene or clean bathrooms in the hierarchy of importance.

In any case, it was time to go. "Okay, that's it. Everyone in the car," she declared. "Right now. It's already seven forty. Aiden, did you remember your cleats?"

He didn't answer.

"Aiden, I'm talking to you!" Sometimes, Perri felt as if she were talking to the wall.

"What?" he said.

"We need to go."

"I'm not finished with breakfast." His mouth still full, Aiden dug his fork back into Lake Syrup.

"Take a last bite and *come on!*" The child loved to eat in ways that made Perri nervous.

"And, Sadie, you, too. Get your coat on *right now.*"

"Aiden's got syrup on his chin."

"Do not."

"Do so."

"You two, *enough!!*" As Perri literally shoved her children out the door, she wondered when she'd turned into a shrieking battle-ax. That had never been the plan.

Even on her "city days," and even with Mike at home, Perri made a point of dropping her two older kids at school before she left for work. She enjoyed seeing them run up the steps and disappear through the double doors. *Occupied for the next six and a half hours, at least.* This was the primary thought that went through her head. Had an earlier generation of parents spent so much time worrying that their children would be bored? Perri had no idea if either Sadie or Aiden actually *liked* school. As many children did, they typically answered "Fine" to the question "How was school?" and "Nothing" to the question "What did you do today?" But neither seemed reluctant to get out of the car, at least. And on occasion, one would excitedly attest to some possibly fantastical development such as "Guess what? Our gym teacher has bird flu!" (Sadie) or "Porter Smith's dad got arrested for *tax elation*" (Aiden).

That morning, after school drop-off, Perri returned to the house to collect her briefcase. She found Noah standing two feet from the TV, his eyes enormous. Mike was sprawled on the sofa behind him, singing along to the opening credits in a rich baritone: "Yoouuurrr backyard friends, the backyaaaard-igaaaannnnns. In the place where we belong, where we'll probably sing a song…" It was cute, sort of. Except not quite. A familiar rush of irritation and impatience replaced Perri's earlier happiness over the music class news. For the eight hours a week that Mike performed childcare, why couldn't he sit on the floor and play with blocks, or show Noah a map of the world, or even bounce a ball his way? It was a competitive world. Chinese kids Noah's age were probably already adding fractions! Perri experienced a familiar rush of fear as well—that her family was falling hopelessly behind in the race to the top.

It was more than that, too.

When Perri was young, the Hellinger family hadn't even owned a TV set. Carol, who considered television to be a scourge on humanity, hadn't purchased one until the mid-90s after her three daughters had left for college and ostensibly only to watch *Great Performances* on PBS, whereupon Bob had gotten hooked on the vintage police drama, *Hawaii Five-O*. And yet, Perri didn't remember feeling deprived—maybe because she and her sisters had been too busy building dollhouse furniture out of matchsticks (Perri), conducting "science experiments" with baking soda and toothpaste (Gus), and painting scenery for Greek tragedies (Pia), which the three of them would then perform in togas made of their own twin sheets fastened over the shoulder with safety pins.

It wasn't until sixth grade that Perri had realized what she'd been missing—and how unusual her upbringing was. After she confused the animated TV show and its eponymous dog,

Scooby-Doo, for a candy bar, her classmates had laughed—and Perri had experienced deep feelings of shame and alienation. When she became a mother herself, she'd been determined that her own kids should avoid a similar fate. But at the same time, she'd secretly suspected that Carol was right and that creativity blossomed in inverse proportion to the amount of screen time allowed. In what was Perri's greatest and (arguably) only rebellion against the Hellinger family, aggressive normalcy had ultimately won out. She'd relented on morning cartoons, and then relented on video games. And yet...

Perri lifted the remote off the coffee table and hit the power button. The screen fluttered into darkness.

"Tttttttt Vvvvvvvvvv!" wailed Noah.

"Sweetie poo," said Perri, lifting him into her arms. "Mommy doesn't want your brain turning to mush."

But the child kept wailing. That was when she noticed the cereal bar—suddenly smeared across the collar of her freshly dry-cleaned silk blouse, mashed strawberries and all. "God damn it!" she cried as she turned back to Mike. "How many times have I asked you *not* to let the kids eat in the living room!" At the ferocity of her upbraiding, Noah cried even harder. Upset to see him upset, Perri felt even more inflamed at her husband. "See what you've done now!"

"See what *I've* done?" He laughed. "I'm not the one who turned off his favorite show, then yelled at him for eating breakfast."

In an attempt to control her rage, Perri breathed in and out, both to a count of three. "I'm late—and I have to go change now," she said finally. She deposited the child on his father's stomach and walked out.

"Are you trying to make this house an incredibly unpleasant place to live in? Or only a *slightly* unpleasant place?" Mike called after her.

The comment stung, and Perri stopped short. Catching her reflection in the mirror over the console table, she was aghast to discover how puffy and ill-defined her face had become with age. She was beginning to resemble a Yorkshire pudding. And what if Mike was right? What if she'd become unbearable to be around? And if she *had* become unbearable, was it mostly because he'd stopped having sex with her? Or had he stopped having sex with her because she was so unbearable? And had she not had perfectly valid grounds for complaining just now, or was she being too much of a stickler? Should she have cut Mike some slack and let the TV stay on?

Perri changed into a short-sleeve sweater. Then she went back downstairs. She hated leaving for work right after she and Mike had had a fight. But she also knew that she'd have to be the one to apologize. Somehow, despite her doubts and melancholy, she couldn't bring herself to do so. She had too much pride. And yet, how badly she wished her husband would come to her just then, put his arms around her waist and tell her how lucky he was to have a wife like her. Stalling, she went to collect the mail. She found the usual bills and catalogues waiting in the basket. She must have gotten six catalogues a day. Sometimes Perri felt as if Pottery Barn and J. Crew were personally stalking her. In the Closet sent out only two catalogues per year. Perri felt it made the experience of receiving one special.

She also found a credit card offer addressed to one Ginny Budelaire. Perri recognized the name as that of the previous owner of the house. At the time of the sale, Ginny Budelaire, then in her eighties, had been afflicted with Alzheimer's disease. So her grown children had sold the place on her behalf. According to their real estate agent, Ginny had been a chorus girl at Radio City Music Hall back in the 1940s. Later, she'd married an Amtrak executive who'd seen her onstage. It had been hard to connect the story with the figure who Perri had caught a glimpse of during her final walk-through with Mike. To Perri's recollection, Ginny Budelaire had been a tiny slumped woman with parchment skin, vacant eyes, and a wisp of orange hair. Perri also recalled the rush of joy and pride she'd experienced that afternoon as she and Mike — grown-ups at last! — had made their way through the house, Mike squeezing her hand and Perri squeezing back. As if coconspirators in a secret pact that was finally coming to fruition. How long ago that all seemed now . . .

It was getting late. Perri had a nine thirty meeting with an investor. She took the envelope into the kitchen with her and, feeling that it was somehow sacrilegious to toss it in the trash, stuck it in her handbag instead. Then she walked back into the living room and gave Noah a kiss good-bye. He'd stopped crying for the moment, if only because the TV was back on. He was also sitting in Mike's lap. "I'll be home by six thirty, seven. Thank you for taking my father to the hospital," she told her husband in a flat and inanimate voice and without making eye contact.

"Sure thing," he replied faux breezily.

A blur of ranch houses and warehouses, anemic-looking poplars and junked car part lots, greeted Perri's eyes through the window of her Metro-North car. Finally, the train slowed into Grand Central. Perri slung the strap of her briefcase over her shoulder and stepped out.

Her office in the city was on the thirteenth floor of a generic glass high-rise on Fifth Avenue in the 30s. Her business partner was a woman named LuAnn, who was older and had once worked as an interior decorator. The two shared adjacent offices. They also employed twenty-three people, more than half of them under thirty. One of them was a graphic designer with a handlebar mustache, an extensive collection of skintight jeans and oversized plaid shirts that he wore buttoned to the neck, and a tattoo of a pizza on his left hand. His name was Troy, and he functioned as Perri's connection to the "next generation." In the Closet's chief demographic was thirty-five- to forty-two-year-olds, but Perri and LuAnn were hoping to expand into the collegiate and postcollegiate market with a lower-priced line called ITC.

At eleven, Perri walked her "nine thirty" to the elevator. At twelve thirty, she did the same with her "eleven thirty." At twelve forty-five, she shut the door, glanced at a framed desk photo of Noah, pushed away a horrific image of him being crushed by an oncoming train (why did her brain taunt her like that?), scanned a sushi menu on the Internet, placed an order, and readjusted her buttocks in her desk chair. But she couldn't get comfortable. Her bones felt creaky, her skin itchy. There was a licorice taste in the back of her throat. Maybe she and Mike needed a vacation, she thought. Just the two of them. Somewhere far away with palm trees and white sand. The only problem was that Perri secretly hated vacations. She felt as if she weren't accomplishing anything. Which, of course, was the whole point — just not to Perri.

Over a yellowtail scallion roll and seaweed salad, she reviewed the previous quarter's sales figures. They were disappointing. However, considering the wider economic situation in the country, they were not as disappointing as they might have been. Also, the pastel wicker keepsake boxes were selling like hotcakes. Maybe recessions brought out consumers' nostalgic streaks?

At two, she met with LuAnn and Troy in the conference room to discuss the upcoming catalogue. (Proposed cover line: *Spring = Spring Cleaning.*) Troy felt it sounded too 1950s — no one cleaned exclusively in the spring anymore, he argued — but LuAnn felt that the phrase had retro appeal. And Perri agreed, clearly irritating Troy, who stomped out with a pissy "Who cares what I think — I'm just a pretentious white guy with facial hair who dresses like a perverted lumberjack and lives in Williamsburg. Right?"

Rather than agree, Perri said nothing.

Returning to her office at two forty-five, she dug her hand into her bag in search of her BlackBerry. She was feeling guilty about her freak-out over *The Backyardigans* and thought she'd send a conciliatory text to Mike, something like "Hope you and N had a good Wheels on the Bus. Sorry I was a big crank this morning." But was she actually sorry? All she knew was that she hated the idea of him sitting there thinking he'd married a shrew. Along with her BlackBerry, her hand emerged with the credit card solicitation addressed to Ginny Budelaire.

Without thinking, Perri ripped open the envelope, grabbed a pen off her desktop, and began to fill out the application form. She wrote in a fictional date of birth that established her as ten years younger than she actually was. She listed her marital status as "single." She picked nine random digits as her Social Security number and copied them out. She checked off the box indicating that her annual family income was between $50,000 and $75,000. Finally, with a loopy theatrical hand and with both the capital G and the capital B dwarfing the back-slanted letters that followed, she signed the form "Ginny Budelaire." Then she stuffed the form into its accompanying envelope, licked it closed, tucked it back in her purse—and dared herself to drop it in the mailbox in front of the Lexington Avenue post office on her way back to Grand Central later that day.

7

TAKING PITY ON HER MOTHER—and with nothing else to do after work now that Debbie had moved out—Gus had been going out to Yonkers to visit Carol every evening or two.

"Let me know if you want me to bring anything else to the hospital," she offered one still-wintry mid-March eve. "Crossword puzzles. Socks. Fresh fruit. My diary for you to read." In high school, Gus had caught Carol doing exactly that, which wouldn't have been a big deal if Gus hadn't used the pages to confess to an undying crush on the captain of the girls' basketball team. Whether her mother realized that P.S. was Penny Showalter was unclear. In any case, she'd never forgiven Carol, who'd never apologized, on the grounds that Gus had left the thing sitting out in clear view.

But for once, Carol let the reference fly right by her. "I'd love some green grapes, actually," she said.

"Easily accomplished," said Gus.

"You're too kind."

"Really, it's no problem."

"I suppose it would be nice to have a few books, as well," Carol went on. "Whatever you find on my bedside table is fine, if you don't mind schlepping back to the house again. I know you're busy —"

"Not too busy to secure you a fictional autobiography of a Roman emperor," said Gus.

"Thank you, my dear. Actually, I wouldn't mind rereading *I, Claudius.*"

"Sure thing."

"Auggie." Carol pursed her lips, her eyes crinkly beneath her mummy-like head bandage.

"Yes, Mom?"

"It's meant a lot to me that you've been here so much, keeping your feeble old mother company."

"It's nothing," said Gus, unnerved though not displeased by the apparent change in Carol's personality. Indeed, as she emerged from the fog of painkillers, she struck Gus as being newly deferential, even polite, where she'd once been rude and overbearing. As a result, Gus and her mother were getting along far better than usual. It was also clear to Gus that she was attached to the woman in some possibly unhealthy way. But she didn't necessarily want to be reminded of that.

At the same time, having been awarded Favored Daughter status, if only for the moment, Gus wasn't about to pass up the opportunity to denigrate her Less Worthy Sisters. "On that note," she began again. "I can't believe how *little* Pia has been out here to see you. I think Dad's really offended." In fact, Bob had never mentioned Olympia's name to Gus. Not that he necessarily remembered Olympia's name.

"Well, he shouldn't be," said Carol.

"Why not?" said Gus, disappointed.

"Pia has a lot on her plate, between her museum job and raising Lola on her own."

"And I don't?"

"I know you do, too."

"Well, Lola is in daycare, like, seventeen hours a day." Gus felt guilty ranking on her sister behind her back — but maybe not that guilty.

"Well, it's not easy for her to get out here," said Carol, "especially without a car like you have. It's a good hour-and-a-half commute by public transit, and she doesn't get out of work until six something."

"What about weekends? What's her excuse then?"

"I don't know about weekends," Carol conceded.

"Well, my reading is that she can't deal with people when they're in need because she's an incredibly selfish human being." No sooner had Gus relieved herself of the long-held conviction that her middle sister didn't pull her fair weight in the family, however, than she found herself doubting her righteousness. After all, it was Gus who had helped herself — twice now — to the petty cash jar in her parents' kitchen while picking up extra clothes for Carol. It wasn't as if she needed the money. Between Legal Aid and Fordham, she made a decent living, even if a full fifty percent of it was stripped away by the government. (Despite being a committed lefty, Gus secretly hated paying taxes and occasionally claimed questionable write-offs on her annual returns, such as dry cleaning for "public appearances." Which, in her case, meant appearing in family court in the Bronx.) But there was a way in which she believed herself to be deserving of those extra five- and ten-dollar bills.

Gus often thought of a story told by her grandmother, Gertrude, who had been a small child during the Depression, as well as the youngest of six. When Trudy's mother, Alberta, had roasted a chicken, the pick of parts would begin with her oldest brother and continue down. Poor Trudy would always be left with the near-meatless back or thigh. (Gus could relate.) Not that in the eighteen years she lived on Edmarth Place Carol had ever served them a freshly roasted anything. Ready-made astronaut chicken was another story. Gus had nevertheless felt that her older sisters had consumed the majority of their parents' riches, such as they were. To Gus's mind, Olympia had been so beautiful and ethereal that everyone had had to tiptoe around her for fear of her breaking in two. And Perri had been so bossy and histrionic that no one had any choice but to do as she said. No wonder that, growing up, Gus had felt as if she'd had to shout to be heard, even over Olympia's silences, which in their own way could be deafening. "Everyone's doing the best they can" was the New Carol's magnanimous reading of the situation.

"Maybe you're right," said Gus. "Anyway, I should get going. I'm heading over to Perri's for dinner."

"Send my love to everyone."

"Will do. Get some rest." Gus paused. "And stop being so nice. Would you?"

"Pardon me?" said Carol, blinking.

"Never mind," said Gus, eyeing her mother sideways as she walked out of her room. "See you tomorrow."

It was only a ten-mile drive, due east, to Larchmont. Driving up Perri's snakelike driveway in her beat-up old Honda Civic, Gus wondered how anyone could stand to live as her oldest sister did. The pressure to keep up appearances must have been relentless. Gus had no such issues. She lived in an utterly utilitarian prewar apartment on the unfashionable northern tip of Manhattan. For Gus, its utter lack of attitude — never mind charm — made it that much more relaxing. You could walk around in it in sweatpants just being yourself, or, better yet, no one at all. You could leave the bathroom door open when you did your business. That was also the problem. It felt utterly empty in there without Debbie. Was it any wonder that Gus had been coming out to Westchester so much, spending time with the very family who purportedly drove her insane?

Mike answered the front door with a "Yo."

"Hey," she said. Gus had long considered her brother-in-law to be a harmless doofus who was unworthy of Perri in every respect. But she didn't really mind him, either. As her eyes ran from his flip-flops to his baseball cap — worn backward, of course — she wondered if he secretly liked being off work, or if he found it emasculating, or if he had any thoughts in his head whatsoever. "What's up?" she went on, stepping past him and into the house.

"Nice pants," he replied. "I admit I never pegged you as the leather type."

Gus was suddenly self-conscious. Debbie had accidentally left behind all her motorcycle gear at Gus's apartment. And Gus had claimed it for herself, even though it was a size too big. It was a sentimental thing, she supposed — maybe an obnoxious thing, too — since she really ought to have returned it. But she didn't feel like it. Not right now. She was still too angry at Debbie for luring her in and spitting her out. That was how it had felt. Not that it was any of Mike's business. "But I always pegged *you* as the Dockers type," she told him.

"They're actually Banana Republic," he said.

"This is a fascinating conversation," said Gus.

She followed him down the hall. She never understood how her sister kept the place looking like a museum when it housed three children under the age of ten. "Gus. You remember my little brother, Jeff, right?" Mike was now saying.

Gus looked up. Leaning against Perri's marble kitchen island was a person who looked just like Mike, only three inches taller and twenty pounds thinner, chiseled where Mike was doughy and possessed of a full head of swooshy brown hair where Mike's was inching backward like a receding tide. His biceps, which were visible below an artfully torn olive green T-shirt, had the rippled appearance of challah bread. His legs, which were poking out of a pair of gray athletic shorts, were sinewy and the same color as a shiny penny. His coral choker had certain qualities in common with a dog collar. Gus had first met Jefferson Sims at Mike and Perri's wedding, more than a decade ago. She'd been a couple years out of college; he'd been a senior on the extended plan at some ski school—she couldn't remember which one. UVM? Middlebury? Or was it somewhere out west like University of Colorado? To her further recollection, he'd also been incredibly impressed with himself for no apparent reason other than his abdominal muscles, which he'd bared on the dance floor by managing to get himself sprayed down with a Champagne bottle, "forcing" him to disrobe. He'd also been accompanied by his girlfriend at the time, an Amazonian blonde who was reputed to be trying out for the Olympic team in giant slalom. Gus had seen him only a handful of times since then and not in five years at least. "How are you?" she said, raising her palm in a wave. Shaking his hand seemed too formal, kissing him on the cheek too intimate.

"I've been well, thank you," he said, squinting and smiling. "How have you been?"

"Could be worse."

"So tell me this, Gus. Do you too reside in the greater Larchmont area?"

"No, I still live in the city, way uptown, in Washington Heights," she told him.

"Washington Heights." He nodded unsurely.

"I promise you've never been there."

"You're most likely correct."

"And you?"

"Of late, I've been a denizen of Breckenridge, Colorado."

"Fair enough."

"But I'm actually considering moving to your neck of the woods."

"When did that happen?" asked Mike, sounding alarmed.

"Just toying with the idea," said Jeff, shrugging. "You gotta grow up some time and become 'the man.' Speaking of which" — he threw an arm around his brother's back — "how's the job search going, bro?"

Mike made an irritated face and shook off his brother. "At least I've had one in the last ten years!"

"I beg to differ!" declared Jeff. "For six long months in the year two thousand nine I toiled in the capacity of chief ski lift operator."

"Scoring free lift tickets in exchange for a couple hours a week lowering the bar is not working. Sorry, buddy."

"Maybe not to you."

"Maybe not to anyone."

"Do you, too, find my brother exceedingly rude?" said Jeff, turning back to Gus.

"I'm staying out of this one," Gus said, laughing as again she lifted her palm into the air.

"Wise move," said Jeff. "Now tell me this, Gus. How exactly have you been occupying your time when not at home in Washington Heights, New York City?"

There was something about his face that seemed to invite confession. Or maybe it was that he kept calling her "Gus." As if he actually knew her. (In a way, she supposed, he did.) And as if he couldn't wait to know more.

"Well, for the past few years, I've been a family law attorney for a nonprofit foundation," she told him. "I also teach at a law school."

"Impressive," he said, nodding as he turned his lips inside out and scratched at an imaginary beard. "Now, Gus, I have one more question for you. What do you make of my brother's outward spread in the six months since we've seen each other?" He grabbed a chunk of flesh from Mike's waist.

"Fuck you, man!" cried Mike, now sounding genuinely pissed as he pummeled his brother on the shoulder.

"I think I'll stay out of this one, too," said Gus, laughing again.

"Another wise move," said Jeff.

"Hey, I've had experience. I was always busting my ex-girlfriend about having a big butt. She dumped me at the beginning of the year." Why had she just told him that? Why couldn't she ever keep her private life private?!

"I'm sorry to hear that," he said.

"It's okay, I'm over it," said Gus.

"So you're single."

"I guess you could say that."

Jeff got a glinty look in his eye. "Would you like to go out for a beer tonight after dinner?"

"Jesus, Jeff!" cried Mike.

"What?"

"I'm getting out of here." Mike shook his head as he turned his back.

"Thanks, but I'm busy," said Gus, still unsure if the guy was joking or not.

"What if I wear a dress?" asked Jeff.

How dare he mock her sexual orientation! "What if I punch you in the face?" she said, temper flaring.

"I might enjoy it."

"You're sick."

"Maybe you like sick," said Jeff, still smiling.

Gus couldn't believe the cheesy and vile way he was talking to her—a near relative, no less! And she had every intention of giving him the finger and following Mike out the door. But something kept her legs motionless. Was it possible that she was somehow attracted to the guy? Or was she mistaking anger for passion? She felt heat on her cheeks and on her collarbone. "This is just a game for you," she said. "Isn't it?"

"Maybe, but maybe not," he replied.

"You want to see if you can pick up a lesbian. Is that it?"

"What was that, Johnny Appleseed?"

Gus suddenly recalled the satchel of McIntosh apples still in her grip. Glancing south, she burst into involuntary laughter. The week before, Perri had made a dig at Gus regarding the frequency with which she'd been dining in Larchmont. Stung by the accusation, Gus had been attempting a gesture that would counteract the impression that she was freeloading. She set the satchel down on the island and sighed in defeat.

At which point Jefferson Sims threaded his fingers through hers. "Admit that was a good one," he said, grinning.

Gus felt as if her heart were an inmate who had gone berserk in solitary confinement. "I admit nothing," she said meekly.

Just then, Perri walked in, causing Gus to jump three feet backward — straight into Perri's marble countertop.

"Hey!" said Perri, eyes popping at Gus. "I didn't even know you'd arrived." She looked from one to the other of them.

Gus had never felt so humiliated in front of her oldest sister — not even when Andy Lyons came over for the first time, and said, "Perri, you never told me you had a little brother." She'd told him, "I'm female, you fuckhead," an oft-repeated line in the Hellinger household in the years that followed — years during which Gus was expected to laugh at her own alliterative "genius," even as she failed to find the encounter funny and, in fact, still felt vaguely humiliated by it. "Well, here I am," she mumbled while biting her lip and rubbing her side. Who knew marble was so hard?

"I was actually showing Gus one of the relaxation techniques I learned in my therapeutic massage class last summer," said Jeff.

"You went to massage school last summer?" Perri asked skeptically.

"Well, not technically. But I have a close friend who works in the field. Did you know the pressure point between the thumb and forefinger holds the key to most common headaches?"

"I didn't know that. Or maybe I did. It's hard to say what I know right now."

"Anyway," said Gus, desperate to restore normalcy. "I brought some apples. I know the kids like them." She lifted the satchel and held it toward her sister.

"Oh, thanks, that was nice of you," said Perri, still eyeing Gus suspiciously as she removed the bag from her grip.

All through dinner, Gus continued to make a fool of herself. She couldn't help it. Jeff was staring at her, and she at him, while a dead weight lodged itself at the bottom of her stomach and refused to lift. Perri's homemade meatloaf, which Gus usually devoured, sat uneaten on her plate. She could barely even follow the conversation. Mike was going on about the real estate market in Larchmont and how it was "holding up pretty well under the circumstances"—unlike Gus, who didn't know if she'd make it through the meal, didn't understand what she was feeling either...

"Excuse me, Gus," Jeff was saying. "Would you mind passing the butter?"

"Of course," she said, swallowing unnecessarily as she reached for the dish.

As the transfer was made, her fingers brushed his, sending pins and needles up and down the length of Gus's arm. Against all explanation, she longed for the guy to lay her down on the carpet and crush her into oblivion.

That night, Gus couldn't sleep for hours. If she was attracted to this man, did it mean she wasn't really a lesbian? And what if she'd *never* been a lesbian? What if it had all been a pose, as paper-thin as a fashion magazine spread, albeit without the makeup and pretty clothes? And what if her sexual orientation all went back to some desperate need to define herself apart from her sisters, who, early on, had monopolized the good girl and femme fatale roles, respectively? That is, what if lesbianism's main draw had been that it was the ultimate noncompete clause?

Even more pathetically, what if her lust for other women had been born of some secret need to replicate in her love life the intense relationships she'd had with her domineering older siblings? One could make the argument that the women to whom Gus had been attracted, beginning with Penny Showalter in high school, and continuing with her first real girlfriend, Jen French at Wesleyan, had managed to combine Perri's bossiness with Olympia's haughtiness. It was also true that, in the years just after Gus had come out at the age of eighteen, being a lesbian had sometimes felt like a series of stylistic gestures that she was trying on for size. She remembered worrying that her hair wasn't sufficiently "dykey," her walk not tough enough — and making a mental note to improve these things about herself.

Or was she not giving her heart the credit it was due? From a very early age — as early as eleven or twelve — Gus had also been aware that she was different from other girls in her class. She would hear them describe the fluttery excitement they felt in the presence of their boy crushes. Gus had never felt that way. It was her girl friends themselves who occasionally elicited flutters, some of them so painful and exciting and overwhelming that the friendships would become impossible to maintain, and Gus would have to preemptively ax them with one or another concocted fight.

Yet at some indistinct point in her late twenties the performance had become her, especially as her career began to mirror her personal proclivities. Eventually, lesbianism became more than a sexual identity for her; it became an entire way of *being* in the world — not just a lifestyle but a cause and a rallying point that needed no explanation. She was committed to women, not only as lovers and partners but as legal subjects whose interests needed defending. And what if her attraction to Jeff was simply a matter of curiosity in the same vein as eating psychedelic mushrooms or flying a single-engine plane? What if she wanted to try it only once? And if that were the case, would it be so terrible to indulge the impulse while she was between partners? Or would she be betraying the things she stood for, even betraying herself?

The problem was—Gus suspected that the answer was yes. It would have been one thing if Jefferson Sims were some self-effacing New Man who shared a common interest in social justice. But by all accounts, he was a cocky, womanizing ski bum.

8

LYMPIA AND LOLA WERE on their way home from Happy Kids when Olympia's phone rang. Her left hand on the stroller, she dug her right hand into her bag and began to fish. How was it possible that she could grasp every object inside it, from her keys to her wallet to her emergency tampon (which had naturally escaped its paper wrapping) without locating her phone until its last ring? Finally, her hand made contact with the familiar expanse of smooth plastic, and she lifted it into the open. Perri's name flashed across the screen, just as it did most every evening of Olympia's life. Not in the mood to talk, Olympia considered not answering, then decided it would be a greater hardship to have to call her back. "Hey, what's up?" she said.

Perri sounded indignant as she relayed the gossip of the evening—how Mike's brother, Jeff, had flirted with Gus at dinner. With the honking horns, Lola's incessant chatter, and her own exhaustion, Olympia had trouble following the story, which sounded unlikely, if not downright apocryphal. It wouldn't be the first time that Perri had concocted a cockamamie fantasy based on flimsy evidence, Olympia thought. Her sister had always been a fabulist of the tallest order. Or maybe the better word was "alarmist." If you lost two pounds, she thought you were dying of a wasting disease. "That definitely sounds weird," she said. "Are you sure?" Then she turned to Lola, and said, "I'm talking to Aunt Perri!... Wait, what happened at school? ... Gossamer had an allergic reaction to bread?!... Sorry, Perri, hold on one more second.... What? No, I'm *not* buying you your own iPhone on the way home.... No, not next year either. Try ten years!... Sorry, Perri, what were you saying?"

"I don't think you're grasping the enormity of this," Perri went on, clearly irritated. "Mike's brother, who literally arrived in New York ten minutes ago, is making the moves on our younger sister, Gus, who supposedly doesn't like men. I found them in the kitchen holding hands!"

"Are you sure they weren't just *shaking* hands?" asked Olympia.

"They were not *shaking* hands! They looked like they were about to kiss."

"Well, the man definitely moves fast," said Olympia, turning up her block, past a bedraggled figure slumped on the sidewalk, wearing a sandwich board that read, HELP ME.

"The man is a snake!" cried Perri.

"Why is that man sitting on the sidewalk?" Lola asked at the same time.

"He's homeless," said Olympia.

"Hardly," scoffed Perri. "Guess who got a quote, unquote *ride* back to the city with Gus?"

"Sorry—I was talking to Lola. We just walked by a homeless guy."

Perri's voice changed. "Oh, *god*. Where are you?"

"On my block."

"Yikes. I didn't know you had homeless people in your neighborhood!"

Sometimes, Olympia suspected that her older sister was acting willfully ignorant and reactionary to irk her. "Anyway, if it's for real, maybe it will help Gus get over Debbie," she said, refusing the bait.

"She's already over Debbie," snapped Perri.

"Well, then, the timing is perfect."

"She's gay, Olympia!"

"If your story pans out, I'd have to say 'bi.'"

"The guy isn't a toxic bachelor. He's a one-man Superfund site."

"Ouch," said Olympia, wondering at the violence of Perri's reaction. Assuming the story was even true — Olympia had her doubts — was her older sister just being protective? Or was it possible that Perri was jealous of Gus? Olympia hadn't seen Jefferson Sims in years, but he was famously handsome. Twenty years later, it was probably also safe to assume that Mike and Perri's sex life wasn't what it used to be. Not that Perri would ever talk about sex. She'd always been prudish that way.

"I'm sorry, it's true!" Perri said defiantly. "We need to get Gus away from him, and fast."

"She's thirty-six years old, Perri," Olympia told her. "I think she can take care of herself."

"She's also in a fragile state emotionally. And the guy has women coming out of his ears. What do you think he was doing in Breckenridge all year?"

"Skiing?"

"Please," said Perri.

"Nailing half-pipes in the terrain park?"

"Very funny."

"Anyway, we're just walking in the door," said Olympia. "Let me call you later."

"Thanks for your help — not!" said Perri.

"What can I do?!" cried Olympia, turning the key in the front door. "Gus has no interest in anything I say, anyway. You're the only one she listens to."

"Mommy, you talk too much," said Lola. "Get off the phone *now!*"

"Listen, Lola's freaking out. I really have to go," said Olympia, happy for once to have her daughter make demands on her time.

"Fine," said Perri, as if it weren't.

"I'll talk to you later."

"Bye."

Olympia opened the door to her apartment and flicked on the lights. At the sight of her and Lola, Clive stood up on his hind legs and let out a noise that fell somewhere between a squeak and a purr. "Hello there, bunny rabby," said Olympia.

"He made a silly noise!" cried Lola.

As Olympia walked over to where Clive now lay and began to stroke his luscious fur, it occurred to her that he was the only male in her life on whose love she could count. Then again, she held him in captivity. By all accounts, rabbits had extremely small brains. She'd also had him castrated. Clive's nose twitched, but for the rest of the evening he was quiet.

9

PERRI HUNG UP FEELING ANGRY. Here she'd called her middle sister seeking commiseration. In return, Olympia had offered nothing but mockery! For Olympia, sex was nothing but a joke, Perri thought. Well, it wasn't a joke to Perri, who had slept with only two men in her entire life, or, okay, maybe three. She sometimes worried about what kind of mother Olympia would make to Lola, especially when Lola hit adolescence. Would she be one of those awful "my best friend is my daughter" types who outfitted their kids with birth control prescriptions before they even reached puberty? To Olympia's credit, she was very affectionate with the child — when not shipping her off to some filthy childcare center all day, every day. Perri tried not to judge working women and, in particular, other working mothers. But how could her sister justify exposing her own flesh and blood at such a tender age to that many germs?! As Perri resumed cleaning the kitchen, her mind boggled.

But she also felt at peace. Secretly, she found loading the dishwasher and wiping down the counters to be: (a) cathartic and (b) more enjoyable than playing Spin Master Air Hogs Zero Gravity Micro Car with Aiden; Singing Pizza Elmo with Noah; or American Girl Doll Gets Hit by a Bus and Buried in a Shoe Box Coffin with Sadie. Not that she was willing to admit so much to her family, lest they take advantage of the confession and never again clear a dish. Just as Perri was banging the drain catch against the inside of the trash compactor, Mike appeared in the doorway. "Thanks for helping with the cleanup," she cracked.

"Perri, why do you think I just walked in here?!" he asked with an exasperated sigh. "If you want to do the dishes before anyone else has a chance to so you can play the biggest martyr, fine. But if you actually want my help, give me a chance. Or just ask me!"

"Whatever," said Perri. "I'm not going to beg you to help around the house!" Why did she give him such a hard time about doing household chores, when some part of her preferred doing them herself? Mike didn't answer but rolled his eyes and shook his head. Who was the outrageous one? Perri wondered. (She no longer knew.) "Anyway, that was an interesting evening."

"Interesting. That's the word," said Mike, opening the fridge.

"You need to talk to Jeff," Perri told him.

"Excuse me?" Mike squinted contemptuously at her while he grabbed a Heineken off the shelf.

"I'm not letting him screw Gus over!"

"Perri," said Mike, raising his palm, as if to indicate that she should stand back. "Organize all the flatware drawers in Westchester. But STOP TRYING TO CONTROL MY FAMILY!" With that, he yanked open the cutlery drawer, grabbed the bottle opener, and pried off the top of his beer.

His family — as opposed to *hers?* After this many years of marriage, was there really any difference! Perri felt unfairly maligned. She also felt misunderstood. She wasn't trying to control anyone. She was just protecting her family. Wasn't she?

Or was it possible that she didn't even understand her own motives? As she ran a damp sponge over the countertops, she wondered if she was worried on Gus's behalf, or on her own — or maybe both. She knew that old chestnut about imitation being the most sincere form of flattery. But what if she didn't want to be imitated? What if she liked the idea of each Hellinger sister having a distinct identity and personal life with no potential for overlap? She knew that when they were growing up, Carol had had a tendency to pigeonhole all of them. She'd heard both Olympia and Gus complain about it. But the labels they'd all been assigned (The Pretty One, The Political One, The Perfect One) had secretly pleased and comforted Perri. Also, what if the things that Perri told Mike in presumed confidence wound up being passed on to Jeff, who told Gus, who told the world?!

There was also the mind-bending fact that Gus appeared to be the object of a Sims brother's lust — Perri had seen the heated way that Jeff had looked at her sister all through dinner — and Perri could no longer claim to be the same. She could never have guessed at the role reversals at work. Growing up, it had been *Olympia,* not Gus, whom Perri had felt rivalrous with. Statuesque yet skinny, Olympia had even managed to sail through puberty with her comeliness unmarred by pimples or braces. She was so pretty that Perri had sometimes been proud to be related to her: it had made her feel glamorous by association. On occasion, Perri would even play up Olympia's looks to her friends, even boyfriends. "Admit you're secretly in love with

Pia," she'd told Andy Lyons so many times in high school that it had become a joke between them — a joke and a way of preempting her paranoia that he actually *was* in love with Olympia. Not that she would have blamed him if he was. Even today, Perri felt like a grim-faced moose in the presence of Olympia. The previous summer, three generations of the Hellinger and Sims families had gathered at a rental beach house in Cape May. In a frenzy of masochism, while Olympia was in the shower, Perri had found herself trying on Olympia's jeans — just to see if she could get them past her knees. (She couldn't.)

And yet, it had never just been about appearances. Perri thought back to their adolescent and late-adolescent years. She and Olympia had been close — up to a point. But there had always been secrets on Olympia's end, secrets that, by the time Perri had found out about them, had already managed to make her feel excluded from the inner sanctum. This had been true even when the secrets had had no bearing on her life. For example, Olympia hadn't told Perri who she was going to prom with until the day of the event. (Perri felt she deserved to know earlier.) It seemed to Perri that her middle sister had no real loyalty to anyone, not even her family. She'd never felt this so much as when, in college, Olympia had become dangerously thin and refused to admit there was any problem. Instead, she'd hurled the accusation back in Perri's face, saying that it was Perri who suffered from body dysmorphic disorder and needed help (and to please leave her alone, she had a class to attend).

Gus's chronic love troubles were another issue. In truth, it had taken Perri a long time to accept the fact that her baby sister was gay. After extensive reading on the subject in the years after Gus had "come out," however, Perri had come to believe that homosexuality was a trait, like left-handedness, athleticism, or perfectionism, with which one was born. After all, growing up, Gus had never shown the slightest interest in fashion or primping—unless you counted the black eyeliner and white face powder she'd favored during her short-lived Goth phase in ninth grade. Until now, Perri's main complaint regarding Gus's love life had been her failure to have met a nice suit-jacketed lawyer and marry in one of the states in which it was already legal. Instead, she always seemed to pick the gruffest, most unkempt women she could find. The last time Perri had seen Debbie, the latter had been wearing painter pants and a "wife beater" undershirt. Why did lesbians want to look like plumbers? Perri had never received a good answer to this question. And now Gus had picked Jeff. Now she wasn't even a lesbian anymore?

"What I don't understand," Mike was saying, "is why you can't just be happy for people."

"You're right," said Perri, blood rushing to her face. "I should be happy for Gus. At least someone is about to get laid." She couldn't believe she'd said that. Apparently, neither could Mike. The last thing she saw before she exited the room was his mouth hanging open like a trapdoor.

Perri dipped her parsley into salt water, placed it on her tongue, and winced ever so slightly at the acrid taste. As in years past, Perri's best friend from high school, Becky Kahn (now Goldstein), had invited the Sims-Hellinger family to a seder at their new-construction Colonial in nearby Harrison. Once a crazed Dead Head who'd attended thirty-eight shows in five years, Becky had gone "modern orthodox" after college, possibly just to spite her hippie parents, who had founded Hastings's first community puppetry theater. Perri herself had little patience for religion and had therefore been secretly relieved to marry "out of the faith" insofar as it had given her an excuse to do none of the above. But she liked the idea of living according to a strict set of rules and half wished that, like Becky, she was someone who could believe.

Except she couldn't. She'd never seen any evidence of God, except maybe once in a California Closets showroom. Bob or Carol, both of them confirmed atheists, had never pushed any kind of formal religious education on her or her sisters. That said, Perri thought it was good for her children to be exposed to all facets of their ethnic heritage. Bob hailed from rabbinical Jews in Vilnius and Carol from shopkeepers in Budapest, while Mike's parents back in Buffalo were twice-a-year Presbyterians of Scottish-Irish origin. On Easter, Mike had taken the kids to church, followed by an Easter egg hunt. And now they'd all come here, minus Noah, who was still on an early schedule (Perri had put him to sleep before they left), and Bob. So there were eight of them seated at the long shiny cherry-wood table, including Becky, her two teenage daughters (against trend in her socioeconomic cohort, Becky had had kids in her twenties), and her husband, Jason, who was wearing a pale pink yarmulke that reminded Perri of her old diaphragm turned upside down. The chairs had high carved backs that looked as if they belonged in a medieval castle and felt somehow punitive. *Becky had always had terrible taste,* Perri thought pityingly as she reached for an etched crystal wineglass with a thick purple stem.

"Sadie, I understand you're quite the reader these days. How about you pose the Four Questions?" asked Jason. Perri swelled with pride.

"No thanks," Sadie replied. "I don't believe in God."

In an instant, Perri's pride turned to mortification. "Sadie!" she cried.

"She doesn't have to do it if she doesn't want to," said Mike.

There was an awkward silence.

"Okay, then," asked Jason, clearly miffed. "What about you, Aiden? Would you care to do the honors?"

"Sure," he said, shrugging.

"Thank you, Aiden," said Perri, hoping Sadie felt guilty.

"Why is this night different from all other nights?" he began in a mumbly monotone, a Haggadah gripped in his pudgy fists. "Why do we eat only matzo on Pesach? Matzo reminds us that when the Jews left the slavery of Egypt they had no time to bake their bread. They took the raw dough on their journey and baked it in the hot desert sun into hard crackers called matzo. Why do we eat bitter herbs at our seder? Maror reminds us of the bitter and cruel way the pharaoh treated the Jewish people when they were slaves in Egypt." He let out a tremendous fart.

Becky's daughters tittered maniacally.

"Rachel, girls, please," bellowed Jason.

Perri's mortification compounded. How had she given birth to such crude and irreverent children? She feared that their poor manners reflected badly on her own parenting skills. She also loved Aiden in particular as if he were her own arm. Sometimes, when he was sleepy, he still curled up in the crook of it and let her stroke his thick velvety brown hair. But he was such a boy — a boy's boy, really. Perri had trouble imagining how, even when grown, he'd ever find a woman to marry him. "Aiden, say excuse me," she told him.

"Don't embarrass the kid," barked Mike. "It was obviously an accident."

Becky and Jason stared at their hands. Perri felt embarrassed on her own behalf now, too. No doubt her friends were thinking that she and Mike were having marital discord. (She supposed they were.) Aiden looked from one to the other of his warring parents, trying to figure out whose side to take. Finally, he mumbled, "Sorry."

"Why don't you continue with the questions, Aiden," suggested Jason.

Aiden cleared his throat and began again: "Why do we dip our foods twice tonight? We dip bitter herbs into charoset to remind us how hard the Jewish slaves worked in Egypt. The chopped apples and nuts look like the clay used to make the bricks used in the pharaoh's buildings. We dip parsley into salt water. The parsley reminds us that spring is here and new life will grow. The salt water reminds us of the tears of the Jewish slaves. Why do we lean on a pillow tonight? We lean on a pillow to be comfortable." With that, Aiden closed his eyes and let his head fall to one side, as if a pillow awaited him there. Except it didn't. Once again, the teenage daughters exploded in hysterics.

"Girls, *enough!*" Jason bellowed in a stentorian tone of voice.

Perri suddenly felt deep loathing for Becky's husband and his superior attitude. Who was he, a man who manufactured radiant floor mats, to chastise her son for finding humor in religion?! Besides, the text *was* kind of idiotic. *We lean on pillows to be comfortable?* Talk about stating the obvious. "Aiden, sit up," said Perri, wishing she could lean her own head on a pillow. The fact was that she felt exhausted by her own life, exhausted by her need to do the right thing and to maintain order. From the earliest age, Perri had doodled perfect cubes, all the lines straight and connecting. But lately, she'd been entertaining the shocking conclusion that alignment didn't actually make her happy and that her need to control things was more of a compulsion than a pleasure. At the age of thirty-nine and eleven-twelfths, she'd also taken up smoking. Thanks to the peppermint-flavored breath spray she kept in her purse, she'd so far kept the habit hidden from her family. But for how much longer could she keep up the lie? *"Aiden, did you hear what I said?"* she bellowed.

"I heard," he said, slowly uncoiling his torso, clearly shocked at his mother's tone of voice.

The previous night, Perri had dreamed that strange men with paper bags over their heads with only the eyes cut out were lowering her naked body onto a white canvas. They painted her breasts and thighs with bright red oil paint, their brushes flipping like dying fish. Then they rolled her across the canvas— rolled and rolled until the ceiling was the wall, and wall was the floor. Then they began to massage her body. They rubbed red paint into her breasts and tummy and then farther down. And she let it happen. That was the fantasy—that just once she surrendered control. "I'm sorry. I have to go," Perri heard herself announcing. "Thank you for a lovely meal." She grabbed her purse and stood up.

"Mom?" said Sadie.

The other guests stared back at her, slack-jawed. Reaching for her coat, Perri left the room, then the house. The moon was nearly full, the air crisp. A dog barked in the distance. She figured she'd call a taxi from the street. Or maybe she'd just start walking. All she knew was that she had to get away. The men were after her—the big bad men wielding five-gallon canisters of Benjamin Moore Ladybug Red. It was a great color for the interior of coat closets, you know...

10

S o, what's your deal, anyway?" Gus asked
over coffee.

"Define 'deal,'" said Jeff.

"Like, I don't know — what do you live for?"

He shrugged, then pushed out his lips. "I don't know. Just
getting by. Trying to have a good time while I still can."

"I guess that's hard for me to understand, since I've never
lived that way," said Gus.

"You always knew you wanted to be a lawyer?"

"Maybe not a lawyer, but I knew when I was pretty young
that this was a fucked-up world, and I had to do my part to
change it."

"Wow," said Jeff, laughing lightly. "I was never that motivated. My only strong emotion was that I wanted to whip
Mike's ass at every sport we played. Which, frankly, wasn't that
hard."

"You're really competitive with your brother. Aren't you?"
said Gus.

"And you're not with Perri or Pia?" he asked.

"We're all a little competitive. But we're nothing alike."

"Nothing alike, my ass." Jeff chuckled again. "Maybe you've got different taste in brothers. But I hope you don't mind me saying, I can tell from a hundred miles away that you and Perri hark from the same gene pool. Never in my life have I met two girls so obsessed with getting shit done!"

The observation discomfited Gus. "I guess I never thought about it that way," she muttered.

"I don't know what your mother did to you," Jeff went on. "But damn. She did a good job. Or, depending on your perspective, a bad job. Honestly, I sometimes worry about my brother. The guy is driven enough. But Perri, man—she's always on his ass! I've never seen anything like it. He lost his job in a recession—big deal. She can't let the man collect unemployment insurance for even a day without bugging him about job interviews. And it's not like they aren't already loaded."

"I didn't know she'd been bugging him. Are you sure?" asked Gus, embarrassed on her sister's behalf and also on her own—because she recognized herself in Jeff's description, giving Debbie a hard time about not trying to climb the ranks of the GLTF.

"Pretty sure." Jeff took a sip of his coffee, narrowed his eyes. "She hates seeing us hang out, too. Doesn't she?"

"I got that feeling," concurred Gus.

"I got the feeling it's freaking *both* of them out—Perri and my brother, that is," said Jeff. "Whatever—too fuckin' bad. I'm a free man." He reached for Gus's hand, stroked it, and smiled. "Besides, I like you."

"I like you too," Gus said, swallowing.

"You ski?"

"Can't say I do."

He gestured with his chin. "I've got a friend who operates the lift at Stowe. Next winter, if we're still hanging, we'll road-trip and I'll teach you."

"Sounds like a plan," said Gus, even as she put the odds at fifty-fifty as to whether they'd make it to the end of the week.

Jeff leaned in. "Dude, it's a whole other world up there. It's just you and the elements — the snow, the ice, the wind — and God, I guess, if you believe in that stuff."

"Do *you* believe in that stuff?" asked Gus, curious.

Jeff released her hand, took another sip of his coffee, got a far-off look. "To be honest, when you're up in the clouds, you kind of feel like you're in heaven already. Know what I mean?" He turned back to her, his head cocked, his eyes squinty.

The political part of Gus had always hated that kind of back-to-nature talk — considered it mumbo jumbo of the highest form. (What good were ski trails to a domestic violence victim in the South Bronx?) Not for the first time, it occurred to her that Jefferson Sims was a total idiot. But another part of her — the part that was currently pulsating below her waist — was ready to follow him off the next cliff. "I can definitely see that," she said, nodding vigorously.

||

OLYMPIA WAS AT WORK when the next call from Larchmont came in. But this time it wasn't from Perri. It was from Mike. In the twelve years since he'd been married to Perri, he'd never once phoned Olympia. She immediately concluded that it was something serious—unless he was planning some kind of surprise party? Olympia was on the other line with a performance artist named Eberhard Fuchs, who was complaining that he hadn't received the promised stipend in connection with his latest masterpiece, *Military-Agricultural Gang Bang.* From what Olympia had been able to tell, the work consisted of Eberhard parading around the gallery space in a Viennese sausage costume, pretending to have sex with a series of giant paper plates with holes cut out of them. Olympia had found the performance offensive. At the same time, the insecure, self-doubting part of her wondered if it was her eye that was at fault and if the genius was apparent to everyone but her. In his home country, Eberhard was a star. "I'm sorry, Mr. Fuchs. Could you hang on one second?" she asked him.

"Pia, I need to talk to you," her brother-in-law announced in a grave tone.

Olympia's first thought was that her mother had had some kind of relapse. "Is my mom okay?" she asked.

"I'm not calling about Carol."

"Then what's going on?" Had something happened to one of the kids? Had Sadie sprouted horns?

"Perri walked out."

"WHAT?!" cried Olympia. Surely there was some kind of misunderstanding. Perri had probably gotten a flat tire on her way back from the Container Store, and AAA was running late. Or maybe she and Mike had just had a bad fight. The few times in recent months that Olympia had seen her sister and brother-in-law together, they seemed to be at each other's throats. Which had secretly tickled Olympia at the time, but didn't seem so amusing anymore.

"She came home early from Passover. We were at her friends' house," Mike went on. "She was acting really strangely. I thought she wasn't feeling well. She was asleep when I got home with the kids. The next morning when I woke up, she was gone."

"Did she leave a note?" asked Olympia, astounded.

"Yeah, she left a note."

"Well, what did it say?"

"That she needs time away from the family." He laughed bitterly. "Lovely."

"Time away, where?!"

"She didn't say."

"And how long does she plan to be gone for?"

"She didn't say that, either."

Olympia still refused to believe it. Women like Perri didn't walk out on their husbands. They built a terrarium, took a spin class. "Jesus," she said. "I don't know what to say. I'm so sorry. But listen, I'm actually on the other line right now. Can I call you back later?"

"Is there any way you could come out here?" Mike asked plaintively.

"When?"

"Now."

"Mike, I'm at work!" said Olympia, bristling. The only people who were allowed to pressure her were Lola and, by no choice of Olympia's own, Viveka.

"What about after work? Olympia, I'm begging you! I honestly can't handle this by myself. I got three kids to deal with. Your dad is still here, too, in case you were wondering. And he's demanding Ovaltine. Like that's really high on my list of priorities right now!"

"Can't Gus come?" asked Olympia, searching for an out. "She's a lot closer, and she has a car."

"She's in court in the afternoons," said Mike. "Plus, she doesn't know anything about kids. The other weekend I caught her trying to teach Noah how to stick paper clips into electric sockets."

"You're kidding."

"Mostly. But not entirely."

"Fine," said Olympia, sighing in defeat. "I have some stuff I need to take care of up here. Then I need to go back to Brooklyn and pick up Lola. We'll try to catch the seven thirty-seven out of Grand Central. That's the earliest train I can manage. Can you pick us up at the station? It's going to be kind of late by the time we get to you."

"Would you mind taking a taxi?" asked Mike.

In fact, Olympia *did* mind. Taking a taxi meant tacking another ten dollars onto the train fare. The actual money was possibly irrelevant. It was the principle. What had Mike ever done for her, other than mock and patronize her at family functions? Olympia hadn't forgotten the Thanksgiving when he'd sidled over to her, and asked, "So, how's the *Sex and the City* lifestyle treating you?" (Smirk, smirk.) As if the sole reason she'd failed to marry and move to suburbia was her fondness for having casual sex in nightclub restrooms. In fact, casual sex had never interested Olympia. She preferred making her men work for the privilege of bedding her; she felt she deserved that courtesy at least.

Just then, Olympia heard a high-pitched sob on the other end of the line. "Mike, are you okay?" she asked.

"I'm not okay, actually." He began to cry in strange, sneezy bursts. "My life is falling apart. First my job. Now my crazy wife walks out on her fortieth birthday."

"Ohmygod, it's Perri's birthday. I completely forgot!!" Olympia gasped, as guilt consumed her. Traditionally, it was Carol who kept everyone abreast of upcoming milestones. (Bob couldn't be counted on to know what month it was — never mind year — unless you meant "light-years.") But Carol was still in the hospital without her Metropolitan Museum of Art page-a-day calendar featuring Edgar Degas's *Dance Lesson* and Vermeer's *Maid Asleep* to consult. "Out of curiosity, had you planned anything for tonight?" she asked.

"I was going to make strip steaks after the kids went to bed," he said.

"Sounds festive," said Olympia, not bothering to disguise the sarcasm in her voice. A part of her suspected that, had Mike hinted that he was planning to make even the smallest fuss over Perri's fortieth, the entire mess might have been avoided.

"It's not my fault Perri hates restaurants!" he cried. "She thinks all the bus boys are urinating in the food."

I bet she wouldn't have hated Per Se, Olympia was tempted to reply but refrained.

"I had a present for her, too," Mike went on.

"And what was that?"

"An Hermès scarf."

Olympia couldn't help herself. "Mike, that's what you give your corporate secretary on the last day of work before the holidays!"

"She loves Hermès."

"Whatever. It's a moot point now. I'll see you later."

After she hung up with Mike, Olympia reconnected with Eberhard. "I apologize profusely," she said, trying to refocus. "Where were we?"

"You morons haven't paid me," he said, sounding even more peeved than before. "That's where we were."

Olympia was taken aback. "I'm sending an email to our billing department right now," she said. "But I'd appreciate it if you didn't call me or anyone else here a moron."

"I'll call you what I like, you *dreckige Hure,*" said Eberhard.

Had Olympia just been called a "dirty old whore" in German? A vast storehouse of rage welled up inside her, then exploded into the open air — not just at every egomaniacal artist she'd ever had to deal with at the museum, but at Mike for making her come out to Larchmont; at Patrick for letting her fall in love with him; at #6103 for not jotting down his first and last names and home address in the "Additional Facts about Myself" section of his profile; at Carol for turning her and her sisters into butterflies in a museum, their wings immobilized, their identifying labels sealed to the wall; at Bob for being impossible to pin down at all; at Gus for not respecting her; at Perri for patronizing her; at the Monsanto Corporation for injecting hormones into cows; and at herself for not being more ambitious, or less defensive, or whatever it was that kept her from even trying to be the things she dreamed of being. "Well, then, I'll call *you* what *I* like," Olympia told the guy. "You're a pathetic old pervert. Honestly, you're lucky anyone's willing to pay you two cents to perform your bullshit, so-called artwork. You think you're so radical. Well, you have the mental capacity of a sausage! I wouldn't be surprised to hear you were a rapist. Also, need I mention that you people were on the wrong side of the war..." Olympia couldn't believe the bile that was coming out of her mouth.

Not entirely unpredictably, the line had gone dead. "If you'd like to make a call," said a recording, "please hang up and try again."

Olympia's heart was now beating so hard that it actually hurt her chest. She felt elated and terrified at the same time. After Viveka found out what had happened, would she get fired? And if she was unemployed, how would she ever afford health insurance for her and Lola? Never mind nice clothes. These questions in her head, Olympia gathered her belongings and headed out.

Maximilian and Annmarie kept typing, as if they hadn't heard, even though they clearly had.

A low ceiling of dense fog hung over the city, obscuring the tops of the tall buildings. It was still unseasonably cold. But Olympia didn't mind. She found the saturnine vistas to be soothing. On Second Avenue, it started to drizzle, and Olympia opened her umbrella. With her other hand, she dialed Perri's cell number. She was curious about where her sister was. She also felt guilty that she hadn't already called to wish her a happy fortieth. And she was keen to let Perri know that, counter to her older sister's impression that Olympia was selfish and unhelpful, she was on her way out to Larchmont that very evening to help take care of Perri's kids. If points couldn't be scored on this count, how could they ever be scored?!

But her sister didn't pick up. Olympia was secretly relieved. In many ways, she found it easier expressing herself to automated answering services than to actual people. Even so, she strained to achieve a tone of voice that sounded subdued without being phlegmatic. "It's Pia," she began. "I just want to wish you a happy birthday, wherever you are. I'm going out to Larchmont to help Mike with the kids tonight. If you want to talk, give me a call. I'll have my phone on. But no pressure. I hope you're doing okay, wherever you are. We're all fine. Bye." She paused before declaring, "I love you." It had been years since Olympia had uttered those words to Perri. And she wondered where the burst of affection had come from and whether it had anything to do with the fact that, for possibly the first time in the history of the Hellinger family, and despite Olympia's career-ruining outburst in the museum, Perri had claimed the Fuck-up Sister trophy for herself.

It was nearly eight thirty when Olympia and Lola arrived in Larchmont. The rain was even heavier in the suburbs than it had been in the city. Luckily there was an idling taxi in front of the station house. Olympia climbed into the back with Lola. The smell of wet rubber filled the cab. As they approached Perri's house, Olympia begrudgingly handed the driver her last ten-dollar bill.

Mike opened the front door. He was wearing jeans, a UPenn T-shirt, and bedroom slippers that appeared to be made of crafting felt. His face was less pink than usual—more like beige with hints of green. "Thanks for coming out," he said gravely.

"Of course," said Olympia, fighting the urge to ask him for reimbursement for her travel expenses.

Aiden was playing Fruit Ninja on his father's phone with the dim-eyed gaze of a professional drunk, his pointer finger frantically waggling. Noah, dressed in tiny elastic-waist jeans and a Yankees jersey, was fast asleep on the couch, albeit at a strange angle, his legs elevated higher than his head. Bob was nowhere in sight and presumably already in bed. Sadie was eating Cheerios and milk and watching *Harry Potter and the Chamber of Secrets*.

"Scary!" said Lola, hiding behind her mother's leg as a giant serpent sank its fang into the boy wizard's flesh.

"Sadie, turn that garbage off," said Mike. "You're scaring your cousin. And you're going to get nightmares."

"No, I'm not," said Sadie, munching away happily. "And it's not garbage." She took another bite. "Besides, it's not like Harry dies. Dumbledore's phoenix, Fawkes, saves him."

Mike narrowed his already sliverlike eyes, shook his head. As if the misery were all-encompassing.

"Speaking of nightmares," said Olympia. "I need to try and get Lola to sleep. Is there room for her in Sadie's bedroom?"

"There's a trundle under her bed. I can get some sheets for it if I can remember where Perri keeps them." He scratched his head, glanced over at Sadie. "Yo, Sade, where does Mom keep the twin sheets for your room?"

"Hall closet," came the reply.

"I'm sure I can find them," said Olympia, walking toward the stairs.

"It's fine, I'll get them," said Mike, knocking into Olympia's shoulder as he tried to beat her to the landing. It actually hurt. Was the man made of rock?

"I can make the bed," she said, following him upstairs.

Mike turned the knob to the linen closet, whereupon Olympia suppressed a gasp. Even the fitted sheets, impossible for the average mortal to tame, had been expertly folded into perfect squares. What's more, a black satin ribbon encircled each sheet set.

"I can't believe this is happening," Mike mumbled as he knelt and sorted through the pile.

"Maybe she's just upset about turning forty," offered Olympia, who dreaded the day herself. "It's kind of a traumatic birthday — at least for women. I mean, George Clooney is allowed to be a sex symbol in middle age, whereas women his age are basically told to disappear."

"Maybe," said Mike. "But — no disrespect to Perri — being a sex symbol was never her thing."

Although Olympia secretly agreed with the assessment, she was startled by his words and by the betrayal that seemed to be implicit in them. "I guess," she replied, struggling to think of something to say that would sound neutral. "So, have you tried calling her?"

"I'm not going to chase after her," Mike announced defiantly. He picked himself up off the floor, one knee at a time, a pale pink sheet set with a French rose motif in his arms. "If she wants to be part of this family, she can come back on her own account."

"Right," said Olympia, even though it seemed to her that he was taking the wrong approach. Wasn't this the time for Mike to show Perri how much she meant to him?

"Have *you* talked to her?" he asked.

"I just left a message," said Olympia.

She followed him into Sadie's bedroom with its outrageous canopy bed, fit for a royal. Again descending to his hands and knees, Mike yanked out the trundle. Olympia, in turn, bent down to help secure the fitted sheet across the mattress. Her face was now a foot away from his. Curious somehow, she found herself glancing over at him. She'd never noticed the yellow-green speckles in his eyes before. "You look like Perri right now," he said, returning her gaze. "I hadn't seen it before just now."

Olympia quickly looked away. The comparison felt too intimate. It felt strangely threatening, too. Olympia still hated to have her looks contrasted to those of her sisters, if only because it brought her back to a time in adolescence when differentiating herself had been paramount. Back then, clothes had often felt like her only weapons. Olympia had lived in oversized Ts, low-slung belts, long winter underwear, and a Levi's jean jacket she'd decorated with campaign-style buttons advertising the names of various West Village boutiques. Perri had favored white canvas Tretorns, bleached jeans, and giant Benetton rugby shirts that she'd paid for with money saved up from her after-school job at a local jeweler's. (Gus, though still in junior high at the time, had already perfected the art of androgyny with the help of Doc Martens, black jeans, and a black leather motorcycle jacket with lots of unnecessary zippers.) Somehow the three of them had still managed to be in and out of one another's closets, pulling things off hangers, cutting deals. "Guess button-flies for your CP Shades mock?" They'd managed to hurt one another's feelings, too. Olympia still recalled the time she'd worn a shirt with a Nehru collar to school, and Perri had addressed her as "Yo, Gandhi." Even though Olympia had considered Perri's own fashion sense to be the antithesis of cool, she'd never worn the top again.

"No one has ever said we look alike before," she told Mike. "It's probably just that we were talking about her."

"Maybe," he said.

"Anyway, I can finish up here."

"You sure?"

"Positive."

Relief flooded Olympia's chest at the sight of her brother-in-law lumbering away.

But there was no escaping him after the kids were all finally asleep. Since Bob was in the guest room, Olympia's bed for the night was the living room sofa. Which was also the TV couch. Then again, it was Mike's house. He plunked himself down in a club chair across from her and cracked open a beer. She was watching *2001: A Space Odyssey*. "You gotta love the nineteen-sixties idea of advanced computer technology," Mike offered at the spectacle of Hal the talking computer telling one of the astronauts that the spaceship was about to malfunction. "Hal," he went on. "How come no one uses that name anymore? Hal Sims. Not bad. Right?"

"You thinking of having a fourth?" Olympia joked.

"Not likely to happen at present, since my wife doesn't appear to live here anymore."

"I'm sure she'll be back," said Olympia, who wasn't sure of anything.

Mike took a sip of his beer and sighed a world-weary "Who knows."

"Speaking of walking out," Olympia told him. "I basically quit my job this afternoon after I talked to you. Like, I'm not sure it's going to be waiting for me on Monday." She had to tell someone.

"No shit."

"Yes shit."

Mike folded down his lips. "Wow. Well, welcome to the unemployed people club. It's not that bad once you get used to it."

"I guess," said Olympia, unconvinced.

"Hey." He paused, took another sip of his beer. "I appreciate you coming out here."

"Of course."

"It's nice having you here."

Olympia couldn't, in good faith, tell Mike that it was nice being there, so she said nothing.

A few minutes before eleven, he wandered off with a "'Night."

"Sleep well," she told him. She watched a few more minutes of the movie. Then she flicked off the power button, curled up under her blanket, and attempted to shut out the world and all its myriad confusions, if only for the night.

It couldn't have been much more than six a.m. when Olympia woke. The kids weren't even up yet. Her back ached. Yet there was something strangely calming, even copacetic, about lying there staring at the ceiling beams. The silence was as heavy as the velvet drapes in the dining room. The morning light was just beginning to filter through the bay window that looked out into the backyard. It was early spring, and crocuses and daffodil buds were poking through the thaw. Olympia thought back to her earliest love affairs. All of them had started in late March or early April. It made her think that human beings were eighty-five percent biologically programmed and, to that extent, completely predictable. As for the remaining fifteen percent, there was no saying where it would lead.

Or where it had led her sister Perri. The Rocky Mountains? Rio de Janeiro? A thought struck Olympia: Was it possible that she really didn't know the first thing about her older sister? What if the roles we assumed in our families had little to nothing to do with the people we actually became in the outside world? A mutual acquaintance in New York had once described Perri as "such a sweetheart," and the description had shocked Olympia. Was that how her older sister came across in public? And was Perri's critical streak reserved only for her younger sisters and husband? And had it really been so intolerable here in Larchmont? Olympia wondered as she gazed around her at the creamy walls, plush carpets, iron chandelier, leather upholstery, and solid wood furnishings. Olympia had yet to graduate from the Ikea stage of home furnishing, the particleboard and MDF interspersed with the occasional flea-market find.

Bob was up next. Olympia saw him before he saw her. He was dressed in his flannel bathrobe, and his upper body was bent at a seventy-degree angle. Scurrying down the hall, his eyes darting this way and that, he reminded her of a frightened bandit. Clearly he couldn't wait to go home, Olympia thought with a heavy heart. And why did it so upset her to see her parents looking needy or vulnerable in any way? Growing up, she'd hear the two of them talking in the kitchen in low voices about how her father had been passed over for yet another plum assignment. Carol would express outrage at the head of the lab. Quietly defensive, Bob would try to justify the decision to make Kit Furlong or Dan Lieblich, rather than himself, the team leader of the Booster Neutrino Oscillation Experiment, or some other initiative. As Olympia understood it, her father, while a young atomic scientist at Los Alamos National Lab in New Mexico, had once been deemed a rising star in his field. There had even been talk of a future Nobel. What had happened since then (to change his fortunes) was unclear. Bob never talked about that period of his life. And Olympia didn't have the nerve to ask, not wanting to be nosey or to upset him.

In truth, it was strange to think of her father having ever had a life outside his wife and three daughters and in a place other than Hastings. Still, Olympia always longed to know more about the man he once was. And had he been a virgin when he'd married Carol? It seemed unlikely, but who knew. Clearly, he'd been a serious nerd. "Hi, Dad," she called to him.

Apparently startled, he froze in place before his head swiveled to face her. "Perr-Gus-I-mean-Pia—what in the world are you doing here?!" he asked, his eyebrows up near his hairline.

"I came out last night," she said. "Lola's up in Sadie's room."

"And where's Perri? She's usually the first up."

"She went on a last-minute business trip," Olympia said, improvising. "Some kind of closet organization conference in San Diego, I think. She would have said good-bye, but she didn't want to wake you."

"I see." Bob furrowed his brow. "Well, it's nice to see you! Maybe you'll come to the hospital with me today to see Mom."

"Of course."

"Though I don't know how we'll get there. Perhaps someone can drive us."

"We'll figure it out," said Olympia, conjecturing that Perri and her Lexus were the glue that kept the Hellinger family from splintering into four disparate units.

Noah and Mike appeared soon after that, Noah in the same Yankees jersey and jeans from the previous night and Mike in the same T-shirt—and now sweats. As the latter lumbered down the stairs, his son hanging off his neck, Olympia could just discern the outline of his penis swinging to and fro. "Morning," he mumbled.

"Hey," she said, suddenly as embarrassed by her own semi-dressed state as she was by his—and glad now that her father was nearby. "Hey, Pops," she said, turning to him. "Do you want me to go get the newspaper for you?" Perri still got home delivery of the *New York Times* and the *Wall Street Journal,* though it was unclear if anyone read them.

"Please," replied Bob.

Olympia took her time walking to the front door, then walking back, so as to avoid sharing counter space with Mike. Indeed, by the time she made it to the kitchen, he was already on his way back upstairs, both bottle and baby in tow.

Sadie appeared shortly after that, followed by Lola.

"Good morning, you two!" said Olympia.

"I want pancakes," said Sadie.

"Me, too," said Lola.

"You're just saying that because Sadie wants them," said Olympia, then realized she was being unnecessarily critical of a not-quite-four-year-old.

"No, I'm not!" cried Lola, sounding hurt.

Olympia couldn't blame her. "You're right. That was bitchy. Sorry," she said.

"What's *bitchy?*" asked Lola.

"Mean," said Olympia.

"Supermean," said Sadie. "I love being supermean!"

"Why?" asked Lola.

"I don't know," said Sadie, shrugging.

At least she was honest, Olympia thought. "Well, if Sadie shows me where the ingredients are, I'm happy to give the pancakes a go," she said.

"Mom keeps the organic buckwheat mix over here," she said, leading her aunt to a pullout pantry that made the linen closet look haphazard. The twist ties that accompanied already-opened products such as rice and pasta appeared to have been color-coordinated to their packaging. What's more, all the cereal boxes were lined up so that no box stuck out farther than any other. Olympia felt as if she needed a double dose of her anxiety medication. It wasn't just the perfection of Perri's pantry that unnerved her. The very idea of cooking filled Olympia with dread and self-doubt. She never understood how other women she knew all seemed to know how to make braised lamb shanks and turnip puree. When had they learned? And who had taught them? Carol, a would-be women's libber in her day, had seen cooking as a form of servitude and had done as little of it as possible while her daughters were growing up. The Hellinger sisters had therefore subsisted on TV dinners, pizza, raw carrots, and macaroni and cheese.

But Olympia's own generation had turned the business of producing edible calories into a higher calling. Not infrequently, Olympia would find herself at dinner parties in Brooklyn where everyone would be sitting around talking about naturally evaporated sea salt or herb-infused olive oil, and she'd feel as if she were visiting from Mars. Neighbors of hers had built a cheese cave in their backyard; another guy she knew in the neighborhood had a giant beehive from which he extracted honey while wearing a black bag over his head that looked eerily like the ones used to humiliate prisoners at the Abu Ghraib prison during the War in Iraq. "Wow, your mom is really organized," Olympia murmured to her niece.

"Yeah, she's kind of a control freak," said Sadie.

"What's a control freak?" asked Lola.

"Someone who likes to be really neat," said Olympia.

"And who freaks out if it's not neat and has to take her medication," added Sadie—to Olympia's shock and fascination. Was her sister on Zoloft too? And, if so, why hadn't she ever told Olympia? Then again, why had Olympia never told Perri about her own prescription? What if the two sisters had more in common than either would ever be willing to admit?

Eggs, milk, and oil all found their way onto the countertop. "Are you girls going to help me?" asked Olympia. "Because, truth be told, Old Auntie Pia isn't much of a chef."

"Can I break the eggs?" Sadie said excitedly.

"Can I mix?" said Lola.

The project was a roaring success. Olympia managed to flip at just the right moment and without excessive splattering. For once, Sadie was being almost sweet. And Lola seemed ecstatically happy to have a "big sister" for the day—so much so that, for a brief moment in time, Olympia allowed herself to imagine they were all one big happy family and that this was her four-bedroom Tudor; her toile-upholstered kitchen nook; even her (god forbid) husband sitting in it, flipping through the Weekend

Journal, Noah on the floor next to him zoom-zooming a toy digger around a pretend building site. Her brother-in-law was no one's idea of tall, dark, and handsome, Olympia thought. But he was all man. His hands in particular had a certain meaty appeal. His wedding ring and neatly clipped nails aside, she could almost imagine Mike as a caveman in prehistoric France, pulling apart an animal carcass.

In the afternoon, they all went to the hospital to visit Carol. At the sight of her broken leg still suspended in traction, guilt consumed Olympia. She suddenly grasped the discomfort that her mother must have been in all that month, as well as her own failure to have made that month any more bearable for her. Olympia couldn't precisely say what had kept her away from Yonkers other than sheer lassitude. If Carol was miffed at her, however, she didn't let on. "It's lovely to see you, Pia," she said, to Olympia's surprise and relief.

Then she relayed the joyous news that, if all went as planned, her doctors were promising to release her on Sunday or Monday.

"Well, isn't that something," said Bob, looking so happy that Olympia thought he might burst.

It didn't seem like a good time to tell Carol (or Bob) what was going on in Perri's marriage, or at Olympia's job. So Olympia repeated her previous lie about how her older sister had left at dawn for a closet conference in San Diego.

"How strange. She didn't mention it when I saw her," said Carol. "But you girls are so in demand! I don't even try to keep up anymore."

Saturday evening, Gus and Jeff came over for pizza. Just as Perri had feared and suspected, the two were now a couple. The thought crossed Olympia's mind that Perri's motives for leaving town included some deep-seated dread of seeing her sister and her brother-in-law romantically entwined. Since Jeff was sitting across from her, Olympia had plenty of opportunity to study his face. *Stunningly handsome* was the verdict, she decided, if in a highly studied way. Clearly, he'd put a lot of thought into making his hair appear as if he'd just climbed out of bed. Or maybe he really *had* just climbed out of bed — with Gus. Or had they not slept together yet? Olympia couldn't tell. Either way, Olympia was surprised to find herself feeling resentful, as well: Why should *she* have to deal with Perri's mess while Gus spent the weekend gallivanting with Perri's husband's handsome brother? Wasn't Olympia supposed to be the Pretty One in the family? Didn't that count for anything anymore?

Or had the tiara been passed down? Olympia had to concede that, if anyone was looking stunning that evening, it was her younger sister, Gus, who had pulled her hair back in a tiny ponytail and was wearing — was it possible? — eyeliner and lip gloss. Until just then, Olympia had never noticed how fine her sister's features were. The loss of her nose ring definitely enhanced the picture, as well. And why was she smiling like that and giggling at everything Jeff said? Olympia liked to think of herself as someone who didn't begrudge others their happiness and especially not her sisters — so long as they didn't gloat. But with each passing minute, she found the sight of Gus and Jeff more and more unbearable.

On account of (a) Perri's glaring absence and (b) the need to keep the truth about that absence from Bob, the conversation at the dinner table that evening was as desultory as it was stilted.

Bob remarked on how tasty the crust was before asking if the rest of them were aware that pizza dough operated on similar principles as standing-wave ultrasound, providing insight into the motors used in micro-actuator technology? No one was aware. At another lull, Olympia asked Aiden, "So, what's your favorite movie these days?" (Having already eaten dinner, the younger kids were in the adjoining den, watching *Mary Poppins*.)

"*Transformers*," he said, without skipping a beat.

"An excellent film," said Jeff. "I thought Megan Fox really brought depth to the character of Mikaela Banes, the all-knowing auto mechanic."

"I guess," said Aiden, who still didn't like girls.

"What about you, Dad?" asked Olympia.

"Let's see. I enjoyed *What's Up, Doc?* with Barbra Streisand. I suppose it was many years ago now. But Carol and I have never laughed so hard in a movie theater. I also enjoyed Woody Allen's *Sleeper*. A very amusing film."

"Interesting choices from yesteryear," said Olympia. "Jeff?"

"Let's see. I remember digging *The Shawshank Redemption* when I saw it. On a lighter note, I definitely enjoyed *Wedding Crashers*."

"That *was* a seriously funny movie," offered Mike, chuckling for the first time all weekend. "That scene when the weird gay brother climbs into Vince Vaughn's bed and tries to seduce him—hilarious."

Gus took the opportunity to shoot her brother-in-law an angry look and mutter "Homophobe" while an apparently newly sensitized Jeff added, "Easy there, bro."

Meanwhile, Olympia's mind traveled at the speed of a flying pizza back to Brooklyn and her black file cabinet, whose bottom drawer she mentally pulled open to reveal the donor profile of #6103. They were *his* favorite movies, too. A coincidence, she hoped. Only, what did that coincidence say about Lola's father? To the best of her abilities, Olympia had blocked out Dawn Cronin's New Year's missive, refusing to believe that her daughter's father could possibly be a second-tier underwear model named Randy from Las Vegas.

Or what if, by some freak chance, it wasn't a coincidence at all? What if Jefferson Sims, in need of cash for a new pair of Rossignols or the like, had paid a few visits to the Cryobank of Park Avenue five or six years ago, en route to Stowe? Olympia suddenly recalled Perri's saying that he'd spent one semester at medical school in the Caribbean before quitting to start a T-shirt and Boogie Board business on Venice Beach. Plus, he was over six feet tall with blue eyes and brown hair. Moreover, #6103 had listed skiing as one of his favorite sports, albeit the cross-country variety.

Olympia thought she was going to be sick. She put down her fork and reached for her wine. "Jeff," she said, swallowing. "I have a strange question. By any chance do you like the Boston Red Sox?"

"The Red Sox?" he asked, squinting.

"Yeah."

He shrugged. "I'm not really a team sports kind of guy. But the Sox are pretty awesome if you like baseball. They've got Big Papi—"

"Right. Excuse me," said Olympia, rising from the table.

Each of her legs seemed to weigh a thousand pounds as she mounted the stairs. Closing the door to the kids' bathroom, she sat down on the toilet seat, pulled an emergency pack of American Spirits out of her handbag, yanked open the window (so

Sadie's and Aiden's monogrammed towels wouldn't reek), and then, her hands trembling, lit up. *Surely she was just being paranoid.* Lola and Jeff looked nothing alike. Or did they? Flipping from one disturbing thought to another, she thought of Patrick and wondered what he was doing just then and if he ever thought about her, ever missed her, ever realized the heartache he'd caused her. She also thought of Perri and how crazy she was to be throwing away this life of bounty, this life that Olympia actually wanted. There, she'd finally admitted it to herself. She was tired of going it alone, tired of pretending to be brave and sleek and free of neediness, like some honey trap in one of her beloved John le Carré spy novels. She was getting too old to keep up the act. Her eyes filled with tears, but she kept them at bay for as long as she could. Then she couldn't anymore and began to weep — not loudly, but apparently loudly enough for Mike to hear.

Whether he was worried and had come to check on her, or just happened to be walking by, she never knew. But there was a knock on the door. "I'm in here," Olympia called out in a thin voice, as she instinctively stood up, lifted the toilet seat, and pitched her cigarette into the bowl. As if she were a teenager about to be grounded, even though, while she was growing up, Bob and Carol regularly pretended not to notice the smoke that billowed out of Gus's bedroom and hers. (Even in middle school, Perri was violently antismoking.)

"Pia?" came the tentative response. "You okay?"

By then she was crying too hard to answer.

Mike cracked the door, peered at her in silence for a few moments, then took a step in and closed the door behind him. From there, he slowly walked over to where she now sat, slumped on the floor beneath the window. "Hey," he said. Squatting before her, he laid a tentative hand on her upper arm.

"I'm okay — thanks," Olympia finally choked out, both embarrassed to have been discovered in such a pathetic state and, in truth, thankful for the sympathy. She wiped her nose with the back of her hand. A fluttery breeze danced in circles over their heads.

"You don't look okay." He handed her a tissue.

"I'm just — it's nothing," she said, blotting her nose and eyes.

Mike stood up, slipped his hands into the front pockets of his jeans, and appeared to examine a bottle of scented moisturizer on the glass shelf over the toilet. Then he let out an acid chuckle, and said, "I thought I was the one who was supposed to be crying."

"Go ahead," said Olympia, laughing herself now, if secretly disappointed that he'd already turned the conversation back to himself. Why were men always doing that?!

"Nah, I'm done with that part," he said, turning to lean his backside into the edge of the sink, one sneaker foot lifted onto its toe. "To be honest, a part of me is kind of enjoying this in some sick way."

"You *are?*" said Olympia, startled by the admission and furrowing her brow.

"I don't know" — Mike shrugged — "maybe everyone wants what they don't have."

"Maybe," she said, unsure what he was getting at.

A few more moments of silence passed between them. Then he glanced sideways at her, visibly swallowed, his Adam's apple shooting up and down his neck like a pinball that couldn't break through to the next corridor. "What about you?" he said in a strange voice. "What do you want, Pia?"

"What do you mean?" she asked, sensing a new intention.

Suddenly he was right next to her, kneeling before her, as if he were about to pray to Mecca. But he wasn't. He was looking right at her, looking at her longingly and clutching her upper arms with his caveman hands. He was so close that Olympia could see the little lines that ran up and down his lips. She could smell him, too. And he smelled like pepperoni and aftershave and beer. And he was warm. She could tell that from his hands alone, tell that he was an ideal furnace to be wrapped around on cold nights in January. "Pia," he whispered. "You're so beautiful. I never felt I could tell you that before now." And his chest was going in and out. And his words felt like the prick of a pin. Olympia winced in pain or pleasure — she could no longer tell the difference. All she knew was that this wasn't supposed to be happening.

Except it was. And in that moment, she wanted so badly to reciprocate, to fall into Mike Sims's chest and let him have her. It had been so long since she'd felt desired. And she felt so comfortable with him. As if they'd known each other their whole lives. (In a way, she supposed, they had.) She trusted him, too; however ironically, he felt like a safe bet. Plus, there was no denying the comfort of his words, familiar words that she still needed to hear, that still made her feel special, even as she acknowledged the hollowness of an accolade that was slipping further and further out of reach.

But she couldn't do it, couldn't do that to her sister. Even if Perri didn't want him anymore, that didn't mean she wanted Olympia to have him. Olympia couldn't bear the thought of incurring Perri's eternal wrath. She had pride, too. And she hated the idea of Perri imagining that Olympia had spent the previous thirty-eight years coveting what her older sister had already achieved, trying to be *just like her.* Also, she didn't want to prove Gus right again; she could still hear her younger sister the night of Carol's accident, saying she'd "always been into married guys." "Mike — stop!" she squeaked in a puny voice, standing up to escape his clutches.

But he stood up, too. Their bodies were inches apart, their groins nearly touching, his beer breath on her neck. "Pia," he said again, his chest cratering. "Let me kiss you —"

She felt so torn — and also, in that moment, so starved for love. Why should she be the only one in the family without it? And Mike wanted her so badly. How could she deny him? Men had their needs. Well, so did women. And it could be just one time. As he moved closer, she felt powerless to everything that came next. She closed her eyes and felt his lips brushing against hers, her breasts melding into his volcanic chest, his crotch hardening against her thigh . . .

"Mommy?" came a tiny voice from outside the door.

Lola!! Olympia felt as if she'd touched an electrified fence and jumped away from Mike as fast as she could. "Coming, sweetie," she trilled. She wiped her lips against the back of her hand, tucked her hair behind her ears, and exited the bathroom, failing to close the door behind her.

"Mommy, have you been crying?" asked Lola. Gus stood next to her, looking probingly at Olympia, then at Mike, who was now standing by the window, his back turned, his head down. Then she looked at Olympia again.

"No, sweetie, just allergies," said Olympia, taking her daughter into her arms and doing her best to ignore her sister's suspicious glances. Except she couldn't. "What?!" she said accusingly, turning to Gus.

"Nothing!" cried Gus. "Lola was just looking for you, that's all."

"Well, here I am."

"Is everything okay?"

"Everything's fine. Why?"

"Sadie says we can have popcorn," said Lola. "But Aunt Gus and I can't find it. And Grandpa doesn't know where it is."

"Well, let's go look for it," said Olympia, shuttling her daughter and sister back down the hall and trying to pretend that what had just happened never had.

This time it was Olympia who lay awake long into the night, trying to make sense of what had happened. In her mind's eye, she could see Perri and Mike walking down the aisle at Lyndhurst Castle, while Eric Clapton's "Wonderful Tonight" played in the background, both of them beaming and round-faced. She also saw herself and Perri as children playing "ship" in their bunk bed. Perri, on the top bunk, was directing Olympia to raise the ladder before the pirates could climb aboard, then berating her for having done it too slowly and at the wrong angle and then placing it on the wrong side of the bed. It wasn't just that Perri was bossy. It was that she seemed to need Olympia to fuck everything up. And Olympia was no longer willing to play the role. It followed that, the more convinced Perri became that she had all the right answers, the more loath Olympia was to reveal any doubts or questions about her life whatsoever, including those surrounding her decision to have a child on her own.

Olympia had also learned her lesson. In her twenties, following a breakup and leave of absence from yet another graduate school, Olympia had admitted to Perri that she felt aimless and depressed. In response, Perri had suggested that Olympia consider an inpatient treatment program for insane people. That, or she should lower her expectations and get a minimum-wage job as a toll taker at the Tappan Zee Bridge. Or maybe Perri hadn't actually said those things. Yet that had been the message with which Olympia had come away. She'd felt judged rather than supported.

Still, she didn't hate Perri. On some level, yes, she was jealous of her older sister's professional success. She also considered Perri to be a semi-absurd figure. At the same time, Olympia had always taken a strange sort of pride in having a sister like her. She even recalled feeling tickled when Perri had married at a relatively young age. It had made Olympia feel grown-up by association. It had also felt like further permission to stray and to fail. Only now Perri had called in sick, and Olympia was being offered a chance to play her sister's understudy. Was that what was happening here? Or did this have nothing to do with Perri? Had Mike been secretly enamored of Olympia all these years? Olympia did a quick mental vetting of their interactions over the last ten years of Hellinger family functions. Sometimes he'd look at her sideways and make provocative, even suggestive comments. But he did that with everyone, didn't he?

Olympia felt confused and agitated. All night, she waited for Mike to appear in the living room. What had happened between them felt like one step removed from incest. Mike was practically her brother! At the same time, she longed for him to climb under her blanket and smother her with kisses...

He never did.

And in the light of early morning, she was glad that he hadn't. The same scenario that had kept her up half the night seemed ill-advised, even absurd. She longed to flee the premises — and her crazy urges — as soon as possible. Unfortunately, she'd already promised Sadie and Lola that she'd take them ice-skating in the morning. So there was no chance of a graceful exit until the afternoon.

At breakfast, Olympia avoided all communication and even eye contact with her brother-in-law, who kept his own distance as well, directing all his conversation at the kids (and Bob).

The skating expedition was yet another exercise in frustration. Sadie had taken lessons and even knew how to skate backward. But Lola was so petrified by the sensation of unsteady ground that, even with Olympia holding her in a full body lock, she refused to let her skates touch the ice. Instead, she lifted her bent knees into the air, and panted, "No, no, no!" while Olympia cried, "Ohmygod, do you have to be such a wimp?" Ten minutes later, her back and brain aching from the strain, Olympia gave up hope and accompanied Lola off the ice.

Back at the house, Olympia quickly stuffed her and Lola's belongings into an overnight bag, while Lola and Sadie played with Sadie's Littlest Pet Shop collection. "Sweetie," Olympia said in a low voice. "I'm afraid we have to go back to the city now."

"No!" cried Lola. "I want to stay with Sadie."

"I know, sweetie. But I have stuff I need to take care of at home. I promise we'll see Sadie again soon."

Lola folded her lower lip over her chin. It was a face that Olympia had seen before, on someone else. But who? "We haven't even had the funeral yet," she said.

"Funeral?" asked Olympia.

"The walrus died."

"I'm sorry for your loss."

"You're not sorry."

"I am. But we have to go."

"I'm not leaving!" announced Lola.

"You *are* leaving," said Olympia, struggling to keep her cool.

"Am not."

"Are so."

"Am not."

Her patience worn thin, Olympia grabbed Lola by the elbow and began to drag her toward the door, Lola moaning in revolt. That was when Olympia caught sight of Bob. Embarrassed by both her display of aggression and the fact that she was leaving already, she quickly released Lola. She'd seen her father lose his temper only once, decades ago, after a family of Italian tourists cut them in the line to buy tickets to the laser light show at the Hayden Planetarium. "Excuse me, you fascist sympathizers, but we were here first!" Bob had said. "So SHOVE IT!" At the time, Olympia had been mortified. But during the years that followed, "Shove it, you fascist sympathizers" had become yet another oft-repeated joke-phrase in the Hellinger family.

"Leaving already?" asked Bob. The sight of Olympia's overnight bag in the middle of the living room must have given her away.

"Unfortunately, I have some work stuff I need to take care of," said Olympia.

"Well, that's a real shame because I just got word that Mom's being released this afternoon," said Bob. "I know she'd be thrilled if you were part of the welcoming party."

Olympia's guilt metastasized. "Wow, I forgot she was getting out so soon," she said, lamenting the timing, even as she was thrilled and relieved to think that her mother was on the mend. It occurred suddenly to Olympia that Hastings via Yonkers was as good an "escape route" as any other. Plus, she couldn't very well leave Mike to deal with getting her parents home from the hospital. "You know what—I can let work slide for a day or so," she said. Never mind that she didn't actually know if she had any work waiting for her next week. "Why don't we go over to Yonkers with you right now and get Mom. Then all four of us can go back to Hastings together. Lola and I will spend the night. The museum is dark on Monday, anyway."

"What a wonderful idea!" declared Bob. "It will be a real homecoming for Mom."

No sooner had Olympia made the offer, however, than she began to regret having done so. Sleeping in her childhood bed always made her feel as if she were nine inches tall. But it was too late. Olympia helped her father pack up his two pairs of pants and rusted beard trimming kit.

Lola was still whimpering when the taxi honked.

Olympia kissed her niece and nephews good-bye. She and her brother-in-law exchanged no such formalities. "Good having you, Bob—and let me know if you need help at the hospital," Mike announced while gripping his father-in-law's hand.

"Will do," Bob replied. "And if you don't mind me saying, you have some handshake there! My right hand feels as if it were just mauled by a brown bear."

"All those years of football training." Mike smiled congenially. Then he turned to Lola, and said, "See you later, Deep Sea Diver."

"Bye, Uncle Mikey," she said lugubriously. Then "Bye, Sadie. I love you."

Sadie didn't answer. Olympia tried not to take it personally.

The three of them walked to the waiting taxi. Mike and the

kids stood on the front step, watching them go. "Bye, Grandpa," Aiden called out.

"Remember, kiddo, develop knights toward the center!" Bob called out the window. As the car snaked down the driveway, Olympia glanced out the window and thought she saw Mike mouth the words "I love you." A roiling, nauseated feeling overtook her gut. Or was she projecting? Maybe he was just telling Aiden to put some shoes on. And why was it that, throughout Olympia's life, all the men to whom she was most attracted were unavailable? Was it possible that what made them attractive to her was the fact that they weren't in a position to reciprocate? Olympia tried not to think about it.

Bob, Olympia, and Lola walked into Carol's hospital room just as Carol was signing release forms. She still had a cast on her leg, albeit a smaller one. She was going to be on crutches, it seemed, for three more weeks. She'd also lost what appeared to be a considerable amount of weight, especially in the bosom. Her favorite plum chenille sweater hung off her like a scarecrow's plaid shirt. Olympia didn't notice the excess fabric until her mother turned around and said, "Pia, what a lovely surprise!"

Olympia was suddenly pleased she'd made the effort. (Everyone liked to play the Dutiful Daughter sometimes.) "Wouldn't miss your homecoming," she said.

"And Lola, too," Carol went on. "Hello, sugarplum. Did you come to see your grandma home?"

"Look, Mommy!" cried Lola, who was excitedly pressing the button that made the bed go up and down.

"Grandma's talking to you!" said Olympia, wishing that Lola had said something charming in reply to Carol's question. Then again, she and Lola were both here, and her other children and grandchildren weren't. Maybe that was enough. "Here, let me put these in a bag," Olympia said, as she began to stuff novels, socks, and a sodden-looking bag of yogurt-covered pretzels into a large brown Bloomie's bag.

"Oh, you don't have to do that," said Carol, waving her hand.

"But I want to."

"Well, then, I won't stop you."

As they started toward the door, a plump Filipino nurse whose name tag read CINDY said, "We're all going to miss you, Mrs. Hellinger."

"Forgive me for saying that the feeling is *not* mutual!" said Carol. "Six weeks in captivity was long enough."

"Mom!" cried Olympia, aghast if not entirely surprised. Gus had been going on lately about how much "nicer" their mother had gotten since the accident. (Olympia and her sisters regularly dissected Carol's personality with all the squeamish fascination of a seventh-grade science class dismembering a fetal pig.) In any case, Carol was apparently back to her feisty old self. Which was comforting news in its own way.

"It's okay," said the nurse, chuckling. "You're not supposed to miss us."

"Well, I'll be delighted if and when I run into you in the frozen food aisle at ShopRite," said Carol. "How's that?"

"That's just fine."

As they walked down the corridor that led to the door, Olympia held one of her mother's elbows—a largely symbolic gesture since she was using crutches. "Good-bye and good riddance, hospital," said Carol, taking a last look at the peach walls and rubber plants before they stepped into a waiting elevator.

"Hear, hear!" said Bob, who hadn't stopped beaming since they'd arrived in Room 310.

Olympia had called yet another taxi to fetch them. When they walked out into the daylight, they found it idling by the curb. The four of them climbed in, Bob in front and the women and Lola in back. Within minutes, Lola was slumped against Olympia's shoulder and on the verge of dozing off. Lola rarely took naps anymore, but Olympia suspected that she and Sadie had barely slept the night before.

They weren't the only ones.

12

MOSTLY SUNNY, *with a high of 85 and a 50 percent chance of a late-afternoon shower. Clearing overnight.* That was the forecast in the complimentary copy of the *Miami Herald* that had been left outside Perri's hotel room door. Now she was reclining in a teak and canvas beach lounger by a kidney-shaped art deco splash pool. Past the point of showing off her thighs to anyone to whom she wasn't related, Perri was dressed in a black bikini top with plenty of support and a paisley-patterned sarong. A five-dollar glass of lemonade bedecked with a striped straw sat on a wrought-iron table to her left, and a self-help book called *Awakening at Midlife,* which she'd ordered before she left, lay unopened and so far unread in her lap.

Lifting her face into the sky, Perri felt for once blissfully indifferent to her own neuroses, including those to do with her skin. (Though, admittedly, she was wearing a medical-grade Swiss sunscreen with a micronized zinc formulation.) She felt indifferent to her future, too: all that existed for her was the delicious if relentless lashing of the sun. She lay there until she couldn't take it anymore. Then she sat up and reached for her lemonade. As she sucked the sweet and cool liquid down her throat, she looked around her at the mise-en-scène — mostly Russian tourists in the act of tanning and flirting. The men had shaved heads and large biceps and were smoking Marlboro Lights. The women had suspiciously circular breasts and were wearing too much lip liner, lending them the appearance of sexy clowns. They were probably in their late twenties, Perri thought, suddenly recalling that she was supposed to be that age, too. Or, at least, Ginny Budelaire was supposed to be that age. Wrenched back to reality, Perri shuddered at her own gall in having checked into the hotel under the other woman's name and with a fictitious credit card to match.

And the credit card was arguably the least of her sins. She'd also walked out on her husband and kids and was about to hook up with her old college boyfriend, Roy Marley. Only, what if she wasn't attracted to him, or he to her? Surely, he'd already seen the snapshots she'd posted of herself on Facebook. But all of them were strategically flattering, three years out of date, shot at dusk, and featured Perri only from the waist up. Then again, she'd finally shed ten of the fifteen extra pounds she'd accumulated over three pregnancies — or four, if you counted her late miscarriage between Sadie and Noah. Having a midlife crisis, it turned out, was the ultimate weight-loss technique. (Grapefruits be damned!) Moreover, Roy was a virtual stranger at this point. If the two failed to hit it off, they'd simply go their separate ways — no harm done. Alternately, if the chemistry was still there, their affair would be Perri's special birthday treat to herself. And no one had to know about it but Roy and her.

And no one *would* know, Perri had already decided. Both of

her sisters had already left messages that, while ostensibly wishing her well, were clearly designed to elicit information regarding her whereabouts. Which is why Perri didn't dare call either one back. She'd always been a terrible actress and feared she'd end up confessing all. She could already picture Olympia quietly gloating over Perri's moral and sexual failures, believing the two of them to be equivalent now. (Gus had long ago relayed her suspicion that Lola's father was Olympia's married ex-lover, Patrick, and Perri didn't doubt it.) But while Perri wasn't proud of her recent behavior, she felt that extramarital affairs were one thing; reproducing with another man's husband was quite another. That is, in her own Ranking of the Righteous, she still believed that she came out significantly ahead of her middle sister.

Or was Perri trying to justify the unjustifiable? Did she actually feel terrible? Lifting her book so it blocked the sun, she began to read: *Many people will attempt to defer or delay this terrifying journey of transformation through addictions that will blunt the pain of the passage. Others will find all manner of avoidance behaviors and devote themselves to constant "doing" so as never to leave even a brief, unguarded moment when the questions that prompt the initiation might appear.* Perri snapped the book shut. She didn't like the author's alarmist tone. Plus, her eyelids were drooping. She decided to head back to her room. Let the record state that it was to be Imperia Hellinger Sims's first afternoon nap in a decade.

While Perri had been out at the pool, her room had been tidied and her bed made. A white brocade spread lay smoothed over the corners of the mattress. The sight of it filled Perri with a sense of well-being, even optimism. She may have been upending the status quo in her life, but visual and sensual order still mattered to her, still calmed her. As she pulled the drapes against the glare, her chest purred with the easy glide of the rings across the rod. Stretching out on the bed, Perri breathed deeply — in, then out. The large size of her breasts had always made it difficult for her to sleep on her stomach. But she'd found a way of reclining on her side with a pillow wedged between her belly and the mattress that approximated the tummy-down position. Lying there, she wondered if she still loved Mike, wondered what that word even meant in the context of a long marriage. She still felt proud when she stood next to him at parties. As if she'd snagged one of the "cool guys." But the romance of their relationship seemed as ancient to her as the black stirrup pants in which she'd lived during her freshman year of college, believing them to be the epitome of chic when, looking back, she probably looked like a hotdog that had gone horseback riding. At the same time, she clearly loved what she and Mike had made together — their family, their home. Was that enough? (If only that had been enough!) At some point, she must have dozed off...

She woke to find her mouth attached to a pool of dribble. She was also aroused. On the chance that she and Roy would make passionate love later that afternoon, however, Perri decided to refrain from using the vibrator she'd hidden in her suitcase inside three pairs of socks. And still, she'd quaked in fear while passing through security! Instead, she got in the shower and soaped up her body with complimentary glycerin soap. By the time she'd finished blowing out her hair, it was nearly one thirty. Roy was due to arrive in a half hour. She dressed in a pale pink twin set and floral-patterned culottes. Then she took the elevator down to the first floor to have a light lunch (on account of her birthday, she'd decided to temporarily suspend her No Restaurants Rule) and wait for her would-be lover. She spotted Roy before he spotted her — ambling over to the reception desk, his aviators still on. At least, Perri thought it was him. He looked exactly as she imagined he'd look after a time lapse of nearly twenty years. Even so, there was something shocking about the sight of him, if only because he was flesh and blood, whereas in the past few months he'd come to seem like nothing so much as a shapeless phantom lurking in her phone. That said, Roy Marley cut an impressive figure in the material world, too. His skin was still taut, his nostrils pronounced. Instead of dreadlocks, he sported a globe-sized, shaved dome. (Probably losing his hair, Perri decided.) He was also dressed conservatively, which she liked, in a light blue polo shirt and tan chinos with only the gentlest of guts to show for his two decades of bourgeois living. Perri considered calling out to him but decided to get closer before doing so. She took another bite of her salad, reapplied her lipstick, then rose from her chair and sauntered over to where he stood.

But as she neared her target, her heartbeat suddenly quickened; her shoulders withdrew into her body; and her stomach crunched into a knot. It was strange, she thought, how, the further one traveled from youth, the more timid one became physically: everything from skydiving to sex with new (or even old!) lovers became that much more terrifying and likely to produce an excess of self-consciousness that bordered on existential dread. Shouldn't it have worked the other way around? When Perri was no more than two feet away from where Roy stood — hunched over the reception desk with a pen — she uttered "Roy" in a low voice that sounded off-kilter even to her ears.

He abruptly turned to face her, his eyes popping. "Perri?!" he said, as if he hadn't seen those Facebook pictures after all. Or maybe he *had* seen them, and she no longer looked anything like them. And he was disappointed. Or pleasantly surprised. Or maybe Perri was just projecting.

"Hi!" she said, laughing nervously as she lifted her palm in salute.

"Heeeeeyyyyyy," he said, taking the two steps necessary to lay a hand on her forearm and kiss her hello — first on one cheek, then on the other. He smelled of airplane pretzels. Then he pulled away. Perri felt his eyes roaming up and down the length of her. "You look good, woman," he said, his eyes crinkling as he smiled.

"Oh, thanks. I try!" said Perri, laughing again.

"You don't need to try," said Roy.

"Well, thanks for that, too." She paused. "I hope I didn't scare you."

"You didn't scare me at all."

"I was just sitting over there eating my lunch when I saw you come in." She motioned at her table. "You're hard to mistake."

"Why? Because I'm black?"

Perri blanched.

Roy burst out laughing, punched her lightly in the arm, and declared, "I'm just kidding!"

"Ha ha," said Perri, suddenly doubting that this was going to work. Racial humor: she'd never been good at it.

"Listen." Again, Roy laid a hand on Perri's forearm. "Let me just get settled in here. And I'll join you in ten minutes. How does that sound?"

"Fine! Great," said Perri, wishing now that she'd waited to approach him. Why was she always in such a hurry? What if

Roy thought she was too aggressive? It had been years since Perri had dated. Come to think of it, she'd never really dated. "Take your time," she added.

Roy abruptly took her hand in his, leaned over it, then pressed his lips to the back of it. His eyes were twinkling when he came up for air. "I'll be there as quick as I can," he said.

"I'll keep a seat warm," Perri said, then wished she hadn't done so. Who said things like that? It sounded as if she were talking about a toilet.

After Roy left, she returned to her salad. But it no longer looked appetizing. The kernels of corn called to mind the rotten teeth of an old man.

Perri was signing the bill — and starting to wonder if Roy Marley had had second thoughts and gotten on the next plane back to DC — when he reappeared. He'd changed into a white polo shirt and sandals instead of sneakers. He pulled out the chair opposite her, turned it around, and straddled it. "So, Perri Hellinger," he began anew. "How have you been these past twenty years?"

There was something so sympathetic about his face, Perri thought. Suddenly she longed to tell all. And why not? He'd known her since she was practically a child! "To be honest, I'm kind of in crisis mode," she said. "Total breakdown on the home front." She took a sip of her water. "But it's not your problem." She waved her hand through the air. "And I promise not to spend the whole weekend talking about it. But I just have to say that it's such a relief to be away for a few —"

"Perri — stop," Roy interrupted her. "How about we just try and enjoy the weekend. Huh?"

"You're right," said Perri, hurt and mortified all in the same breath. Roy had come to Florida to help her cheat on her husband, she saw now — not to help her figure out the second half of her life. "Waiter!" she called out in too loud a voice. Several other diners glanced in her direction, scowling. Finally, a waiter appeared. "I'll have a piña colada," she told the guy. "And can you make that with freshly squeezed pineapple juice?"

"Now you're getting the idea." Roy smiled approvingly.

"We serve only freshly squeezed juice," snipped the waiter. Then he turned to Roy. "And for you, sir?"

Roy ordered a light beer.

The waiter disappeared. Perri and Roy talked about the weather. They ordered another round. Then they got drunk and began to talk about old times. "Who was that guy in Delta Upsilon with the four-foot-high American flag bong?"

"You mean, Marty Weinstock?!" Roy let out a belly laugh. "Dude was high, twenty-four/seven!"

"Marty Weinstock — that's right," cried Perri. "God, that guy really was a wastrel. I don't know how he ever graduated, *if* he ever graduated."

"I've actually been in touch with Party Marty. He's making a shitload of money now designing golf courses all over the Southwest."

"You're kidding?! Like, he decides how big to make the sand pits and stuff?"

"They're called bunkers, my dear."

"Like Hitler's?"

"Something like that."

"I gather you play golf, too."

"Damn right I do. Handicap is a seven."

"And when you're not golfing, what do you do?"

"Nothing as exciting as designing bunkers."

"Well, maybe I'll find it exciting."

"I'm a vascular surgeon. About twenty percent of my work is helping patients with life-threatening vascular abnormalities. The other eighty is lasering off the varicose veins of middle-aged ladies who come to me feeling bad about their legs and wanting to wear shorts and tennis skirts again."

"How charitable of you," said Perri, suddenly self-conscious about her own imperfect gams, which she crossed beneath the table, before asking, "And are there discounts for old friends?"

"Depends on whether that old friend really needs help. Which, in turn, requires a full inspection of the affected area." Roy smiled suggestively.

"I see," said Perri, her heart suddenly beating in her throat.

They wound up in Perri's room. No sooner had she opened the door than Roy backed her against it and began to kiss her neck. Then he pressed his groin into hers and began to massage the sides of her breasts. Perri was so aroused that she felt dizzy. This is what it felt like to be desired as a woman, she thought. Before long, Roy pulled her onto the bed, unfastened her culottes, and began to wriggle them down her hips. "You are one hot mama," he said.

"You're not so bad yourself," she panted as she pulled him toward her.

But he had other ideas in mind. After scooting his body down to the foot of the bed, he began to kiss his way up her legs. Perri moaned in anticipation of the ecstasies to come.

But midway up her thighs, he paused before he murmured, "Hello, Spidey."

"Excuse me?" said Perri, lifting her head.

Roy's own head emerged as well — from between her knees. "I was just saying hello to a cute little spider vein. You know, you can have these removed."

"EXCUSE ME?!" Perri cried again. Shocked and outraged, she raised her body into a sitting position and instinctively covered her thighs with her hands.

"Sorry, it's my profession," said Roy. "Hard for me not to look."

"Well, you're not at work! And I'm not a patient!" The lust drained out of her like contrast dye after an MRI. The moment was ruined. She looked across the room. A narrow beam of sunlight reflected on the carpet reminded her of Aiden's once-beloved Star Wars light saber, and then of Aiden himself. She wondered what he was doing just then, and a spasm of heartsickness radiated through her chest. She thought of Mike, too, in his favorite UPenn T-shirt, running through the yard with Sadie on his shoulders, yelling, "Special delivery!" Was it possible she missed *him,* as well? And what if her desire to flee Larchmont had mostly to do with her need to show Mike the extent to which he took her for granted? Maybe that was all this was, Perri thought — a way of getting Mike to figure out how to press Start on the washing machine. "I think you should get dressed," she told Roy. She knew she was being cold, but she couldn't help it.

Roy's boxers were still on, but his erection had distended them into a miniature tent. "Baby, come on," he moaned with a stroke to her calf. "I was just being funny!"

"Please get off me," said Perri, scooting her leg away.

"Jesus, Perri, I'm sorry! Okay?" he said. "I didn't realize you were so sensitive on the subject."

"I'm not."

"So what's the big deal?" he asked. As if he didn't understand.

And why should he have? Perri thought. He knew nothing about her. He was a stranger, after all. She turned away, so she was facing the wall. "I'm sorry, Roy," she announced in her most officious PowerPoint presentation voice. "It was my mistake. I never should have invited you down here. I'm a married woman with three children. If you'd like, I'll reimburse you for your airfare."

Roy's patience had worn out. "I don't want your fucking money!" he cried as he lunged for his pants and furiously fitted his legs inside them. "And I don't appreciate being treated like a man-whore!" He laughed bitterly. "I should have remembered from college. You had great tits, but you were bonkers then, too — following me around the frat house with a goddamn sponge mop! That's why I ended it, if you want to know."

Perri felt heat on her face. "*That's* why you ended it?!" she said, turning back to him. All these years, she'd wondered. Now she had her answer.

"Yes," said Roy, fitting his arms through his polo shirt. "If you must know."

Perri felt humiliated. How dare he accuse her of being crazy! It was true that their relationship had coincided with her OCD years. It was also possible that the reason she fell in love with Mike was that he didn't judge her for applying baby wipes to toilet handles. "You should leave," she said.

"Gladly," he said on his way out.

"Can you please close the door behind you," said Perri.

"As Her Royal Wing Nut wishes. Oh, and you heard it here first: you dress like a fucking flowerpot. Or maybe I should say *crackpot*."

That was the last thing Perri heard Roy Marley say — before the door slammed shut. Then she broke down in sobs. How had she made such a mess of her fortieth birthday and of her life? she wondered. And was her outfit really that bad? Mike never noticed what she was wearing. She supposed that was another check mark in his favor.

13

SEX IS A SNEEZE. Sex is the meaning of life. Which one was it? Gus and Jeff had made another date for that evening. He was supposed to pick her up at her apartment. Then they'd go get dinner somewhere on the Upper West Side. At least, that was the plan. But they both knew it wasn't really about dinner. It was Sunday, already late in the day. Standing before her closet, Gus felt stymied by the question of what to wear. The options weren't exactly myriad. Black corduroys or black jeans? Black blazer or gray? Gus had always felt sorry for people who cared about clothes — people like, well, her older sisters. Being fashionable seemed like such a colossal waste of energy and time. For what purpose? She felt the same combination of pity and noncomprehension regarding her sisters' obsessions with home decorating. Once you got the sofa, the TV, and the bed down, all the rest was, to Gus's mind, window dressing.

And yet, at that moment, the paucity of clothing choices available to her left her feeling impoverished. She wondered what she'd missed out on in life. Then she hated herself for feeling that way — hated Jeff, too. She'd been fine before he'd shown up, hadn't she? She ought to go down to the Cubbyhole for the night, she thought, and try to meet someone. But then she'd always hated pickup bars. It was about as warm and welcoming in those places as it was in family court. She and Debbie had met through a mutual friend. And they'd been buddy-buddy for several years before they'd hooked up. But Debbie wasn't around anymore, Gus reminded herself. Debbie was with Maggie Snow now. Or so Gus had heard. Not that she cared — at least not that much. Besides, Gus couldn't stop thinking about Jeff. She finally settled on black jeans and a gray blazer.

The doorbell rang at seven. Jeff was holding a bouquet of wilted tulips whose conical paper enclosure Gus recognized as harking from the Korean grocer on her corner. For a brief moment, she imagined that she'd unwittingly joined the cast of some passably amusing romantic comedy starring Kate Hudson. Before long, it would be revealed that they were actually on a stage set on the Warner Brothers lot. "Pretty," she said, taking the flowers out of his hands. "Unfortunately, I don't own a vase anymore. Ex-girlfriend took them. But I guess you can always use a jar. Right?"

"You crack me up," he said. He was wearing jeans, Nike slides, and some kind of windbreaker, zipped all the way up to the neck. His legs were slightly bowed. Gus hadn't noticed that before. And why was it that, as soon as she got close to someone, she started finding faults, being critical? It was her mother in her, she supposed. Though, to be fair, Carol was rarely critical of her own daughters, who could do no wrong. It was the rest of the world that was full of morons.

Gus was standing at the sink, filling an old jam jar with water, when Jeff came up behind her and put his hands around her waist. Suddenly nervous, she barely formed the words "You move quickly."

"I'm just being friendly," he murmured.

Too friendly, was Gus's feeling. "So, where do you want to have dinner?" she asked, slithering out of his grip.

But Jeff wasn't giving up yet. Again, he moved closer, threaded his index finger through her belt loop and smiled his insinuating smile. "What if I say I'm not hungry yet?" he asked.

Gus hesitated. Wasn't this why she'd invited him over? And what if there wasn't another opportunity like this in her lifetime? Her eyes scanned the drab furnishings in her living room — the old Door Store sofa, the Mexican tapestry hanging over it. She'd purchased the latter on a trip to Oaxaca with her ex-girlfriend Jen. It was her apartment's one nod to the Decorative Arts. It was also ugly and tattered. "You can say anything you like," she said, her heart in her stomach.

"Let's go in the bedroom," Jeff said in a low voice.

"Fine," said Gus, terrified. She wondered if Jeff knew it was her first time with a man (and hoped he didn't). "Do what you want." She'd never said those words before, never voluntarily offered to cede control. She had that in common with Perri, she thought — an obsessive need to control others. Where had the instinct come from? Neither of her parents were really like that.

"Or what you want," said Jeff, pulling her toward him.

The size of him — the size of his body against hers — somehow astonished her. And his lips tasted like green olives. Gus closed her eyes as Jeff carried her into her bedroom, where he slowly pried off her nondescript outfit and went to work on her. Or, at least, Jefferson Sims's version of work.

·   ·   ·

The next morning at the office, Gus found herself unable to concentrate. She kept going over what had happened the night before, trying to figure out what it all meant and if she'd enjoyed it and if it had changed her in some irrevocable way. She kept this up even as she conducted an interview with a client. The phone interrupted both lines of inquiry. "Excuse me," she told Marta Johnson. Then she picked up the receiver.

"Gus?" came the trembling voice. It sounded like Perri. But it couldn't possibly be Perri—

Except it was Perri. "Perri?!" said Gus.

There was a sob on the other end of the phone.

"Ohmygod—where are you?" said Gus. "Are you okay?"

"I'm not okay, actually," Perri choked out.

"Okay, calm down," said Gus, beginning to panic herself.

"Why should I calm down?" cried Perri. "You've never been calm a single day in your entire life!"

"Fine. Sorry!" said Gus, taken aback by the accusation even as she acknowledged that Perri was probably right: for the Hellinger sisters of Hastings-on-Hudson, the joys of Zen were mostly unknown.

But then, Gus was only trying to be helpful. And it wasn't as if she'd had experience in this area. It had always been her oldest sister who had been the voice of reason and comfort in the family. Still, it was flattering to think that Perri had called her, not Olympia, first. Or had she already called Olympia? Gus knew it wasn't a competition. Yet she couldn't help but hope that she'd been number one on the list.

Perri cleared her throat. "I'm actually calling for legal advice."

Gus was shocked—already? "You mean, like, divorce-lawyer advice?"

"No, regular-lawyer advice." There was another sob on the other end of the phone. "I got a credit card issued in the name of a dead person. And I used it to pay for my hotel."

"Right" was all Gus could come up with. She couldn't believe what she was hearing. Olympia was supposed to be the one who was irresponsible with money—not her well-heeled MBA oldest sister with her stock portfolios and SEP-IRAs, full-term life insurance and pending IPO.

"I'm such an idiot." Perri wept into the phone.

It was hard to argue with the conclusion. Even so, Gus told her, "You're not an idiot—you just made a mistake. This is what you need to do. First, go down to the lobby and tell the hotel you want to put down a different credit card for your stay. Substitute a real one for the phony one."

"But then Mike will know I'm in South Beach," moaned Perri.

Gus registered her sister's location—and felt vaguely disgruntled. The last time she'd been on vacation somewhere sunny was probably 1996. Then again, to Gus's secret shame, she hated traveling and could never wait to come home from wherever she'd gone. The problem was that she felt bad about that fact—felt she ought to be the type to be backpacking through the Andes. But the truth was: she didn't actually want to go anywhere. It was yet another thing that she'd always envied about her sisters—the casualness with which they (and in particular Olympia, at least before she'd had Lola) traveled around the world. "What's worse?" she said. "Getting hauled to jail or getting hauled back to your four-bedroom Tudor in Larchmont?!"

Perri didn't answer.

"I rest my case," said Gus. "Anyway, after you resettle the

hotel bill, call the airline and try to do the same thing. Then call the bank that issued the bad credit card and tell them you want to cancel it."

"But what if, for identification purposes, they ask me for my Social Security number, or something?" Perri sniffled. "I can't even remember the number I wrote down on the application. I filled it out as a joke — sort of — at least at first."

"Well, then, tell them you're traveling, and you can't remember it. Assuming you succeed, cut the bullshit card up into a million pieces and never mention this to anyone ever again."

There was silence, followed by another sniffle, and then a mousy "Okay, I'll try."

Gus felt nervous for her sister. What if word leaked to her company? What if she got prosecuted and thrown in jail? She was also tickled and proud to think that Perri was actually planning to take her advice. "Now, what the hell are you doing in Miami Beach?" she asked, determined to secure information in exchange for her expertise. Fair was fair. Though of course in families, Gus had learned, there was no such thing as fair.

"*South* Beach," Perri corrected her.

"Same difference."

"I'm getting sun."

"Alone? On your fortieth birthday?"

"I invited a — friend. But it didn't work out."

"What friend?"

"Mmmm Yyyy Oooo Bbbbbbbbb!!!" It was the same acronym that Perri had brandished countless times and in the same singsongy voice, albeit mostly between the ages of six and sixteen.

"Sorry! I was just asking," said Gus, defensive again.

"And I was just answering. By the way, everything uttered

during this phone call needs to stay between us—and not just the business about the credit card."

"Of course!" said Gus. "But, honestly, you haven't even told me that much."

"That's because there's nothing to tell. Nothing even happened. Or, at least, not that much." Perri let out yet another hiccup-like sob. Apparently, she was back to personality A. Or was it B? "But it's over now. He's gone."

"Hey, you don't have to justify yourself to me. I'm not judging you!" said Gus. But, in truth, she *was* judging. Judging and despairing. How could Perri be doing this to her credit rating—never mind her marriage? She was supposed to be the Settled Sister. If she abdicated the role, who would take her place? It seemed to Gus that at least one of the three of them needed to uphold traditional values. Olympia, independent to a fault, didn't show any signs of upholding anything these days, except maybe her own right never to be held accountable. And Gus was a single lesbian! Or, at least, she had been one until recently. Now she didn't know what she was—only that she felt delirious and something like happy. It was a little disturbing that Jeff had no ambitions in life, but it was also refreshing. Besides, other skills he possessed—skills he'd demonstrated the night before—more than compensated for the lack.

At the same time, it made Gus feel disloyal, even traitorous, to have slept with a Sims brother at the exact moment that her oldest sister was fleeing hers. Growing up, Perri had frequently played the role of Gus's "other mother." It was also to Perri that Gus had first come out during college. (Perri's response had been characteristically insulting and, at the same time, reassuring: "Duh," she'd said. "You think everyone doesn't already know that?") In the past few days, Gus had sought out a similar vote of approval for her relationship with Jeff. But Perri's insistence that "Mike and I are both really happy for you" had sounded hollow. Gus had concluded that her oldest sister must have found it all too close for comfort.

In any case, Gus didn't blame Perri for having fled. Clearly, Mike didn't have her best interest at heart. What he and Olympia were doing in the bathroom with the door closed, two nights earlier, was anyone's guess. But Gus suspected that it had nothing to do with flossing.

"Anyway, tell everyone I'll be home by dinner. I'm about to rebook my flight," Perri announced in a newly businesslike tone.

"Um, I don't think that's such a good idea," said Gus, suddenly concerned on Olympia's account. Or was she simply making trouble because she could? "Why don't you spend a few days relaxing and come back midweek?"

"Why?!" screeched Perri, sounding alarmed. "Did Mike say something? Does he not want me back?"

"No!" said Gus. "It's nothing like that. It's just that— everyone's been a little weirded out. Instead of surprising them, why don't you give them time to readjust to the fact that you're coming back. I'll tell them I spoke to you—and that you're just taking a break and you'll be home in a few days."

"Gus. Tell me the truth. Did something happen?" Perri demanded to know. "You're really freaking me out. Did Mike hire a hooker, or something?"

"Not that I know of—"

"Excuse me," came a voice from across Gus's desk. "Are you ever getting off the phone? I've got bills to pay."

Gus gasped in horror. She'd been so riveted by the details of Perri's midlife crisis that she'd forgotten she was in the middle of an interview! "Listen, I have to go. I'll call you back. Okay?" she told Perri. Then she turned back to Marta, and said, "I'm so sorry. Where were we?"

"You asked me whether I ever saw my ex giving alcohol to our baby," said Marta. "And the answer is, yeah — once, I saw him mixing Wild Turkey in with the formula."

Gus duly noted the detail on her questionnaire form. Then she paused, realizing that she couldn't begin to concentrate on anyone else's man problems when the ones in her own family were so vast. "Actually, I'm wondering if we could finish this interview at some later date. The truth is, I've got a bit of a Wild Turkey crisis in my own family. I hope you'll forgive me."

"As you like." Marta shrugged, clearly miffed as she rose from her chair.

Gus rose, too, apologized again, collected her belongings, and followed Marta outside.

Every year, it seemed, springtime in New York grew shorter — until summer seemed to follow directly on the heels of winter. That day, which happened to be the last in April, was as sticky as any in July. Gus walked by Jimbo's Hamburger Palace, her nostrils filling with the heady scent of grease, then managed to traverse the traffic nightmare that was the intersection of 163rd Street, Hunts Point Avenue, and Southern Boulevard without getting flattened by a sixteen-wheeler. As she grew farther away from a parked car blasting salsa — and closer to the subway entrance — she dialed Jeff. She knew she wasn't at liberty to tell him what Perri had told her. Yet she somehow felt that he should at least *know* that Perri had called. After all, he was the brother of Perri's husband. Until further notice, he was also

Gus's boyfriend. It was also true that Gus was excited to have "inside information" and couldn't bear not to advertise that fact to her close relations. Plus, she just wanted to hear his voice, just wanted to know it hadn't all been a dream...

"Hey," she said. "It's me." Jeff had already gotten himself a job filling in for a traveling tennis pro at the Midtown Tennis Club. (He'd been second singles at Pepperdine before transferring to the University of Colorado at Boulder.)

"Hey, baby," he said. "I'm just about to head onto the court. What's up?"

Gus felt disoriented. She'd never been called "baby" before in her life — wasn't sure she ever wanted to be again. "I heard from Perri."

"No joke. Where is she?"

"I can't say."

"What do you mean you can't say?"

"I promised her I wouldn't."

"Wait, didn't you just call me?" Jeff sounded peeved.

"I know, I know. I'm sorry," said Gus, now wishing she'd never dialed.

"All right, well, I should go."

"No, wait!" cried Gus. She hated the thought that he might be mad at her, didn't want him to hang up yet. The sex had made her needy. It always did.

"What?" he said.

"All right, fine. She's in Florida," Gus told him. "But that's ALL I CAN SAY!" Why was it so hard keeping one's mouth shut when talking to someone with whom one had recently exchanged bodily fluids?

"The Sunshine State — interesting. *Por qué?*"

"Just—I don't know—so she can get some sun."

"By herself?"

"Don't make me answer that."

"Okay, not by herself."

"I didn't say one way or the other!"

"Yes, you did. By refusing to say that she was alone."

"Okay, fine, but the other person is already gone."

"So it was a one-night stand?"

"I have no idea. But please, Jeff—I'm *serious* about you not saying anything to Mike." Realizing how much she'd said (without actually saying anything), Gus was beginning to panic. It hadn't been her intention to have been the first link in a long gossip chain. What's more, if Perri found out that what she'd revealed to Gus in confidence had gone straight back to Jeff, who would likely tell Mike, Gus might have to join the Witness Protection Program. Though at least Gus hadn't said anything about Perri using a bogus credit card...

"Gus—Mike is my brother," Jeff announced in a righteous tone. "And he's in a lot of pain right now. I'm only going to tell him what I think he needs to know."

"Yeah, well, your brother is no angel, either," said Gus. "You might want to ask him what exactly he was doing with my middle sister in the kids' bathroom last weekend with the door locked."

"What in Jesus's name are you talking about?!"

"Just that he and Pia were in there together for, like, a half an hour. And I kind of doubt they were comparing plucking techniques. Though you never know."

"Interesting," said Jeff.

"Ohmygod, what have I done?!" gasped Gus, suddenly

cognizant that she'd now sold out pretty much the entire family. "Next thing you know, I'm going to tell you about Perri's fake credit card."

"You just did."

This time, when Gus gasped, no sound came out. How had she become such an incorrigible loose lips? In her professional life, she was a model of discretion. In fact, she made a point of protecting the privacy of her sources. But in her personal life, it was as if she were still a teenager, trying to get her sisters' attention at the breakfast table in Hastings with scandalous tidbits about their classmates.

"Listen, babe," Jeff said. "I should go. Private lesson waiting. But that was superfun last night."

"I had fun too," said Gus. "But, Jeff?"

"Yes, milady?"

"I was serious about not telling Mike everything I just told you. I'm actually begging you."

"I like a woman who begs for it."

"Jeff, I'm serious!"

"I'll do my best."

Was it any wonder that Gus descended the steps to the subway feeling as if Hades awaited her?

14

AS MANY TIMES AS Olympia returned to her childhood home, she never grew acclimated to the sight of it. It seemed somehow impossible that it should still exist with the same people in it, the same furniture she remembered too. Most of her friends' suburban parents had downsized to condos after their nests had emptied — not the Hellingers. It was midday. Lola was asleep upstairs. Olympia wandered into the kitchen. She found her mother peering into the cupboards.

"Is there any coffee?" Olympia asked her.

"Should be, but I'm actually looking for the Ovaltine," said Carol. "Oh, here it is!"

"What is it with you and Dad and the Ovaltine?" Olympia muttered as she lifted the kettle off the stove.

After the water boiled, and Olympia poured out two hot beverages, she and Carol sat down at the kitchen table. "So, what have I missed?" Carol asked with a breezy sigh.

For the first time in ages, Olympia saw an actual person sitting across from her, as opposed to her Annoying Mother — a person who wanted to believe her life mattered and that she was indispensable to those around her. It seemed suddenly ludicrous that everyone should be lying to her. Olympia took a deep breath and announced that Gus had fallen for Mike's brother, Jeff, while Perri, far from being at a closet conference, had walked out on Mike on her fortieth birthday and was currently in an undisclosed location.

Carol sat listening with popping eyes, her cup suspended in midair. When Olympia had finished speaking, she took a sip of her Ovaltine, and declared, "My goodness — well, I don't know what to say. Between you and me, I never thought Mike was worthy of Perri. He's a Republican, you know."

"I know."

"But they have three kids."

"The split might not be permanent."

"And I bet that brother of his is a Republican, too. It tends to run in families."

"As far as I can tell, all the guy cares about is skiing. And now, I guess, Gus."

"And is Gus in … love with him?"

"I'm not sure she's 'in love,' but she clearly likes him."

"The heart is a mysterious thing," Carol said, sighing again, as she gazed out the window. "And here I'd finally come to accept that I was the mother of a gay person!" She turned back to Olympia. "And what about you? Who does your heart belong to these days, other than to Lola?"

The question startled Olympia in its very directness. Meeting her mother's gaze head on, she thought of how infrequently the two of them spoke about anything meaningful — it was all quips and barbs — and how little time they'd spent together in recent years apart from Perri or Gus. Who knew when the next time would be? And who knew how many years her mother and father actually had left? Ten? Twenty? Twenty-five at the absolute most? In that moment, Olympia resolved to come clean about her own life, too. "If you want to know the truth," she said with a trembling heart, "I've been in love with the same man for five, maybe even six years. We broke up before Lola was born. He runs a community center for disadvantaged kids. The problem is…he's married and his wife is"—Olympia swallowed hard—"a paraplegic. So he can't leave her." She held her breath while waiting for the onslaught of disapproval that she'd always assumed her faithfully married mother would direct at her.

But to Olympia's surprise, all Carol said was "That does sound complicated. I'm sorry."

Carol's reticence, in turn, spurred Olympia onward. "Complicated is one way of putting it," she said, somehow knowing she'd live to regret what she was about to say, yet unable to stop herself. "So complicated," she went on, "that when I wanted to have a baby four-plus years ago, and he was the only guy in my life, I decided to use"—Olympia paused—"a sperm bank instead."

"A SPERM BANK?!" Carol cried.

Olympia was already regretting her confession. "I thought it would be less complicated," she said. "I was wrong about that, of course. But at the time…"

Carol's contorted face suggested horror, bewilderment, and disappointment all in one. It was the same expression she'd had when Gus had "come out" nearly twenty years ago—only a more extreme version of such. It was one thing, apparently, for a gay person to admit that she couldn't help being gay, quite another for a heterosexual person to admit to willfully subverting reproductive norms. "But couldn't you have waited to see if you met someone else?" she stammered.

"I was turning thirty-five. How long was I supposed to wait?" asked Olympia, her lower lip now quivering.

Carol didn't answer.

15

PERRI HAD ALWAYS LOVED BREAKFAST. It was her favorite meal of the day. When Mike traveled for business, she'd treat herself by eating cereal for dinner after the kids went to sleep. Now she lay sprawled on her hotel bed, feasting on room-service waffles (at four o'clock in the afternoon, no less) and trying not to fret about the fact that Gus had discouraged her from returning home. What accounted for Gus's negativity? Seeking distraction from her worries, Perri flipped on the TV. *The Real Housewives of New Jersey* were having some kind of altercation. As Teresa overturned a table onto Danielle, Perri felt a momentary jolt of smugness in the knowledge that the lives of reality TV stars were infinitely tackier and more dysfunctional than hers would ever be.

However, the sound of her ringing phone — and the sight of the name "Sims, Michael" flashing across its screen — undermined that certitude, reminding Perri that she'd dumped her husband and kids so she could have sex with a vascular surgeon in South Beach. She dreaded the thought of the conversation

LUCINDA ROSENFELD

to come. But if there was any hope of repairing the damage, it
needed to be had. It was why she'd left Mike a teary message,
twenty minutes earlier, apologizing in a general way and asking that he call her. "Hello?" she said in a mealy voice.

"You went down to Florida to have an affair. Is that it?" he
barked.

"WHAT?! Who said that?"

"I have my sources."

Perri was aghast and inflamed. So it had taken Gus not even
five minutes to betray her? There was no other explanation. She
wanted to break one of Gus's legs. "Well, your sources are
wrong," she told him.

"Yeah, right," said Mike.

A sob climbed the length of Perri's throat, and she felt powerless to keep it inside. "It's already over," she said. "And nothing even happened. But I'm sorry anyway. I'll be sorry for the
rest of my life."

"So, who was it?" asked Mike, seemingly unswayed by his
wife's display of abjection. "Some pool boy you met down
there? The sixteen-year-old with the handlebar mustache from
the office?"

Remorse mingled with rage. "What do you care?" cried
Perri. "It's not like you want me anymore!"

"Is that what you think?"

"Yes." He hadn't denied it, had he?

"So you had to go fuck someone else?"

Perri felt as if she'd been punched in the stomach. "I didn't
f-word anyone." It pained her in particular to have to use the
word as a verb, even in an abbreviated form, but she saw no
other way to counteract the charge. "And for the record, I'm
lying in bed *alone* right now eating waffles. Okay?"

"Well, good for you. I hope you have a lovely and romantic getaway. And at the end of it, do everyone a favor and don't come back."

Was he serious? "Mike! PLEASE!" Perri was crying so hard now that she felt as if she couldn't breathe. What had she done? And how had they arrived at this point? Hadn't they loved each other only a short time ago? She could no longer even remember what she was doing in Florida.

"Please, what?" he said.

"Forgive me!"

"I can't. I'm sorry."

"Mike, we've been married for—" she began. But the line had already gone dead.

As the tears rolled down her cheeks, Perri redialed her home number. She stopped after the fourth digit, realizing there was no point. Mike wouldn't pick up. Besides, there was an even more urgent call she needed to make just then—to her youngest sister, Gus, to tell her that she was never speaking to her again for as long as she lived.

Gus and Perri had never really had a big blowout before. True, Perri had been less than amused when her sister had shown up for her wedding twelve years earlier wearing a light blue men's tuxedo. Perri had begged Gus to wear a dress, even offering to buy her one of her choice at Nordstrom's, no expense barred— to no avail. But the whole incident had been more of an eye roller than anything else. This time was different.

"What's up?" asked Gus.

"This is Perri," she began in a shaky voice, "and I just want you to know that I'm never speaking to you again."

"What?!" said Gus.

"I spoke to you in confidence this morning, and you betrayed me. You told Mike every single thing I told you. You told him I had an affair, too. Which, by the way, is patently false. But what do you care about the truth?"

"Oh, Jesus," she said.

"That's the best you can do?" said Perri. "Invoke the name of a God you don't believe in?"

Gus sighed heavily. "Perri, I swear—I didn't mean to say anything. Jeff dragged the whole thing out of me, and then he swore he wouldn't tell Mike. I'm seriously going to kill him."

"Do what you like!" Perri shot back. "It won't make a difference to me, since our relationship is OVER, a relationship that, by the way, I once considered among the most treasured entities in my life."

"Perri—PLEASE!" Gus let out a gasping little yowl.

Perri's first instinct was to comfort her sister, just as she'd done so many times before. In order not to do so, she had to remind herself that she was the victim, not the other way around. Perri wasn't going to let Gus off the hook without further berating, either. "When I think of all the times I was there to hold your hand," she went on, "like when you thought you needed a sex change, freshman year of college." Perri paused to catch her breath and wipe the spittle that had found its way onto her chin.

"You've been a great sister," moaned Gus. "I didn't mean to upset you. Please don't cut me off."

"Why shouldn't I?" cried Perri. "You sold me out. I turned to you in a vulnerable moment, mistakenly believing you'd have more compassion than Pia would. It turns out I was wrong."

"You weren't wrong."

"Really?"

There was a pause. Then, in a newly defiant voice, Gus announced, "I'm not the sister who's getting cozy with your husband the second you leave."

"Ex-*cuse* me?!" cried Perri.

"Let's just say that a certain two people spent a lot of time in the bathroom together with the door closed the night after you left."

Perri was momentarily speechless. What in the world was Gus trying to imply? Had her husband been unfaithful, too?! "And which two people would that be?" she asked.

"You figure it out. One of their names starts with O — and the other with M."

For a full minute, Perri was speechless. Was Gus serious? It sounded implausible. But what if it wasn't? What if her husband had spent the previous twelve years believing he'd married the wrong sister? And what if Olympia, consummate flirt and known saboteur of others' marriages, had tried to sabotage Perri's marriage too? Perri's thoughts turned to the entirely inappropriate outfit that Olympia had worn to her wedding, which had basically consisted of two pasties attached to a loincloth. "Good-bye, Augusta," Perri said finally. "I hope you have a nice life. You won't be hearing from me again."

"Perri — WAIT!" cried Gus.

But Perri had already hung up, just as her husband had hung up on her, ten minutes before. As far as she was concerned, both sisters were now lost to her. She picked the phone back up and dialed Olympia's number to inform her that she, too, had become a nonperson.

16

UST AS OLYMPIA WAS EXITING THE KITCHEN, following her unpleasant confession to Carol, Perri's name flashed across the screen of her phone. Happy for the distraction from her own problems, Olympia took the phone into the living room with her, and said, "Hello?"

What she wasn't expecting was the fusillade of vitriol that greeted her left ear. "For nearly forty years, I've stood by you!" said the furious person who was apparently Perri on the other end of the line.

"Perri?" said Olympia.

"In high school, when everyone was calling you a slut, I told them to go jump in a lake!"

"*Jump in a lake?* I don't think anyone's used that expression since the nineteen-fifties," said Olympia, her casual banter belying her now pounding heart. Had Mike told Perri about their sort-of kiss?

"And when you were struggling in your twenties," Perri went on, "I sent you that check for five hundred dollars—which, for the record, you never paid back. But that's beside the point."

"Well, then, what *is* your point?" asked Olympia, now fearing the worst, even as she felt enraged. Perri had some nerve in raising the issue of Olympia's ancient, unpaid debts! Besides, what was five hundred dollars to a rich person?

"My point is that whatever secret hostilities you've been harboring toward me for the last thirty-eight years, this is one shitty way of expressing them! Though on that note, if you really want my idiot husband, you can have him." She let out a high-pitched laugh. "Really, he's yours!"

Olympia's heart rate had gone berserk. So Mike had told her, she thought—*the bastard!* Clearly, he'd just been using her to get back at Perri, Olympia decided. He'd caught Olympia at a vulnerable moment and turned that vulnerability into a cudgel to use against his jealous wife. What a fool Olympia had been to fall for it! Even so, she wasn't ready to hand him (or Perri) the victory just yet. "So, now I'm taking the hit for the fact that I had to haul my ass all the way to Larchmont after work on Friday because you decided to split on your family and on Dad?" she said. "Only to have your husband come onto me in the bathroom out of nowhere and, to be honest, to my complete and utter horror. I wasn't going to tell you, because I didn't want to embarrass you." Olympia realized that she wasn't being entirely honest. But maybe her version wasn't *that* far from the truth?

"That's not what I heard happened," said Perri in a more subdued voice.

"Well, what *did* you hear happened?" asked Olympia.

"Gus told me that—"

"Gus?!" Olympia felt heat on her face. So it had been her younger sister, not Mike, who had betrayed her. Olympia couldn't believe it. Or maybe she could. Growing up, Gus had been her most loyal and consistent playmate. The two of them had even had their own secret society—the Kangaroo Club (headquarters: Bob's shoe closet). But now Olympia wondered if she and her younger sister had ever been as close as she'd thought. She'd never forgotten that Gus had "come out" as a lesbian to Perri rather than to her. Clearly, Gus had been Perri's Chief Confidante (and Snoop) all along.

"Well, she saw everything," Olympia heard Perri saying.

"Well, if you want to know what *actually* happened, why don't you ask your estranged husband," said Olympia, her anger welling up.

"How dare you presume to know my marital situation!" declared Perri.

"Well, how dare *you* presume to know what happened when you weren't there!"

"I don't want to have this conversation anymore."

"Me, neither."

"Then let's hang up."

"Fine with me. Happy fucking birthday."

"Thanks—and f-f-fuck you!"

Olympia hung up the phone stunned not only by her sister's fury, but by her use of the f-word, itself a rarity if not a first. Turning to leave the room, she found Carol standing there next to the hunk of gnarled wood that passed for a coffee table. Tears shimmied in her eyes like water sloshing around the bottom of a rowboat. At the sight of them, Olympia felt even more wretched. The only thing more awful than having a screaming fight with one's sister was feeling as if one had simultaneously ruined the life of one's parent. "What?" said Olympia. "Why are you staring at me like that?"

"Be angry at me all you want," Carol answered in a shaky voice. "But please don't fight with your sisters. You'll need them someday — after Dad and I are gone."

It was too heavy a concept to entertain in daylight (and without alcohol). So Olympia turned the conversation back to her mother. "Well, why do you think we fight?"

"You're all strong-willed, I suppose. I don't know." Carol shook her head, bit her lip.

"Yes, and did it ever occur to you that all your labeling and comparing and boasting has made us all insanely competitive?"

"I never compared you," insisted Carol.

"Well, maybe you never compared us directly. But telling us all how perfect and successful Perri was all the time; and how passionate and committed Gus was in her quest to raise a thousand dollars for the starving children of Biafra; and how beautiful and artistic I was — didn't exactly help." Olympia wasn't even sure if she believed half the things she was saying, but the words tumbled out of her mouth now as if her life depended on it. As if they'd waited four decades to come out (maybe they had).

"I'm sorry for being proud of you!" cried Carol.

"Proud — or not as proud as you wish you could be of me?" asked Olympia.

"Proud of you just the way you are."

"Well, there are ways of being proud that don't turn us all into caricatures."

"You defined yourselves. I had nothing to do with it. Dad and I gave all of you the same opportunities."

"But you were always push-push-pushing for us to *achieve* something, *be* something! It made all of us neurotic messes. You want to know why I never made it as an artist? Because the expectations in this family were too high. I couldn't handle any kind of rejection. And you know why I never found a great guy and got married? No one was ever good enough, because you taught me to believe that I was special in some way, better than other people. And you taught me to be critical, too. That's why I'm being such a Huge Bitch right now."

This time Carol didn't answer. She pursed her lips, hung her head.

Out of accusations, and filled with shame at all the people she seemed to have hurt and disappointed in one day, Olympia ran up the stairs and into her childhood bedroom, or what was left of it. Now it was more like a storage locker. In one corner there were *National Geographic* magazines piled nearly to the ceiling, their skinny yellow spines cracking like late autumn leaves. In the other corner was a picture window with views into the Romanos' backyard, with its neatly planted azalea bushes all in a row like Civil War soldiers ready to do battle. Growing up, the Hellingers had been the North to the Romanos' South, with disputes regularly breaking out over everything from overly bright Christmas lights (the Romanos) to maple trees whose untrained branches created unwanted shade (the Hellingers). The previous fall, however, Carol had been delighted to announce that a new family had moved in, a young Serbian couple with a baby. Meanwhile, the Romano elders, who'd once toiled in the chemical factories on the Hudson, had retired to the Gulf Coast of Florida with the proceeds from their house sale. A happy ending for all, if only . . .

Stretching out on her old twin bed, which was half covered with garment bags, Olympia felt exhausted and disoriented. It wasn't just the thought that she no longer knew anyone who lived on Edmarth Place with the exception of her own parents.

It was the fact that she was no longer on speaking terms with anyone in her family with the exception of Lola and Bob, neither of whom were fully verbal. For the second time in twenty-four hours, tears cascaded down Olympia's face and dripped into her mouth. She'd never felt so alone.

But single mothers don't have much time for self-pity. Minutes later, Lola appeared in the doorway, claiming to be hungry and demanding spaghetti—and wondering why Mommy's eyes were all red.

"Mommy's got hay fever again," Olympia told her. "But I'm fine now." And so she was, because she had to be.

Five minutes after that, three generations of Hellinger women (Carol, Olympia, Lola) were back in the kitchen, talking about trivial matters in strained voices ("Does she want butter with that?"), when the doorbell rang. "This darn leg," said Carol, trying to lift herself off her chair.

"Don't bother. I'll get it," said Olympia.

"I want to come!" said Lola, rising too.

"Eat your pasta," said Olympia, pushing her daughter's tiny shoulders back down.

"Maybe it's the boogeyman," offered Lola, before exploding into giggles.

"At this point, I wouldn't be entirely surprised," said Olympia. On her way out of the room, she snuck a glance out the bay window, which afforded views of the driveway. Parked behind Carol's Honda was a navy blue VW Jetta, seemingly fresh off the assembly line. No doubt some faculty member from Hastings High, coming to check on Carol or some such, Olympia thought. But what if it wasn't? For a fleeting second, she imagined that Mike had sent a hit man to kill her off, so he'd never have to see her again, never have to face the temptation. She could already see the headlines: "Sister Murdered in Love Triangle Drama." Then again, the Internet had killed the newspaper headline. Now they came and went every two hours. It was sad in a way, Olympia thought. She cracked the door.

Standing there, her shoulders thrown back and chin lifted, was an extremely attractive Asian female, about five feet eight inches, of indeterminate age. She was wearing a trench coat, a black V-neck shirt, black pants, and ludicrously high, very expensive-looking, black patent leather stilettos. Her shiny black hair hung practically down to her waist; a tiny butterfly barrette held it off her forehead. Fine lines fanning out of the corners of her mascara-caked eyes were the only evidence of time's passage. "I'm so sorry to bother you," she began with a smile that fell somewhere between shy and officious. "My name is Jennifer Yu. And I'm looking for Robert Hellinger?"

It had become a beautiful spring day. Even the crabgrass in the front lawn looked verdant and lush. Birds called to one another. Olympia could have sworn they were saying, "The-o-dore, the-o-dore." (Theodore?) In her twenties, she'd dated (that was a nice word for it) a bartender named Theo who had green-tinted glasses, was obsessed with anal sex, and called her "O." As if she were the protagonist of that dirty French novel from the 1950s with which everyone in college was obsessed. Olympia couldn't imagine what this "Jennifer Yu" could possibly want. She held no clipboard containing a petition, no flyer to indicate a fund-raising request. Olympia was stumped. It was her impression that the only people who ever came calling for her dad these days were the UPS man and, on occasion, Bob's old friend and onetime bluegrass band mate, Jim, a mustachioed biochemist who moonlighted on the mandolin. Feeling protective of her father, Olympia assumed her haughtiest art world voice, and said, "May I ask what this is in reference to?"

Jennifer lifted up her shoulders. As if it pained her to have to admit "It's sort of a personal matter."

A personal matter?! Bob Hellinger didn't have a personal life. Or at least he didn't have one outside of Carol. Olympia's imagination ran wild with the possibilities. Was Jennifer some kind of nuclear activist about to deliver a Unabomber-inspired package that, when opened, would blow up in her father's face, punishment for all the years he'd spent splitting atoms? The strangest part was: there was something familiar about the woman's smile. Olympia wondered if they'd met somewhere before, maybe at an art opening or wedding or even day-care holiday party? In that event, she didn't want to be rude. "Oh, right," she said. "Well, do you want to come in while I go get him?"

"It's fine. I'll wait outside," she said.

"Okay, well, I'll be right back." Olympia left the door ajar.

But as she climbed the stairs to Bob's study, she wondered if she should have closed it, even locked it.

She found her dad fiddling with her old Rubik's Cube, his legs elevated and extended on the desktop, his satellite radio tuned to what sounded like a Quebecois station. Olympia had studied French for ten years but couldn't understand a single word apart from *oui*. She'd never had a gift for languages. Maybe she'd never had a gift for anything. "Dad," she began. "There's a woman here to see you."

"A woman? What kind of woman?" he asked, looking up.

"The kind with two breasts."

"Ho-ho. I mean, who is she?"

"Beats me," said Olympia, shrugging. "She says it's personal."

"How strange." His brow knit, Bob turned down the volume on his radio, let down his legs, and pulled himself up and out of his leather chair. "Maybe she's an old colleague from Nevis. What color hair?"

"Black, and shiny. She looks Asian, or maybe part Asian."

Bob made a final adjustment to Olympia's old Rubik's Cube, producing two simultaneous rows of orange. "That's better!" he declared.

"And she's waiting outside," said Olympia. "So can you hurry up?"

"Here I am."

The stairs creaked and groaned as the two walked single file down them, Bob in front. Though it was Olympia who reopened the door to its full capacity.

Jennifer was bent over Carol's lilac bush, apparently enjoying the scent of its fledgling blooms. At the sight of Olympia and Bob, however, she quickly straightened her posture, then extended her arm to Bob. "Are you Robert Hellinger?" she asked, blinking.

"Indeed I am," said Bob, meeting her hand. "And you are...?"

She pursed her lips primly and said, "Jennifer Yu." Then she released his hand. "My mother was an old...friend, I believe. Shirley Yu?"

"Shirley Yu from Los Alamos?!" Bob looked somewhere between fascinated and horrified.

"She worked there until the early seventies. We moved to Palo Alto after that."

"Well, I have to admit I haven't heard her name in, well, it must be forty years!" He let out an ostensibly jolly laugh that revealed jagged edges.

"My mother died in the early nineties — just after I finished college — of breast cancer."

Bob stopped laughing. "I'm very sorry to hear that. I didn't know."

Jennifer glanced away from the house. Olympia's eyes followed. A squirrel darted across the front yard like a flasher at a Broadway show. "I've spent many years looking for my father," she said. "She never told me who he was...only that he was a postdoc at Alamos named...Bobby." She turned back toward Bob. "It's taken me many years to figure out who Bobby was."

Just like that, Bob turned ashen. "You're not saying—"

"I'm saying exactly that."

"That I'm your father?!"

"Most likely so, yes," she said quietly.

"But how can you be sure?"

"I hired a private investigator. There was only one Robert working in the lab as a postdoc in nineteen sixty-eight. And it was you."

Bob tried to form the word "incredible," but he couldn't get past the syllable "cred."

"Which means I'm your half sister," Olympia cut in. The words seemed to be coming out of someone else's mouth. And yet her own lips were forming the words, and it was her own voice that emerged, albeit a squeaky and strangulated version. Her father had slept with a woman who wasn't her mother? It seemed impossible. And yet, if Jennifer Yu was to be believed, she and Olympia were living proof of it.

"I guess that's true, too." Jennifer smiled almost sweetly.

"It's Olympia, by the way," Olympia said, extending a hand. It seemed only right and, at the same time, so incredibly wrong. Olympia's whole identity was founded on being sandwiched between two sisters and therefore desperate to escape, yet somehow unable ever to do so. Finding out now that the top slice had slid off to make room for yet another sister left her feeling exposed to the point of nakedness. Her only consoling thought was the realization that, if this woman's story panned out, Perri would be stripped of her title as Sister Superior. What's more, Olympia might find out she got along better with Jennifer Yu than she did with her original sisters. At the moment, she couldn't get along any worse.

"Call me Jenny, please," said Jennifer.

Just then Carol appeared in the doorway. Perhaps predicting conflict, Jennifer was suddenly all business; whatever softness she'd displayed with Bob had been extinguished like a birthday candle after the song had ended. "And you must be Carol Hellinger," she said quickly.

"And who are you?" said Carol, who kept her hands on her crutches.

"I'm Jennifer Yu. I've been looking for your husband, Robert—or, rather, Bob—for years." She smiled a strange, almost giddy smile, it seemed to Olympia. As if she relished the opportunity to destroy someone else's family, just as her own family had been destroyed before she'd ever had the chance to see it whole. "I believe I'm his daughter," Jennifer went on.

"WHAT?!" screeched Carol. She turned to Bob. "Is this true?"

"I—I don't know the answer to that," he said, his eyes on his Wallabies. "I can't honestly remember that far back."

Carol glared at Jennifer. "When exactly were you born?"

"June thirteenth, nineteen sixty-nine," she answered.

Carol looked aghast as she turned back to Bob. "But that's only a week after our wedding!" There was silence. Bob wiped his brow. Carol looked as if her brain were about to burst out of her skull. "You filthy swine!" she snarled at her husband. And then, since she couldn't stomp off, she hobbled away down the slate path that led to the street.

"Mom," cried Olympia, her own irritation rendered null and void by her mother's distress. "Don't leave." She grabbed her mother's sleeve.

"Why not?" said Carol, shaking her off. "I just found out that my husband of nearly forty-one years is a liar!"

"You don't know that for a fact," Olympia said quickly. "And, come on, whatever happened, it was a long, long time ago. And you know Dad loves you." Did Olympia even believe the things she was saying? Did it matter? In that moment, all she wanted was for the family to be whole again, for everyone to be talking to everyone else as if they were mild nuisances to whom they were eighty-five percent resigned to tolerating and even, on occasion, finding amusing — not mortal enemies they wanted to see struck dead by lightning.

"And he apparently loved his secretary, or whoever she was, too!" declared Carol. "Unless it was what we used to call a one-night stand. Which is an equally disgusting thought to entertain." Olympia was now blocking her mother's way. Carol poked her calf with her crutch. (It hurt.) "Let me walk, please."

Sighing, Olympia got out of the way, then returned to the front step, whereupon Jennifer cleared her throat, as if to remind everyone of her existence. (They didn't need reminding.) "Well, it sounds like you all have a lot to discuss," she said, in what struck Olympia as an inappropriately upbeat voice.

"I'm actually here for the year — up at Columbia Presbyterian."
She extended her business card to Bob. "If you'd like to be in
touch, and I hope you will, here's my contact info. I'm living on
the Upper West Side."

Bob took the card out of her hand as if he were receiving a
parking ticket. "Thank you — Jennifer," he said lugubriously.

Jennifer next turned to Olympia. "And it would mean a lot
to me if I could meet you again, Olympia." She handed over
another card.

"Of course," said Olympia, quickly scanning it. It read, "Jennifer Yu. Associate Professor of Pediatric Oncology, Mayo
Clinic, Rochester, Minnesota." Another telephone number, presumably Jennifer's cell phone, had been written beneath the
printed information in tiny, precise, right-slanted numerals.
Both her handwriting and her French-manicured fingernails
were Neatness Incarnate. How would Perri ever cope with a
sister who was even more "together" than she was? Olympia
wondered. For a moment, she almost felt sorry for her — until
she remembered that Perri wasn't speaking to her.

"I understand there are three sisters?" asked Jennifer.

"There are," said Olympia.

"I'd love to meet them, too."

"Of course."

"Well, I should be going."

"I'll be in touch for sure."

"Great. Well...bye now." Jennifer started back to her car,
handbag held firmly against her slender side.

As Olympia watched her go, she tried to hate her for disturbing the family peace. But then, at present, there wasn't
much peace for her to disturb. And none of this was Jennifer's
fault, Olympia thought. She hadn't asked to be born any more

than she or Gus or Perri had. And it was only natural to want to find out who your father was: How could Olympia pass judgment on Jennifer's mission when she'd been making similar inquiries on Lola's behalf? And she seemed perfectly nice. She was also stunningly attractive. It was on that last count that Olympia felt hostility rising within her. It seemed grossly unfair that Jennifer should get to be impressive *and* beautiful.

Jennifer slowly backed her Jetta out of the driveway and pulled out onto Edmarth Place. Then she was gone. Alone now at Bob's side, Olympia searched for something apt to say to fill the space but came up with nothing. Her embarrassment at the mere fact of her father's sexuality was too deep. She thought back to the time in late childhood when she'd accidentally walked in on him in the changing house of a family friend's pool. He'd had one leg in his bathing trunks but his genitals had been fully exposed. And the sight of them, flapping between his legs like a sprig of giant wrinkled raisins, had shocked and disgusted her. "Sorry," she'd mumbled and quickly turned her back — and he'd done the same. But it hadn't been quick enough. Even hours later, Olympia had been too mortified to look him in the eye. Somehow, the whole thing had felt like her burden, just as it did now...

Just then, Carol reappeared, audibly weeping. *If only Perri were here to take charge,* Olympia thought. Except she wasn't. She was busy destroying her own family. Bob wasn't in any position to comfort his wife, either. It was therefore left to Olympia — despite her lingering anger over Carol's reaction to the news of Lola's paternity — to escort her mother inside, take her into her arms, and cradle her head against her shoulder, supporting her weight as best she could. "Mom, it's okay," Olympia said, patting Carol's coarse hair. "Forty-one years was a long time ago. And Dad loves you. You know that. And the woman died of cancer."

"We were already engaged." She wept.

"Well, maybe Dad wanted to have a"—it pained Olympia to have to use this phrase, but she couldn't think of an alternative—"*last hurrah* before he tied the knot. It *was* the late sixties."

"Shirley Yu was an ugly slut who answered the phone!" cried Carol.

"Carol, please," murmured an agonized-sounding Bob, who was now standing in the corner.

"I know, I know, women didn't have the same opportunities back then. We were all basically glorified secretaries. That, or schoolteachers." She laughed bitterly. "But she should have left my fiancé alone." She paused, swallowed. "I'm sorry, of course, that she died a premature death."

"But not that sorry," offered Olympia.

"If the woman hadn't died and left the child with no family, the child might not have felt compelled to come find us," said Carol. "So I'm sorrier than you even know." She blotted her eyes with an ancient Kleenex she must have located in some pocket.

"Mom, the child is forty and has a name," said Olympia.

"*Jennifer*—fine." She spit out the word as if it had cooties.

Bob sheepishly touched his wife's arm, and muttered, "Carol."

But Carol was having none of it. "Don't touch me," she said.

"I just want you to know that I've been true to you ever since our wedding night."

"Maybe I'll let you guys talk this out," said Olympia, taking a step backward. There were some things that daughters didn't ever want to hear their parents talk about.

"Or we can never talk about it again," said Carol.

Bob looked helplessly from his wife to his daughter. And Olympia looked helplessly back. She wanted to feel angry at her father too. But she felt as sorry for him as she did for her mother (and herself). *We've all made mistakes,* Olympia thought: Who was she to judge? "Well, maybe you'll feel differently at some later point," she said to her mother.

"I doubt it. Meanwhile, I still haven't had lunch." Apparently done with the topic, at least for now, Carol began to totter in the direction of the kitchen. "There must be something to eat in this house —"

"Maybe Lola and I can do a big grocery shop before we leave," offered Olympia.

"In the meantime, I can order us some pork lo mein from New China," Bob said, tagging after her. "Or I can pick up a carton of eggs and some English muffins. Whatever you'd like."

"I'd like you to be honest with me!" cried Carol.

"I *am* being honest with you. It was so many years ago, Coo-Coo," said Bob, employing one of his affectionate old nicknames for his wife.

"Don't call me that..."

Olympia let them go. Detouring to the living room, she was surprised to find Lola standing there. Upon closer viewing, Lola was using a nail scissors to cut up Carol's copy of *I, Claudius.* Scores of tiny triangular paper scraps littered the floor. "I'm making confetti," she explained. "For my birthday party."

There were crimes — and there were crimes. Olympia saw that now as she'd never seen it before. "Cool," she said. "The only thing was—that was Grandma's book. And it's going to be a little hard to read now."

"Who was the lady at the door?" asked Lola.

"Just an old friend of Grandpa's," Olympia replied, before removing the scissors from her daughter's hand and placing them on a high shelf, out of reach.

On further reflection, Olympia found the revelation about Jennifer Yu's existence far too distressing to handle by herself. She needed her real sisters. That much was clear. It was also true that, while she prided herself on being the opposite of a gossip, even she had to admit there was something exciting about having explosive news to relay. Unfortunately, the only sister to whom she was currently speaking was Jennifer herself. Later that day, the two exchanged friendly if generic emails. "It was great to meet the Hellingers!" Jennifer wrote. "Great to meet you, too," Olympia felt compelled to write back. But surely Gus and Perri needed to be notified about this major new development in the family. It seemed unlikely that Carol would provide them with an unbiased picture, or that Bob would provide them with any information at all. Olympia also saw that it was in her interest to tell them sooner rather than later. With any luck, the sensational revelation of Bob having sired a fourth daughter would dull the news that Olympia had picked Lola's father out of a sperm bank catalogue.

Even though Olympia felt betrayed by Gus, she decided to begin with her younger sister on the grounds that she was less likely to hang up on her. She waited until Lola, Bob, and Carol had all gone to sleep that night.

Gus picked up on the first ring. "It's Olympia," she said quickly.

"We're using our full names now?" asked Gus, with a quick laugh.

"In about five minutes, we're not using any names," said Olympia, inflamed all over again.

"And why is that?" asked Gus.

"Because you ratted on me to Perri, and I'm not actually speaking to you?" Olympia could feel her heart beating through her shirt. She'd always hated conflict. But she'd reached a point in her life where she wasn't always able to repress her rage for the greater good.

There was silence on the other end of the phone, then a long sigh. "She told you that I told her I saw you and Mike in the bathroom on Saturday night?"

"Yes, in the bathroom at the same time. *Big deal.* I was upset about something, and he was trying to be nice. Whatever you think you saw, you're wrong. So, how about minding your own business next time?"

There a long sigh. As if the imposition had been on Gus. "I'm sorry, okay?" she finally replied. "She had me backed against a wall. If it's any consolation, she's furious at me, too, for telling Jeff about her South Beach fling."

"It's no consolation at all, actually." (Though in truth it was.)

Suddenly there was a choking sob on the other end of the phone. "Ohmygod, now you both hate me!"

"You should have thought of that before you went around blabbing," said Olympia, unmoved.

"You're right, I should have. I'm sorry. I'll never say anything again. It's like my whole life is upside down, ever since Jeff walked into it. I don't know what I'm doing. Even my clients are furious at me."

"So you're blaming Jeff?"

"I'm not blaming Jeff. I'm just—"

"My heart bleeds for you."

"Pia, please!"

"I'm actually calling about something else," said Olympia.

"You are?" There was a relieved-sounding sniffle on the other end of the phone.

"A woman showed up in Hastings this afternoon looking for Dad."

"What kind of woman?"

"That's exactly what Dad asked."

"Well, what's the answer?"

"A woman named Jennifer Yu who says she's Dad's daughter from an earlier relationship. That's the polite way of putting it. The less polite way is that Dad and Mom were already engaged at the end of nineteen sixty-eight, when Dad apparently thought it would be fun to go screw his secretary at Los Alamos."

"What?!"

"So if the story pans out, we basically have another sister, who's actually older than Perri by ten months."

"Holy crap," gasped Gus, tears apparently forgotten. "Does Perri know?"

"Not yet."

"Well, she's going to freak. I mean, I'm freaked too. But whatever. I guess I'm not entirely surprised. All men are basically dogs. Right? I just happen to be dating one of them." She laughed.

"You're right. Let's make this about *you,*" said Olympia, anger returning.

"I didn't say it was about me!" said Gus. "I was just saying that it turns out Dad was kind of a dog, too."

"I guess. It was also forty-one years ago. Anyway. I have to go call Perri and tell her the news. Though thanks to you, she'll probably hang up on me before I actually have a chance to tell her."

Gus sighed again. "Pia, I'm really, really sorry."

"Thanks — and go fuck yourself." If Perri could use the f-word with Olympia, it seemed only fair that Olympia could hurl it at Gus. Gus had betrayed her. Olympia didn't know if she could ever feel close to her again. She hung up the phone, knowing that the next call would be much harder.

That Perri didn't pick up the phone when Olympia called didn't entirely surprise her. It didn't displease her, either. At least Perri couldn't hang up on a recorded message. Olympia took a deep breath and said, "I know we're not speaking anymore because you mistakenly believe that I'm hot for your husband, but I thought you'd want to know that a woman just showed up in Hastings claiming to be our fourth sister. Call me if you want to hear details."

The phone rang approximately sixty seconds later. "Hello?" said Olympia, hoping against all reason for the near-instantaneous make-ups of her childhood, when the bitterest of tugs-of-war and screaming matches over toys and clothes would lead directly back to giggling camaraderie. Back then, nothing ever seemed to stick.

"Excuuuuuuuse me?" was Perri's opening line.

Olympia proceeded to tell her older sister what she'd already told her younger one.

"And why should I believe anything you say?" was Perri's response.

"So don't believe me," said Olympia.

"Dad cheated on Mom? *Our* dad?"

"They weren't married yet. But they were engaged."

"Is this some kind of April Fools' joke? Because if it is, I don't see where you get off trying to be funny."

"I wish it *was* an April Fools' joke," said Olympia. "No such luck."

There was silence. Then Perri cried: "The philandering frigging bastard!" Perhaps realizing the hypocrisy of *her* complaining about straying spouses, she added, "That's no way to start a marriage, engagement, whatever. If this is true, I'm never speaking to Dad again. And I'm never speaking to the ho's daughter, either."

"Just like you're not speaking to me?" ventured Olympia.

"I'm only speaking to you because you called here leaving a message that our entire family is a lie. After I hang up, we're going our separate ways for a long while. I'm honestly done with our relationship, done with your sabotaging and undermining, done with all of it."

"Whatever you want," Olympia said dryly. As if her sister were just being difficult. As if it were all a big joke. But what if Perri wasn't kidding, and this was it? What if the two of them were to be estranged forevermore, their daughters never to bury an American Girl Doll or Littlest Pet Shop Walrus again? Olympia saw the poverty of a life with no sisters. Yes, their endless calls and messages sometimes felt like a burden. But she'd also probably miss it bitterly if and when they stopped prying.

"I was actually thinking that maybe you, Gus, and I could get together another day and talk about everything," she said in a pained voice, figuring she had nothing left to lose.

"You mean, talk about her — or us?" asked Perri.

"Both, I guess," said Olympia, encouraged. At least she hadn't said "No."

"Sorry, not interested," said Perri and abruptly hung up.

Yet again, tears sprang to the corners of Olympia's eyes. It was turning out to be the worst weekend of her life, even worse than the one when she and Patrick broke up. At least then she could say she had her family to be grateful for. She thought back to Perri's parallel-parking lessons in late high school — how she'd barked instructions and withheld praise but nonetheless turned out to be an expert teacher. After failing her driver's test two times, Olympia had finally passed.

But thirty seconds later, the phone rang. It was Perri again. Had she had a change of heart? "Hey, it's me," she said gruffly.

"You called back," said Olympia, relieved.

"No, it's just someone who sounds exactly like me," said Perri. It was a tone of voice that Olympia knew well from even before high school. (Perri might as well have just said "Duh.") "And when exactly were you hoping to host this Sisters' Summit?" she asked.

"I guess that depends on when you're coming back," said Olympia, treading carefully.

"I haven't decided yet. Not that it's any of your business!"

"Well, let me know when you decide."

Perri cleared her throat. "I'll probably be back midweek."

"So what about next Sunday for lunch?" asked Olympia. "Location t.b.d."

"I'll do it on the condition that we discuss only the situation concerning this Jennifer person," said Perri.

"Fine. Should I invite her to join us later in the afternoon?"

"Over my dead body!"

"Okay, I'll hold off. But for the record, she seemed pretty nice."

"Nice, my ass. What kind of woman shows up uninvited to someone's home, claiming to be someone's long-lost daughter! Is there no such thing as email? Never mind the U.S. Postal Service."

"In case you were curious, she's a pediatric oncologist at the Mayo Clinic."

"Oncologists are a dime a dozen," said Perri. "Plus, they all go into it for the money. Big Pharma showers millions in bogus speaking fees on those people for promoting their bullshit drugs."

"I didn't know that," said Olympia, allowing herself a brief smile. She'd been right. Big Sister wasn't taking the Jennifer news very well.

17

O N EVERY AIRPLANE THAT Perri had ever boarded, she believed she'd die in a fiery crash. She considered that familiar line about air travel being safer than car travel to be bullshit: people could live through car crashes; falling out of the sky was another matter. And even if the chances were one in a million, who was to say that she wouldn't be that one? After her Delta flight careened onto the tarmac at JFK and ground to a halt, Perri breathed a sigh of relief. Her second thought was that she hated men. It wasn't just that her husband had come on to her sister, or that her would-be lover had made fun of her legs. It was that her father had lied to them all about the existence of a fourth daughter. Not for a minute did Perri believe that he had no knowledge of the pregnancy. When women were expecting, they couldn't wait to tell the world.

Her third thought — after alighting at the Delta terminal — was what a terrible impression the place surely made on foreign tourists who were arriving in the United States for the first time. The carpets were threadbare, the ceiling low, the light dim. Two sparrows glided across Perri's field of vision, just beneath the ceiling, barely skimming the heads of several travelers. Really, it was an embarrassment. So was the fact that this woman who claimed to be the fourth Hellinger sister had apparently been the one to inherit their father's love of science, rather than Gus, Olympia, or Perri herself. Perri would have had a perfect 4.0 in high school were it not for Chemistry, in which she'd received an ego-shattering B–, having had a mental block about the difference between hydrogen and helium...

The taxi line stretched long and far. Waiting in it, Perri found herself so impatient with its glacial pace that she actually cut the old lady in front of her. Finally, she was at the head. "Larchmont," she told the driver. But once in the car, she felt trepidation at the thought of returning home. Mike was so furious at her. And she was so furious at him. Whatever happened next, it was sure to be ugly. Despite her fears, however, Perri still had a need to "win the fight" which trumped all other emotions. On the ride home, she rehearsed her lines. Maybe she'd begin with "Whatever crimes I committed against you, at least I didn't try to screw your brother!" But then he'd surely counter with "Yeah, but your other sister did." So maybe the better approach was "We're even now. Are you happy? Except what you did is so much worse." He'd profess not to know what she was talking about, at which point she'd spring on him her knowledge of the shenanigans that had gone on in the kids' bathroom Saturday night. And then what? They'd call divorce lawyers?

An hour later, the taxi turned onto North Chatsworth. Perri glanced out the window. Fluffy little clouds interspersed with bright patches of blue had taken over a formerly overcast sky. She thought of cauliflower sitting untouched on Aiden's dinner plate. The child hated all vegetables; there was no disguising them, either, not even in cakes and muffins as Jessica Seinfeld had advised in her ridiculous cookbook. As they rounded the corner onto Perri's block, the sun peeked out from behind the scrim, lending her home an enchanted glow that made it look like an illustration in a children's book.

The taxi snaked up the driveway, then came to a stop behind the Lexus. The driver removed Perri's three suitcases from the trunk. (She'd never seen the point of packing lightly.) She paid the man, and he sped off. *Ring the bell or use her key?* That was the next question. It was Tuesday, Mike's day at home with Noah, and she fully expected that father and son would be home from music class by now and preparing for Noah's nap. For dramatic effect, and so as not to scare everybody, Perri decided to ring the bell.

To her surprise and relief—or was it disappointment?—her nanny answered the door. "Dolores!" Perri cried. "I didn't know you were working today."

"Mr. Mike has to go to the city," she said. Dolores had the habit of calling all adults by their first names, then attaching a "Mr." or "Mrs." She also had an overfondness for the present tense. Then again, she was bilingual, and Perri wasn't. So who was Perri to make fun of her English? "Noah, your mama is home," she called into the kitchen.

"Mommy!" cried Noah, appearing in the hall and rushing toward her on his short legs.

At the sight of him, Perri felt her chest collapsing around her heart. Scooping Noah into her arms and holding him close, she wondered how she could ever have gotten on a plane without him. She also wondered how such an ogre as her husband could have played a role in the creation of such a heavenly

LUCINDA ROSENFELD

creature — never mind one who looked exactly like him. "I'm
sorry I've been away," she told him. "I missed you so much."

Mrs. Dolores gazed disapprovingly at her. Or was Perri projecting? "Mommy home," Noah said.

"I'm home indeed — home forever," said Perri, before she
turned to Dolores and asked, "Do you know where Mike is?"

"Mr. Mike says he has to go to work."

"That's interesting," said Perri, talking mainly to herself,
"since Mr. Mike is out of work." She turned back to Noah.
"Sweetie, do you want to come upstairs with Mommy while I
unpack?"

"Mommy, Mommy, Mommy," he said, squeezing her nose
between his two fingers.

"Nice to see you, Noah," Perri said in a nasal drawl, causing
Noah to burst into giggles.

Small children's love was so unconditional, Perri thought
wistfully as she climbed the stairs to the master bedroom. One
day, of course, Noah would probably turn into a lying bastard
like her husband and father. (In the previous twenty-four hours,
Perri had nearly managed to convince herself that her *own*
extramarital flirtation had never actually occurred.) But why
ponder that grim outcome now?

Perri sent Dolores home, albeit promising to pay her for a
full day. She wanted to spend time alone with Noah, even as
she looked forward to his nap. He went down at one. Then she
puttered around the house, unpacking, tidying, looking at wedding photos of her and Mike, and feeling strangely resigned to
the end of their marriage. And wasn't that what was happening
here? Perri didn't want to get divorced, but it seemed unlikely
that she'd ever be able to forgive Mike, or he her. It was the kids
who complicated matters. How would Perri ever forgive herself

for allowing the family to be broken up? She was no better than Olympia! Just recently, she'd read an ominous article in the *Times* about how test scores were lower among kids who lived in single-parent homes.

At three o'clock, she fastened a still half-asleep Noah into his car seat and went to pick up Aiden and Sadie from school. "Hey," said Aiden, hoisting himself into the backseat. As if his mother had never been gone.

"Hi, sweetie," said Perri. "How was school?"

"Fine," he mumbled.

Sadie, however, refused to play dumb. "Daddy says you went on vacation without us," she said. "Is that true?"

"It wasn't quite a vacation," Perri told her quickly. "Though I was in Florida."

"I don't like it when you go away like that," she said.

In the rearview mirror, Perri could see her daughter sulking. The expression reminded her suddenly and almost eerily of Olympia when she was pissed about something. Sadie was beautiful like Olympia too, Perri thought with pride and anxiety. Was it possible to be intimidated by your six-year-old? "I'm sorry," she said, her stomach constricting at visions of the future, when she'd be "going away" all the time in accordance with the custody arrangements she and Mike would need to draw up. "I should have said good-bye before I left. I won't do it again."

Sadie glowered but said no more.

When Mike finally walked into the living room at eight fifteen that evening, Perri was seated on the sofa with her three children nestled around her, reading *The Trapp Family Book,* a Christmas present for the kids from "Uncle Jeff," who had apparently picked it up on one of his ski trips to Stowe, Vermont. Surely, she looked like the perfect picture of motherhood, she thought—all the better to shame the man! Or did he have no shame? Glancing over at her husband out of the corner of her eye, Perri saw that he was wearing a suit and tie, which surprised her. (A job interview?) He was also staring straight at her. Feigning oblivion, she kept reading. "One morning Captain von Trapp received a letter from the German navy department asking him to take over command of one of their new submarines."

"Hey, kids," Mike said in a low voice.

"Hi, Daddy," they mumbled, without looking up.

"What are you doing here?" asked Mike.

Perri looked up from the book, as if noticing him for the first time, and said, "Oh, hi."

"Are you guys in a fight?" asked Sadie.

"Shush," said Perri, folding the corner of the page down and standing up. "We'll read more later. Why don't you go play Angry Birds while I go talk to Daddy for a few minutes."

"You want us to play games on your iPad?!" asked Sadie, screwing up her face.

"Just this once."

"But what about all those Chinese kids whipping our butts in standardized testing?" asked Aiden.

"We'll let them beat us tonight."

"Cool!" he said.

"What do we have to talk about?" Mike asked Perri on the way out of the room.

"Please, Michael—not in front of the kids," she muttered.

"Now I'm *Michael*?"

"Can we please talk about this elsewhere?"

Grimacing, he followed her into the kitchen, where he

leaned his backside against the countertop, crossed his arms, and said, "I told you not to come back here."

He really did hate her, Perri thought. And maybe she couldn't entirely blame him. But could this really be it for them? "This is my house, too," she said, her hand gripping the handle of the dishwasher so she wouldn't fall over. Mike didn't answer. Perri figured there was nothing to lose by telling the truth. This could be the last conversation they ever had without a lawyer present. She took a deep breath. "Look — I freaked out. I admit it. Okay? Maybe it had something to do with turning forty and being upset that my life was half over. Or maybe it was because" — Perri swallowed hard — "you never want to have sex with me anymore. But whatever I did to hurt you, it pales in comparison to what you did after I left. After all the stories I've told you about Pia undermining my confidence, did you really have to pick her, of all people, to hit on?"

"That's not what happened," Mike said flatly.

"No?" said Perri, catching a glimpse of his crotch and idly wondering if he'd gotten an erection when he kissed her sister. The thought both repulsed and fascinated her.

"No. She was just" — his mouth was forming words, but nothing was coming out — "there. And I — I didn't know what I was doing." He hung his head.

"I see," said Perri, realizing in that moment how desperately she wanted to believe him, wanted to be reassured that it had all been a big misunderstanding, wished they could start from scratch...

"Also, I've been under a lot of stress lately. Okay?" Mike went on. "In case you hadn't noticed, I lost my job a few months ago. Which is a nice way of saying I was fired. It was pretty humiliating, frankly."

"You were laid off, not fired," said Perri.

"Semantics," said Mike.

"But it wasn't your fault. The whole banking system ground to a halt last year!"

"You and I both know that's not what happened. The recession was in two thousand and nine. I got fired at the beginning of *this* year — just as things were looking up again, at least in the financial sector."

Perri wasn't going to argue. "Well, you said having time off was a blessing in disguise. I remember you using those exact words."

"Give me a fucking break," he said. "I love the kids, but you think I want to hang with them all day?! I've never been so bored in my entire life as I was constructing that underground mining station with Aiden. Maybe you don't understand this, Perri. But a man's confidence is tied up in his work."

"And not a woman's?"

"Not as much. Women take pride in other things, too."

"Is that right?"

"And it's not like you were very supportive."

"I was very supportive!"

"You were bugging me about job interviews my second day at home!"

"No, I wasn't."

"Also, it wasn't like you instigated anything on the other front."

"I'm a woman! I don't instigate."

"Why not?" Mike shrugged. "You order me around in every other part of my life."

Perri considered this possibility — that their moribund sex

life was simply a matter of her not being bossy *enough* — and thought he might have a point. But she had other complaints. "Maybe that's true," she said. "But my frustration wasn't just about sex. All these months you've been home, you never bought milk once."

"You didn't ask me to!"

"How do you think milk gets into the house? You think it miraculously appears via our backyard dairy farm?!"

"Fine. Sorry. I've been a little distracted. Or depressed, actually, if you really want to know the truth."

"You? Depressed?!" Perri said with a laugh. It was a new concept for her to entertain. She'd always imagined that guys like Mike didn't get depressed.

He shook his head and let out a short laugh himself. "This is all pretty ironic."

"Why is that?" she asked.

"Because" — he allowed himself a half smile — "I actually got rehired today."

"What?!"

"Good old Credit Suisse. The private banking division needed fresh blood — you know, someone to help a bunch of bajillionaires diversify their holdings. The base salary is lower, but what the fuck. Institutional stock sales are about to go the way of the phonograph. In a few years it's all going to be done on computers."

"Wow — that's great," said Perri in a lackluster voice.

"What, private banking's not good enough for you?!" Mike's face tensed. "Is that what this is really about? You wish you'd married a Wall Street star and instead you got a cog in the machine?"

"No, no! It's not that at all." She stared at her feet, bit her lip. "I'm sure you'll never believe this, but it was just the thought of you being gone all the time again."

"I don't believe you. You're right," he shot back, even as he seemed relieved. "What do you care if I'm gone?"

"I care because"—Perri swallowed again—"I'm assuming— or, rather, hoping—that we're going to continue to be a family." With that, she met Mike's eyes, tried to smile. "At least, I hope so."

But he looked away, toward the convection ovens. There was silence. Then he said, "To be honest, I don't know what I want right now."

Perri felt as if her stomach were falling out of her body. It was really happening. She couldn't believe it, or maybe she could. Would she die alone? Would Mike marry Olympia? That might actually kill her. "Well, maybe we could go talk to somebody about it," she said in desperation.

"About what?" asked Mike.

"Our marriage."

"Jesus, Perri. I'm an Anglo-Saxon male! You think I want to sit around talking about my feelings!"

Was he trying to be funny? (Was that a good sign?) "You'd rather just be in an unhappy marriage?" she asked him.

"I'd rather order a pizza. I'm starving," he said on his way out of the room. Apparently, he was done with the subject, at least for now.

Not knowing what to think, Perri followed him back into the living room.

At the sight of their downcast faces, Sadie asked, "Are you and Daddy getting divorced?"

"Don't be ridiculous," said Perri, ripping the iPad out of her hands. But her words were more confident than she was.

"But you said—" began Sadie.

"I changed my mind. Where are your Kumon workbooks? You should be doing three pages a night, at least."

"The Asian kids—right, Mom?" said Aiden, sighing.

"Exactly my thought," said Perri. "Actually, it's bedtime. I want you upstairs right now! It's a school night. And I want everyone to floss. No excuses will be entertained."

"Does Noah have to?" asked Sadie.

"No, he's a baby."

"That's not fair."

"Life's not fair. Not fair at all."

That night, Perri and Mike slept next to each other, but not even their ankles touched.

18

S O MUCH HAD HAPPENED in one short weekend that Olympia woke up Tuesday morning, in Brooklyn, wondering if it had all been a dream. Did Viveka expect her back at work? She hadn't received a call or message over the weekend telling her *not* to come. So she figured her job was still waiting for her, assuming she still wanted it. But *did* she still want it? Unable to answer that question, she found herself filled with anxiety. She dressed in her usual museum uniform (all black). Then she dressed Lola in *her* uniform (all pink). The two ate a quick breakfast. Then, just as she'd done hundreds of times before, Olympia wheeled Lola to Happy Kids Daycare.

They'd made it three blocks and were crossing Hoyt Street when a Lycra-tights-clad biker appeared out of nowhere and nearly mowed them down. "Watch where you're going, asshole!" yelled Olympia. She had no idea if the guy had heard her — maybe he was already too far ahead? — but for a brief moment she felt thoroughly gratified by her outburst. Then she

---

remembered Lola's ears and was racked with guilt. She really had to stop swearing in front of her daughter.

Luckily, this time, all Lola asked was: "Mommy, why are you yelling at that man?"

"Because he nearly ran us over, sweetie," Olympia told her. "And also because, even though Mommy believes global warming is a dire threat, she also thinks that the guys who ride around Brooklyn acting as if they're in the Tour de France just because their carbon emissions are lower than mine are really annoying."

When Olympia arrived at work, later that morning, she encountered a monastic level of quiet. Annmarie and Maximilian failed even to greet her with a *Guten Morgen,* as they usually did. Instead, they kept their eyes on their screens. The door to Viveka's office was closed. After twenty minutes, Olympia couldn't take it anymore, and muttered, "Jesus—it's like a funeral home in here." Still, Annmarie and Maximilian didn't answer. Clearly something was amiss. "Also, is there a reason no one's talking to me?" Olympia asked.

Annmarie looked at Maximilian. Maximilian looked at Annmarie. Finally, Maximilian spoke: "Viveka said you were to retrieve your belongings and exit the building immediately."

"Right," she said. So that was it. Humiliated and relieved in equal parts, Olympia began to empty the contents of her desk. The only question left was whether she should say *Auf Wiedersehen,* or screw you—or some combination of the two—to her boss. Her bag packed, Olympia decided to knock on Viveka's office door. Receiving no answer, she turned the knob anyway. She found Viveka leaned over a birth control wheel with a giant magnifying glass. For a split second, Olympia actually felt sorry for her.

"Have you not heard of knocking?!" Viveka screeched as

she snatched the disk off her desktop and slipped it into the pocket of her parachute pants.

"I did knock."

"And I did not answer. Which means you were not welcome to enter."

"I just wanted to say good-bye," Olympia told her.

"My family fires you," said Viveka.

"You can't fire me because I'm already leaving," Olympia pointed out.

"Well, you will not be receiving a recommendation from me," said Viveka.

"If you don't give me a recommendation, I'm going to tell everyone in the art world that you're blind." Olympia couldn't believe her gall. Was she blackmailing the woman? And if so, was that okay?

Viveka narrowed her eyes at her. "Good luck finding your sperm donor."

Olympia winced before she regained her composure. "Good luck finding Tuesday's pill," she said. "And good luck promoting crappy, misogynist art. Oh, and for the record, Eberhard Fuchs called me a *dreckige Hure*. Which is why I freaked out on him."

"Do you not have a bastard child?"

"You're a terrible person."

"Eberhard is a visionary. Please close the door behind you."

"There's just one thing."

"What?"

"You have two different gladiator sandals on. I thought you might want to know."

Viveka looked down at her feet, then back up at Olympia, her face contorted. "EXIT THE PREMISES!!" she cried.

After she left Viveka's office, Olympia said farewell to Maximilian and Annmarie.

"Good-bye," they muttered in unison.

"I just have one question before I leave," Olympia said, pausing at the front door. "How come you guys never smile?"

"What do you mean by smile?" asked Maximilian, stony-faced.

"Never mind," said Olympia. She shut the door behind her and exhaled.

The unemployment rate was close to ten percent. In two weeks' time, she'd have no source of income. Plus, she had a daughter to support. But she had enough savings to make ends meet for three months at least, and she could always apply for unemployment benefits. Maybe she'd finally be able to devote herself to her watercolors. But first, she was going to treat herself to a café au lait at her favorite Eurotrash bistro on Madison Ave. She'd read the newspaper and catch up on what was going on in the world. The truth was that she was tired of thinking about herself, tired of thinking about the Hellinger family too. She needed a week off. She'd be seeing her sisters again on Sunday, anyway.

19

US FELT ALMOST AS anxiety-ridden about what to wear to the Sisters' Summit as she had been when selecting an outfit for her rendezvous with Jeff. Today's choice had come down to: her court outfit (i.e., a men's suit) or one of her new "girlier" ensembles, if only so her sisters would find her easier to relate to. Right now, they were treating *her,* not Jennifer Yu, as if she were the interloper fourth sister. Multiple messages to both Perri and Olympia had gone unreturned. Meanwhile, Gus was no longer speaking to Jeff, ostensibly for the crime of having told Mike exactly what she'd asked him not to, but also because she'd suddenly become repelled by the very idea of him. The one time they'd spoken since Gus had chewed him out, Jeff had claimed to be suffering without her. Though Gus had read between the lines that he'd already started flirting with a SoHo housewife whom he'd met at the tennis bubble. And so, while she felt sorry for him, she didn't feel all that sorry. Clearly, he was obsessed with her only because she'd dumped him.

Figuring that it was in her best interest to remind her sisters of her "old self," Gus settled on black jeans, a striped boatneck jersey with a shredded bottom, and a black suit jacket. She was already in her car when she glanced at the radio and realized that she was running ahead of schedule. In need of a time killer, she detoured south to Fairway. Gus had never cared much for cooking, but she enjoyed strolling down the produce aisles of upscale supermarkets, examining the brightly hued pyramid-shaped pilings.

She liked to examine the customers, as well. She was feeling up a Georgia peach when she became aware of a man standing next to her with a strong nose, a sculpted chin, lightly freckled cheeks, and golden brown eyes. His light brown hair had an auburn tint. He was wearing a canvas jacket, blue jeans, and tennis shoes. Objectively speaking, he was cute, if in a slightly weather-beaten way. Not that Gus was interested! She'd had enough of men for the moment and possibly forever. But something kept her gaze fixed. He must have seen her looking. "Hard as a rock," he muttered while attempting to gain traction in a peach of his own. Was he flirting with her?

"Yeah, these things are tough," said Gus. Even worse, did he think she was flirting with him?! She cleared her throat. "I know this sounds like a line, but you look so familiar."

"Oh," he said, seeming amused as he lifted his eyebrows. "Well, I'm Patrick." He stuck out his free hand.

"Gus," she said, meeting his, while her mind thought: Patrick? *The* Patrick?! Was *that* why he looked so familiar? "Wait, do you know my sister Olympia?" she asked, squinty-eyed.

An emotion that resembled anxiety crossed with wistfulness and softened by time came over his slim face. He parted his lips, then pressed them together again. "Olympia Hellinger?"

"That's the one."

"I know her well," he said, nodding. Having placed his peach back in its pyramid, he'd taken to pulling at his ring finger, on which — Gus couldn't help but notice — there was no ring. Which also seemed strange. Wasn't the whole tragedy of Olympia's love for Patrick Barrett that he was married to a woman he couldn't abandon because she'd bungee jumped off a volcano, or something? "We go a ways back, actually."

"I *know*," Gus said pointedly. So he would know that she knew. Patrick pursed his lips and looked even more uncomfortable. "Hey, I'm not here to judge," she went on.

"Thanks," he said, half smiling. In doing so, dimples formed in his cheeks, and his eyes sloped down as if to meet them. The expression was uncannily like Lola's. Or was Gus's mind playing tricks on her? Her heart raced with excitement and fear at the thought of exposing a closely guarded secret. "Well, please send her my best," Patrick continued.

"I will," said Gus. "You know — she has a kid."

"Right," he said vaguely. "I heard something about that."

"She's turning four next month. Her name is Lola." Gus paused. "Do you want to see a picture?"

Patrick looked shell-shocked at the request. "Sure," he said. Not that he had a choice. Gus had already whipped out her phone and was scrolling through her digital album. She stopped at her favorite shot of her niece, grinning in a pink party dress with a heart decal, and stuck it in Patrick's face.

"Sweet," he said. Then, "A redhead, no less."

"I wonder how she got that," Gus shot back.

"What do you mean?" asked Patrick, his face scrunched up.

Gus didn't answer, lifted one eyebrow.

"I'm honestly not following," said Patrick.

Gus shot him another pointed look and left it at that. How

could he not suspect what she did? "Anyway, sorry to bother you," she said. "Go ahead with your shopping." But no sooner had she given Patrick permission to flee than she had second thoughts. What if she never saw the guy again? Moreover, her middle sister was still barely speaking to her. What did it matter now if Olympia got even angrier? For that matter, what if Gus's meddling were to bring love into the life of her romantically challenged sister, who would be eternally grateful for said meddling and resume speaking to Gus as if she were a human being, not a piece of dung? It had taken the events of the past few weeks for Gus to realize how much her sisters mattered to her and how dependent she was on their alternately comforting and critical presences. "I was just wondering," she added. "Do you have an email address I could use if I wanted to get in touch for any reason?"

Patrick visibly recoiled, as if she'd just announced her intention to become his stalker. "Um, sure," he said cringingly. Who could blame him? Patrick rattled off the address.

"Great!" said Gus, making a mental note of the address. "I mean, thanks. Oh, and it was nice running into you."

"Same here." He scurried away. Gus grabbed two unripe peaches, tossed them into her cart, silently repeated Patrick's email address to herself, and pushed away, toward the cheese section...

He had to be Lola's father, she was thinking as she examined a hunk of fresh mozzarella. The only question was whether her sister realized this, or not. Carol had recently broken the bizarre news that Lola was a sperm donor baby. But Gus suspected that the "revelation" was just another of Olympia's elaborate ruses, designed to throw off those who dared to seek the truth.

· · ·

The Hellinger sisters had finally decided to conduct their summit in Hastings because it seemed like the most neutral of all potential locations. The only problem was, of course, the presence of Carol and Bob, who were still barely speaking to one another. But at Perri's request, Carol had begrudgingly agreed to sit next to her husband for the duration of a community performance of *Death of a Salesman*. (She considered Arthur Miller to be the only twentieth-century playwright who came close to achieving Sophocles's grasp of catharsis and remorse.) It was Perri who opened the door to Gus that afternoon. "You're late," she said in a voice as cold as the instant ice packs she kept in her freezer by the dozen.

Gus glanced at her watch. "It's only two minutes after one."

"Well, that's two minutes late," said Perri.

"That's not actually late, but whatever," said Gus.

"I guess it depends on your perspective."

"I guess," said Gus, noting that her oldest sister's obsession with promptness was almost as pathological as her middle sister's inability to arrive on time. In fact, Perri had the maddening habit of showing up early and then asking where everyone was. "Speaking of late," Gus went on. "What's Pia's ETA?"

"Naturally, she sent word of a delay." Perri made mock air quotes around the word "delay."

"Well, I might as well make myself a sandwich, then," said Gus. She followed Perri into the kitchen. "Is there anything to eat in this house that isn't Ming Dynasty stir-fry?" It was one of the Hellinger sisters' favorite themes of recent years — i.e., how their parents' never threw out the Chinese food containers that cluttered the fridge.

"Beats me," said Perri, refusing to play along.

It was the first time that Gus had seen Perri since Perri had returned from Florida. Her scoop-neck T-shirt was scooped practically to the waist, while her skirt was so short that her crotch was visible through her underpants when she sat down. Gus was no expert in fashion, but it seemed clear to her that, if her sister was going to wear minis that mini, she needed to wear shorts or tights underneath. Under the circumstances, however, Gus decided to keep her opinion to herself. Instead, she crammed her Fairway groceries in the fridge, then made herself a peanut butter and jelly sandwich with some questionable Jif.

Perri sat in silence reading *Fortune* magazine. Forty minutes went by.

Finally, Olympia arrived. She was wearing dark sunglasses and clutching a high-end shopping bag. "Sorry I'm late," she said, removing her glasses and shaking out her luxurious mane like a movie star sitting down to lunch at Nobu. Upon closer viewing, however, she appeared to have some kind of huge zit on her forehead.

"Since I'm not officially speaking to you," began Perri, "I can't ask you the question I'm tempted to ask you right now. Which is 'Why bother apologizing for being late when you're always late?'"

"Great unofficial question," said Olympia, pouring herself a glass of water.

"And since *you're* not speaking to *me*," Gus said to Olympia, "I guess there's no point in asking you the question I'm dying to ask you, either," said Gus.

"And what's that?" said Olympia.

Gus couldn't help herself. "What's on your forehead?"

"Could you be any ruder?" asked Olympia.

"Probably not," conceded Gus.

"It's a hive."

"That must be itchy."

"It is."

"I have another question, too. Were you serious when you told Mom that Lola's a sperm-bank baby?"

"I was," said Olympia, blasé even under fire, it seemed to Gus.

"What?!" screamed Perri.

"Mom didn't tell you?" asked Olympia, sitting down at the table. "Wow, that's a first."

"Mom told me nothing. Are you serious?" Perri turned to Olympia, her eyes as large as billiard balls.

"Serious as the day is long," said Olympia.

"I don't believe you."

"Then, don't…So moving along to more important matters — what do you want to do about our other sister?"

"Half sister," said Perri.

"Half sister—fine," said Olympia, clearly relieved to have moved the topic away from herself.

"That is, if she's not a complete fraud," Perri added.

Olympia released a porcine snort. "Honestly, I can't imagine anyone *wanting* to be a member of this family."

"Has there even been a DNA test?" asked Perri, ignoring the implied rebuke.

"I could arrange for one," said Gus. "My office uses this place up in Riverdale. I was actually just on the phone with them yesterday. Actually—" An idea suddenly sprung into Gus's head that had more to do with Lola Hellinger's father than with Jennifer Yu's.

"Actually, what?" said Perri.

"Nothing," said Gus.

Perri turned to Olympia. "Since you're the only one who's met her, how about you ask her if she'd take one?"

"You want *me* to ask her to spit in a cup?" said Olympia, recoiling. "It's kind of an off-putting way to start a relationship, no?" She took a sip out of her own cup...of water.

"Who says anyone wants to start a relationship?" asked Perri.

"No one's talking about being best friends with the woman," said Olympia. "But now that we know she's out there, I don't see how any of us can go back to the way things were before — and pretend she doesn't exist."

"Well, I'd be perfectly happy with none of us ever making contact with the woman ever again!" said Perri.

"Why? Because you can't bear not being the oldest sister who's always right about everything?" Olympia shot back, her jaw jutting.

"Come on, you guys," said Gus, relieved to find that she was not currently the object of her sisters' ire, even as she rued the day that she'd ever tattled on one to the other.

"No, because I think this woman has some nerve just showing up like that and upsetting Mom!" said Perri. "What ever happened to writing letters?"

"Well, I think we should check out her creds first," said Gus. "If her DNA doesn't pan out, we don't even need to be having this conversation."

"I agree," said Perri.

"Fine with me, too," said Olympia, shrugging. "I just don't want to be the one who asks for saliva."

"She's a doctor," said Gus. "I really don't think she's going to be squeamish about bodily fluids. But if you can't deal, I'll ask."

"I'd appreciate that," said Olympia.

"And what if, by chance, her DNA is a match with our father, who I'm also not speaking to until further notice?" asked Perri.

"Then we invite her out to come meet us," said Gus.

"Oh, Jesus," said Perri.

"Sounds like a plan to me," said Olympia. She and Perri separately got up to leave.

That was it?! "Wait!" cried Gus, heartbroken at the thought of them all going their separate ways again. She wasn't entirely sure what she'd expected to happen at the summit — only that their meeting wasn't supposed to end this soon. "We have other things to talk about."

"Like what?" asked Olympia, all business as she cleaned her sunglasses with a dishcloth.

Gus felt her eyes filling with tears. "For one thing, I wish we could go back to the time when you guys didn't hate me — or each other. But that's a separate matter."

"Well, you shouldn't have betrayed my trust," said Perri.

"Or tattled on me for something I didn't do," added Olympia. "Though, to be honest, I'm so exhausted right now that I don't even have the energy to be mad at you."

"Too much shopping?" quipped Perri.

"I actually haven't been shopping in about two months," Olympia scoffed, clearly offended again. "That bag I was carrying is filled with hand-me-downs for Lola from my friend, Danielle."

"Well, you couldn't be any more tired than I am," said Perri. "Noah woke up at four forty-five this morning."

"I thought you wake up then anyway."

"No, I wake up at *five* forty-five."

Olympia released a long sigh. Then she said, "Perri, do you

even hear yourself? You're always competing with me over whose life is harder. Honestly, it's really tedious."

Seemingly stunned by the accusation, Perri stared silently back at her sister, her mouth ajar. It was so quiet in the kitchen that you could hear the ticktock of Great-Uncle Abe's old mantelpiece clock in the dining room. Finally, she spoke: "Well, you always act as if I have it so much easier than you because I live in a big house in the suburbs and have a husband. Or used to." She grimaced.

"I never said you had it easier," said Olympia, sighing. "Obviously, we all have our challenges."

"What if we all make the decision to forgive each other and try to get along," offered Gus.

"Fine with me," said Olympia.

"Who's fighting?" said Perri.

There was more silence, interrupted by the distant hum of a leaf blower. Or was it a chain saw? Gus took a deep breath. "I just want to say again that I'm sorry I blabbed to both of you about the other one. A part of me was just sick of all the secrets. We're sisters. Why do we have to hide so much from each other? I'm not trying to excuse my behavior. Maybe what I did was immature. I'm just telling you where I was coming from. I was also kind of out of my mind with the whole Jeff thing. Which, by the way, is officially over. Anyway"—her voice cracked—"I love you both a lot. And you, not Jennifer Short-last-name, will always be my mean older sisters who I worship and resent."

Gus thought she saw tears spring into the corners of Perri's eyes. Or was she projecting through her own?

"Thank you for saying that," Perri said quietly. "And I'm sorry too—for burdening you with more private information than you could apparently handle. I should have remembered you were an incorrigible gossip." She smiled quickly at Gus, then turned to Olympia. "I'm also sorry the whole mess in Larchmont fell on your shoulders." Pausing, she flared her nostrils and looked away. "Though, to be honest, it's going to take me a little more time to get over whatever happened between you and Mike. Not that I actually *understand* what happened, but—"

"Pia left the table upset that night," Gus cut in, determined to make the story go away once and for all. "And Mike said he was going to go upstairs and see if she was okay. That's all it was."

Perri looked from one to the other of them, clearly trying to suss out if she was being taken for a ride.

"But I should have kicked him out of the bathroom more quickly than I did," Olympia muttered, her eyes now in her lap. "I'm sorry for that too. He was clearly missing you, and I was as close to a substitute as he could find."

"Thank you for saying that. I appreciate it," said Perri. "I'm glad we cleared the air. Now, if you'll all excuse me, I have a tennis lesson to attend." She stood up, again revealing the shortest skirt known to man, and threw her canvas tote over her arm.

So it was a tennis outfit! For Gus, the world was starting to make a little bit of sense again...

At work the next day, Gus tried to put her family drama aside and concentrate on the career that, until further notice, she'd chosen. First, she went to court and asked for a protective order on behalf of a battered woman. Later in the day, she arranged for a shelter to take in another client in need. Then she jumped on a train, went down to Fordham, and gave a lecture about the landmark Baby M case and its meaning for contract law. Gus had been home for only five minutes, maybe ten, when the bell rang. Assuming it was a restaurant deliveryman (the couple next door ate take-out nearly every night of their lives; then again, so did Gus), Gus bellowed "Wrong bell" into the intercom.

The static was so intense that it was impossible to hear the answer. "Who?" Gus asked again.

This time, the answer was clear: "Debbie."

Debbie, as in Debbie Medallo, her ex-girlfriend?! What in the world... In the months since she and Gus had broken up, Gus had somehow convinced herself that Debbie had completely forgotten she'd ever existed.

Gus buzzed her up, then walked into the hall to wait for her. She didn't want Debbie coming into her apartment. That privilege had been revoked the day that Debbie had walked out. Finally, the elevator doors opened, and Debbie stepped out— in an old pair of painter pants and a T-shirt that read, NAOMI HIT ME. Despite the advertised slogan, there were no bruises on her face. But there were circles under her eyes. And her cheeks looked sunken—her butt smaller, too. Had she been dieting? "What are you doing here?" asked Gus.

"I need to talk to you," said Debbie, her hands in her pockets and her mouth downcast.

"What about?" asked Gus.

"Can I come in?"

Gus grimaced before issuing a chilly "Fine." She pushed open the door to her apartment and stepped aside.

Debbie entered first. Gus followed. The TV was on, but with the mute button pressed. "Please don't tell me you're watching *Say Yes to the Dress*," said Debbie, chuckling wryly.

"Wait, let me get this straight," said Gus, her outrage building along with her embarrassment. "You screw me over. Then you show up here, uninvited, to mock my choice in shows?!"

"Sorry," said Debbie. She sighed heavily. Then she turned back to Gus. "I showed up here to tell you — I'm not okay."

"Who is?" said Gus, wondering what this was about. Did Debbie need money or something?

"I'm serious," said Debbie.

"Well, what do you want me to say?"

"Nothing. I don't want you to say anything." It was Debbie's turn to grimace.

Gus was suddenly cognizant of how much she missed having a confidante. "Well, in case you were interested, which you're probably not, my life sucks right now, too."

"I am interested," Debbie said simply.

"That's a new one."

"No, it's not."

"Well, for one thing," said Gus, taking Debbie's declaration at face value, "my sisters are barely speaking to me right now. I'm, like, the family pariah."

"What did you do to them?" asked Debbie.

It wasn't the retort that Gus had been expecting, or hoping, to hear. Debbie had never been supportive, Gus thought. Not that it mattered now. "Nothing that concerns you," she told her.

"At least you have a family," said Debbie, who'd grown up among distant relatives in Texas after her mother and father had died in a car crash when she was still a toddler.

"More than I ever wanted," said Gus. "A week ago, I also found out there's a fourth Hellinger sister — thanks to my father's philandering in the late nineteen sixties." Why couldn't she ever keep her mouth shut?

Debbie seemed strangely unimpressed. "Huh — weird. But

I guess, from where I'm sitting, the more family, the merrier," she said, shrugging.

Gus was suddenly reminded of Debbie and her girlfriend's rumored plans to adopt. "Speaking of families, I heard you and your special friend were about to make your own beautiful lesbian one," she said, her voice slathered in sarcasm.

Debbie looked at her shoes. "Maggie and I broke up."

So she'd come to Gus for sympathy? "Bummer," Gus said blithely. "So what happens now? You have to ship the baby back to Myanmar?" She knew it was a tasteless thing to say. But then, after all the heartache that Debbie had caused her, didn't she deserve to be ridiculed?

It was Debbie's turn to be offended. She narrowed her eyes and set her jaw. "We hadn't even gotten the baby yet. And that's not how it works, and you know it. Also, it was Mongolia."

"Well, I don't know much about adoption," offered Gus.

"You just teach classes on the legal ramifications," Debbie shot back. There was silence. Outside, a car alarm moaned like a sick dog. Finally, Debbie blurted out, "Look, I'm here because I want to get back together. Okay?"

"You want to *what?!*" said Gus, not sure if she was hearing correctly.

"Get back together."

Gus wasn't buying it. "Because you can't bear to be alone for a single day?"

"Because I miss you." Debbie paused, hung her head. "It was only ever a sex thing with Maggie. We never got close — not like you and I got close." She looked up again, met Gus's eyes.

Excitement and jealousy, outrage and disbelief, swirled around in Gus's head. "You mean, you miss fighting?" she said.

"That's not the relationship I remember," said Debbie.

"Well, which relationship do you remember?" Until just then, Gus hadn't realized how hurt and furious she still was. The thought flashed through her brain that her entire affair with Jeff Sims had simply been an attempt to seek vengeance on Debbie.

"The one where we were snuggling on the sofa with a bowl of popcorn," mumbled Debbie, "watching women-in-prison movies."

"Except you didn't love me, never have," said Gus, her heart now pounding. "But that's just a minor matter. Right?"

Debbie visibly swallowed. Then she looked at the wall. "It was never that. You just put so much pressure on the whole topic."

"So it was all my fault," Gus said defiantly. But inside she cringed at an image of herself badgering Debbie, demanding yes or no answers to questions that were more complicated than that. Debbie was right about that part at least, she thought: Gus had a way of harping on things until they turned toxic. Well, in the past few months, she'd taken the opposite approach, taken more steps backward than she could count. She wasn't even sure if she was a lesbian, anymore!

"Not all your fault," said Debbie. "We just got into a bad rut. The more you asked for, the more I withdrew."

"And what's going to prevent you from withdrawing again?" asked Gus.

"Maybe we can both try harder to keep the channels of communication open and not play on each other's weaknesses. You know I need my space. And I know you can get insecure."

"I see," said Gus, recoiling at the description of herself, however accurate it was.

"Also, I promise to buy toilet paper more often."

"So you're inviting yourself to move back in?" The nerve was astounding, Gus thought.

Debbie looked hopefully at her. "If you'll let me, I'd like to try."

"To be honest, I don't know what I want right now," said Gus. And it was true. She was just beginning to adjust to life on her own. And she still had so much anger at Debbie; it was hard to say when, if ever, she'd be able to let it go. And she'd never felt so needy in a relationship as she had with Debbie. Why would she want to repeat that experience? Then again, it was Debbie who was the needy one right now. But how long before they reverted back to their old roles? And who was to say that, in six months' time, they wouldn't find themselves in the same bad place as before? "All I know," Gus told her, "is that when I heard you'd left me for that bitch from Lamda Legal, I felt like someone had put a bullet through my chest."

"I'm sorry," said Debbie. "I was tired of being criticized. That was part of it. I felt like nothing I did was right."

"Well, I'm sorry you felt that way," said Gus.

Debbie stood up. "Gussy," she said. "Take me back. I'm begging you. You're my family — not Maggie. I was just sick of all the fighting. It seemed like we didn't know how to have fun anymore."

"And what makes you think we'll have fun now?" asked Gus.

"Because" — Debbie gulped — "I love you."

"Is that right?" asked Gus, her eyes filling with tears at all the accumulated hurt and longing. "Well, maybe I love you, too." With that, she fell into Debbie's arms and wept. If that made Gus a masochist, so be it.

At midnight, the two could be found eating defrosted burritos on the living room sofa and reminiscing about their lame week in Provincetown the previous summer — they'd accidentally booked a room for Bear Week instead of Women's Week — when Gus saw Jeff's name flash across the caller ID screen on her phone. She didn't pick up. "Fucking telemarketers," she said.

"You know, you can put your name on a no-call list," said Debbie. "I have the number somewhere."

"Oh, yeah?" said Gus. She figured Jeff would get the message eventually, if he hadn't already.

20

O N   T H E   M O R N I N G of the Second Sisters' Summit, Perri woke to find the sun sparkling in a cloudless blue sky. The weather gods had cooperated. She'd been hoping to do the meal outside. That wish, it seemed, would be granted. She'd also made arrangements for Mike to take all three kids to Rye Playland until midafternoon. After the Lexus pulled away in a cloud of juice boxes and sun visors, Perri sighed with pleasure at the quiet around her. Then she got to work setting the table.

She'd already decided on the color scheme (Provençal-inspired yellow and blue); the centerpiece (forsythia branches clipped from the garden); and the menu (*croques monsieur* made in her new sandwich press). If Jennifer Yu didn't eat ham, Perri thought, that was too bad! A tossed green salad and walnut brownies would round out the meal. Perri was also planning to mix up some homemade lemonade. Keen to convey how comfortable she was in her own life and skin, she'd dressed for the occasion in a new jean skirt, yellow sandals, and breezy floral silk-chiffon blouse. Not that she was feeling particularly comfortable about anything. But in the weeks since the world as she'd known it had ceased to exist, she'd become more resigned to the idea that there was only so much you could control on this planet. Possibly, you couldn't control a damn thing.

The previous week, Gus had arranged for both Bob and Jennifer to spit in cups. She'd then had the globules analyzed at a lab. The results had come back five days later and had indicated a match. Which meant that Jennifer was indeed Perri's *older* half sister. How could she turn the woman away? And how could she ever forgive her father? It wasn't just the crime of cheating on Carol for which Perri held him accountable. It was the fact that he'd stripped Perri of her entire identity, as the elder stateswoman of the Hellinger Sisters. It was as if she'd found out the world was flat after a lifetime of having been told it was round. Jennifer's earlier date of birth wasn't the only thing that rankled Perri. From the information she'd gleaned via Google, her new sister was the most distinguished and impressive Hellinger sister of all: a Harvard Medical School graduate who spent her days saving children with cancer. How could Perri begin to compete? All she had to offer society was creative solutions to closet clutter. It was enough to make Perri want to hide in one of the storage boxes she marketed and never come out again.

But in couples counseling in Mamaroneck, "Dr. Jane" was encouraging both her and Mike to face their fears and also to be more honest and open about them with each other. (Wary of running into someone he knew, Mike had begrudgingly agreed to attend ten sessions on the condition that they didn't see a therapist in Larchmont.) They'd been to only two sessions so far. Yet it seemed to Perri that a lot had already been accomplished. Mike had admitted that, on account of his job loss, he'd felt inadequate. Perri had conceded that, following the birth of her third child, she'd begun to doubt her own attractiveness. Both she and Mike had also confessed to having at least flirted with the idea of extramarital affairs. To Perri's horror, Mike had copped to coming on to her sister Olympia after Perri disappeared to Florida, though only after she gave him "welcoming signals," whatever those were. Perri realized she'd probably never learn the truth about what had happened that night in the kids' bathroom. Meanwhile, she'd admitted to meeting up, albeit consummating nothing, with Roy Marley in South Beach. "Jesus Christ — not Rasta Roy!!" Mike had bellowed at the revelation.

"Can you try not to be racist?" Perri had countered. "The guy is from Chevy Chase, Maryland. Okay? And his father was an orthodontist."

"Whatever. The guy was an asshole twenty years ago and he still is! And he tried to fuck my wife."

"People. People," Jane had interrupted them in her soothing therapist voice. "Let's concentrate on saying constructive things to each other. Using profanity is not constructive in this situation. Perri, why don't you go first and apologize to Mike for saying something that was purposefully hurtful."

"Why do I have to go first?" Perri had whined.

"Because I asked you to," Jane had replied, further convincing Perri that she was on Mike's side. Even so, she'd gone ahead and apologized (though it had almost killed her to do so). Perri had also taken Jane's advice that she and Mike try to "reengage with their courtship years." The night before last, they'd gone on a proper dinner date in the city and had even played footsie under the table. But while they were waiting for their tuna steaks to arrive, Mike had started humming Bob Marley's "No

Woman, No Cry." Footsie had soon deteriorated into shin kicking. "That's really not funny," Perri had declared. Not surprisingly, they'd eaten dessert in silence. However, later in the evening, on their way back to Larchmont, they'd had their first real post-breakup laugh talking about the skinny kid on Aiden's Little League team who'd lost his pants while running to second base. And in the parking lot, after their date night, they'd kissed.

They'd also decided to get a live-in au pair to help with the extra housework and childcare. (Dolores had announced that she was planning to move back to Colombia that summer to be closer to her family.) Perri had only one stipulation regarding the new person: no one from Sweden, Norway, Finland, or France. Preferred countries of origin: Bulgaria, Romania, Albania, and Moldova. The agency had promised to come up with a name by the following Monday.

She and Mike still hadn't made love. But maybe, some time soon...

Jennifer Yu had been invited for one p.m., Perri's "real sisters" for twelve thirty. Or, rather, Perri had invited Olympia for noon with the assumption that she'd be at least a half hour late, as she always was. With any luck, Olympia and Gus would show up at the same time and well before Jennifer did.

So much for planning well... The bell rang at twelve sharp. Praying it was the FedEx guy—Perri hadn't even washed the parsley yet!—she opened the door and found Olympia wearing practically the same outfit that she herself had on: a jean skirt, flat sandals, and a billowy chiffon blouse. "Oh, it's you!" said Perri. "Looking like me."

"Nice outfit," said Olympia, seemingly taken aback, as well.

At least this time, Perri didn't have to worry about being mocked for her sartorial choices, she thought. And yet the sight of Olympia standing there, looking like a clone of her, only a comelier version, made Perri's blood pressure rise. Had Olympia been wearing the same shade of lip gloss the night that Mike tried to kiss her? She wondered. And when, if ever, would Perri be able to forgive her sister and husband for their transgressions? "Same to you," Perri said quickly. "Meanwhile, what are you doing here already?"

"You told me to come at noon."

"But I meant twelve thirty."

"Then you should have said twelve thirty."

"But you're always late."

Olympia rolled her eyes. "I'm not *always* anything—you're as bad as Mom with the constant labeling!"

Perri flinched at the charge. In truth, she'd always identified with Carol's need to define what was what. And, at the same time, she liked to imagine herself as being a more refined version of their mother, who had all the social graces of a buffalo. "Fine. Come in. It'll be a little while before Gus and What's Her Name arrive."

"You mean, our *half sister, Jennifer?*" said Olympia.

"Whatever. She doesn't have my last name. Until that happens, she's What's Her Name."

Olympia followed Perri into the backyard, where she sat down on the wooden swing beneath the giant oak and raised her face to the sun. "I didn't feel like talking about it when I saw you in Hastings, but I quit my job," she said. "Or, I guess you could say, it quit me."

"Huh," said Perri, not all that surprised. It seemed to be a biannual occurrence. "Well, congratulations, or I'm sorry—depending on how happy you are to be out of there."

"I'm happy actually. I might take some time off from looking for a new job and devote myself to painting. For as long as I can afford it, that is."

"That sounds like a good plan."

"I hope so."

"You don't like committing to one thing for too long, anyway."

Olympia dug her toes into the dirt, so the swing came to a stop. "You really hate me, don't you?" she said, squinting at her sister. "Like, you fundamentally dislike everything about me."

Perri was caught off guard. She'd never really thought about it that way. "Look, I don't hate you," she said, balling up a paper napkin. "But, to be honest, it hasn't been easy thinking about my husband making a pass at you."

"It hasn't been easy for me, either," said Olympia.

"Oh, really?" said Perri, dubious of the claim.

"Over the years, I've gotten a lot of attention for the way I look—I admit it," Olympia went on.

Could her sister's ego be any larger?! "And?" asked Perri.

"And I feel like this thing with Mike has just reinforced your impression of me as some dumb bimbo or, even worse, evil temptress." Perri was about to deny the charge, if only to deny Olympia some of the sexual potency of which she so clearly thought she was in possession—when Olympia declared, "That's not who I am. I'm actually a pretty sensitive person. And it's been hard for me, watching you and Gus become such successes, while my career, if you can even call it that, has been one big flop."

"You're an artist," said Perri, surprised to find herself taking pity.

"An artist?" Olympia laughed. "Wow, thanks. I think you're the first person ever to call me that. In New York, you actually have to *sell* art to be able to call yourself an artist."

"No, you just have to be talented." Perri couldn't imagine why she was being so nice.

"Gee thanks," said Olympia. She paused to watch a squirrel stick its nose into the ground. "If you want me to be even more honest, it's not your husband I covet" — she motioned with her chin toward the garden —"it's this. You have a real home out here. I'll never have anything like this. For one thing, I'll never be able to afford it."

"But I thought you'd rather die than have two point three kids and live in suburbia," said Perri, surprised by Olympia's admission. "That's what you always said."

"I never said that," said Olympia.

"Well, you implied it," said Perri.

"Well, maybe I changed my mind."

Just then Gus walked in. "Twin alert," she said, noting the clothing coincidence.

"Hey, at least I'm not wearing a hood ornament around my neck," said Olympia, dabbing at her eyes.

"It's not a hood ornament," said Gus. "It's a laughing Buddha. It's supposed to be a good luck symbol. He's the patron of the weak and poor." She paused. "Debbie gave it to me."

"*Debbie?*" asked Olympia.

"Wait—are you trying to tell us that you and *Debbie* got back together?!" asked Perri.

"I'm not trying to tell you anything," said Gus. "But yes, we got back together."

"Wow — congratulations," said Olympia.

"You're kidding — that's fantastic news!" cried Perri, who

could hardly contain her relief. She hadn't realized how much she'd detested the idea of Gus and Jeff being a couple until she discovered they definitely weren't anymore. That phase of Gus's life appeared to be over, thank goodness. The Sims family was once again Perri's private domain to love and loathe. Who could have guessed that Perri would have been so happy to think her youngest sister was a lesbian, after all?

A short while later, the doorbell rang. There was only one person left who it could be. Perri took a deep breath, sucked in her stomach, and strode to the door. Olympia and Gus hung back in the hall, near the console. A beautiful and elegant Asian woman soon appeared in the doorframe, backlit by a gleaming sun. "Hello," she said. She was wearing a lightweight beige power pantsuit to outpower all of Perri's previous attempts to exude sanguinity, capability, and calm. A single gold bangle hung from her wrist. "Welcome. You must be Jennifer," she said, meeting the woman's outstretched hand and scanning her face for signs of her father. (She could find none.)

"And you must be Perri," said Jennifer. "It's a pleasure to meet you finally."

Just then Olympia appeared at Perri's side and greeted Jennifer with kisses to both cheeks. As if they were already old friends. The gesture made Perri wince. Then it was Gus's turn. To Perri's surprise and fascination — she could finally see her baby sister for the person she was in the outside world — Gus went into full attorney mode. "It's nice to meet you in person, finally," she said in a richly textured and self-assured voice. She shook Jennifer's hand with two of her own, then draped an arm over Jennifer's knifelike shoulder blades and escorted her down the hall and into the backyard.

"What a beautiful house and garden you have," said Jennifer, turning to Perri.

"Thank you," said Perri, pleased by the compliment. "Can I get you some fresh lemonade?"

"That sounds delicious." Jennifer took off her suit jacket and carefully folded it over the back of a patio chair, revealing a pristine sleeveless blouse that showed off her well-toned upper arms.

Five minutes later, Perri returned with a sparkling glass pitcher and skinny glasses embellished with drawings of summer fruits. Jennifer and Olympia were now seated on the patio set. Gus stood nearby, her hands in the pockets of her black men's pants. Perri poured four drinks, dropped lemon wedges in each one, and took her own seat—at the head of the table. "So where do you live?" she asked Jennifer. "If you don't mind me asking."

"Not at all. I live in a suburb of Minneapolis called Eden Prairie," said Jennifer.

"It must be freezing," said Perri. She couldn't believe she was talking about the weather.

"In the winter, yes."

"And do you live—alone? with family?" Was that too personal a question to ask your own—sister? Perri couldn't help but notice the lack of any gemstones on her hands...

Jennifer cleared her throat. "I'm actually separated, as of recently."

The news startled and, in truth, secretly pleased Perri. So Jennifer Yu's life wasn't all success stories, after all. "Oh, I'm sorry," she said as compassionately as she could.

Jennifer smiled tightly. "It's fine. It's very amicable. My ex and I have a daughter who's turning eleven this month, and we share custody."

"Funny. I have a son who just turned ten," volunteered Perri, feeling competitive once again. It didn't seem entirely fair that Jennifer's daughter was a whole year older than Perri's oldest son.

"Oh," said Jennifer. "That's great."

"He and his younger sister and brother are out with their father right now."

"Three kids!"

"Yup." Perri laughed proudly. "Three crazy kids!"

"And I have a daughter who's about to turn four," volunteered Olympia.

"Four is such a wonderful age," said Jennifer. "I still remember Lily asking the funniest questions."

"And I'm a lesbian and have no children," said Gus, not to be outdone.

"Cool," said Jennifer, still nodding.

"So where exactly did you grow up?" asked Perri.

"In Northern California."

"And for college?"

"Stanford," said Jennifer. "Many years ago now." She laughed.

"Hey, I'm no spring chicken myself," said Perri. "My twentieth reunion at Penn is next year."

"Penn! Very impressive, too," said Jennifer.

"Thank you," said Perri, smarting. The "too" had sounded patronizing. It also felt like permission to ask her own rude question. "So forgive me for asking this, Jennifer, but I don't quite understand why your mother never told our father she was pregnant."

There was silence. Olympia and Gus both visibly drew in their breath. Jennifer took a sip of lemonade. Then she put down her glass, and said, "I honestly don't know the answer to that, and my mother is dead. So I can't ask her."

"I'm sorry," said Gus.

"She died a lot of years ago now," said Jennifer. "But thank you."

"And do you mind me asking when you decided to find out who 'Bob' was?" asked Perri.

"I'd thought about it in my twenties," said Jennifer. "I got serious about the idea in my thirties, after I had Lily. I wanted to be able to tell her who her other grandparents were. So a year and a half ago, I hired a private investigator."

"A private investigator?!" Perri envisioned a black sedan with tinted windows trailing Bob across the aqueduct on his ten-speed.

"There was no other way to find you guys," Jennifer said with a quick laugh. "I actually sat on the information for a while. Then, when I got offered the fellowship in New York, it felt like fate." She laughed again—nervously this time, it seemed to Perri.

"Right" and "Hmm," the Hellinger sisters murmured in unison.

"Do you want to see a picture of Lily?" she asked.

Again, they concurred in triplicate.

Jennifer pulled out her phone, scrolled to a photo of Lily wearing a short white skirt and swinging a tennis racquet, black pigtails flying, and passed it around.

"Adorable," said Olympia.

"Is your daughter in New York with you?" asked Perri.

"She's with her father right now. She had a tournament this weekend."

"Tournament?" asked Gus.

"She's a tennis player," said Jennifer. "She's actually ranked number one right now in the twelve and unders, Northern section. Which basically means Minnesota and the two Dakotas."

"Impressive," Perri said miserably. Sadie's only athletic achievements involved the Hula-Hoop. And Aiden, while a decent slugger, didn't *run* to first base so much as *jiggle*. "I'm actually an aspiring tennis player myself."

"Well, she's flying here to meet me after the school year ends. Maybe she could give you some tips!"

"Great!"

"She's actually going to start sixth grade in the city this fall."

"Where?" Perri couldn't help but ask.

"Spence. They don't usually take transfer students, but we got lucky."

"Wow. Gwyneth Paltrow's alma mater!" said Perri, bristling again, this time at what she felt to be Jennifer's subtle gloating.

Just then, Jennifer choked up. Dabbing at her eyes with her knuckles, she looked from one to the other of them, and said, "You know, when I was growing up, I always dreamed of having a sister. I actually had an imaginary one—named Priscilla."

"That's sweet," said Perri, guilty to have had such negative thoughts about this woman who had clearly grown up with so little and accomplished so much and who wanted so badly what she and her sisters possibly didn't even want themselves.

"That's funny," said Gus. "Because I had an imaginary brother named Vance."

"Well, we're all yours if you want us!" said Olympia. Perri wished her sister would speak for herself.

They ate and talked more about their children. What other

neutral topic was there? Finally, Jennifer stood up. "Anyway, I should probably be heading out."

"So soon?" asked Perri, who actually couldn't wait for the woman to leave. She was even chicer than Olympia. She had great hair—a thick shiny affair that went halfway down her back and didn't appear to have been colored. (Perri had started dyeing hers the year before.) Her good works put Gus's to shame. And she was even more put together than Perri—and, for all Perri knew, made more money too. Plus, her daughter was a tennis prodigy, of all things! Worst of all, Jennifer Yu was perfectly pleasant. Perri couldn't even hate her—that was the most infuriating part. Though Perri *did* hate her—for forever destroying her picture of her parents as the most happily married people in North America. Never mind her picture of her father as a space cadet par excellence. It turned out the Led Zeppelin–style shirts weren't just for show; Bob had actually had the rock 'n' roll lifestyle to match, Perri thought—or, at least, as close as you could get to one and still be a particle physicist. There was also the picture of Perri herself to consider. Was it possible that she and Jennifer bore a resemblance? Outsiders were always commenting that the Hellinger sisters looked nothing alike. But maybe Perri had finally found her doppelgänger, albeit the size-two, half-Chinese version...

They walked Jennifer to the door. "Definitely let me know when Lily is back in town," Perri told her. "I'd love to get her together with my kids." Did she really mean this?

"Definitely," said Jennifer. "You could also come visit us in the city. We're here through next summer at least."

"Sounds great," said Perri. "Bye!" They all kissed on the cheek. Or air-kissed.

Closing the door behind her, Perri felt as if her lungs had had their first taste of oxygen in an hour.

After Jennifer left, Olympia and Gus followed Perri back outside, where they made a few feeble efforts at helping her clear the table. (Perri blamed Carol for not giving them chores as children and instilling a greater sense of obligation.) It was Olympia who spoke first. "Maybe it's just me," she said. "But I feel like it's kind of a relief to have a new family member — someone new to talk to. I don't know —"

Perri sometimes wondered how she and Olympia could have been created out of the same pool of DNA, yet see the world in diametrically opposed ways.

"I wonder why she and the hubby broke up," said Gus.

"Maybe it annoyed him after a while that he was married to Little Miss Perfect saving kids with cancer," volunteered Perri.

"Yowza!" Gus laughed. "Someone's feeling a tad antagonistic."

"Well, I think it's kind of sad," said Olympia. "We need one happy couple in this family. Mom and Dad are barely speaking. I don't dare ask what's going on with you and Mike."

"Then don't," snapped Perri.

"What about me and Debbie?" asked Gus. "We don't count because we're lesbians?"

"You only got back together, like, yesterday," said Olympia. "Talk to me in three months."

"Well, if you're so pro–happy couples," said Gus, "how come you never have a boyfriend?"

Olympia turned noticeably red. "Everybody knows I can't keep a relationship going," she stammered.

"We do?" asked Perri.

"What? You just noticed that I haven't had any love in my life since forever?"

Except with my husband, Perri was tempted to add, but refrained. Instead, she asked, "So, what's the issue? It's not like you can't get a guy. You're only completely gorgeous." She laughed at the absurdity of the situation.

"The problem," Olympia began in a trembly voice, "is that I've been in love with the same man for many years, and he's not available."

Perri's whole body tensed up. She didn't mean Mike, did she?

"You mean Patrick?" asked Gus.

Olympia turned to Gus, squinting. "How did you know?"

Perri sighed with relief.

"Why do you always act surprised when your own sisters seem to know things about you?" asked Gus.

"I don't know," said Olympia, laughing bitterly. "I guess I just always assume my private hell is my own private hell."

"There's no such thing as private," harrumphed Perri. "At least not around you guys—a lesson I learned only too well this past month."

"Very funny," said Gus, a strange look coming over her face. "On that note—Pia, there's something I feel like I need to tell you."

"What?" said Olympia.

Gus paused, her mouth forming words but nothing coming out. Finally, she said, "Remember those pet goldfish we kept in the Kangaroo Club?"

"Yeah."

"Remember how I said they died? Well, they died because I flushed them down the toilet. I was sick of feeding them, but I knew you'd be mad. So I didn't tell you...till now."

"You, Devotee of All Lowly Creatures, sent our club mascots to a watery grave?!" cried Olympia.

Perri couldn't resist. "Shit happens," she said.

It was a fairly random addition to the conversation. But somehow, in that moment, it was the funniest line that any Hellinger sister had ever uttered. Suddenly the three of them were not just laughing but doubled over on the floor and nearly convulsing, with Perri leading the pack. When she finally caught her breath, she panted out "I say we toast to that," burst into further hysterics, then crawled over to her freestanding wine refrigerator, where she retrieved a bottle of good Champagne. She'd been saving it for a special occasion. What was this if not one? Perri popped the cork and poured out three brimming goblets, which she distributed to her sisters. "To 'shit happens!'" she said again, lifting her own glass into the air.

"And to the Hellinger sisters," said Gus, clinking her own glass against those of Perri and Olympia.

"Old and new," said Olympia.

"But mostly old," said Perri. "And in my case, really old."

"Please," said Gus. "You're only forty."

"Does anyone have a cigarette?" asked Perri.

"You smoke?!" cried Olympia, clearly appalled. "It's so bad for you."

"*You* smoke!" cried Gus, echoing her middle sister.

"But I'm the Family Fuck-up," said Perri.

"Well, I only smoke when I'm having a nervous breakdown."

"I thought you already had yours," said Gus.

"I'm not quite done."

"If you're really desperate, I have a joint in my bag," said Olympia.

"You mean, like, a marijuana joint?" asked Perri.

"No, a pizza joint," said Olympia, rolling her eyes. "What do you think?"

"I might be persuaded to partake," said Perri, nostrils flared.

"I wish I had my video camera," muttered Gus.

"Let me get my bag," said Olympia.

When Mike walked in the door a half hour later, three kids trailing behind him, all three Hellinger sisters were lying on their backs on the kitchen floor giggling maniacally about the time that Carol sent Bob to the pharmacy to buy maxi-pads and he came home with adult diapers. "What the hell is this?" Mike said now, waving his hand in front of his face to clear the smoke. "I thought you guys were all on the outs."

Olympia jumped up and fled as if she'd just seen a ghost. "Thanks for lunch, Perri," she called on her way down the hall.

Thanksgiving was going to be really awkward, Perri thought. Then again, who cared? "Mom, you look really weird when you laugh," offered Sadie.

Perri assumed the fetal position. Whereupon Noah toddled over to her, and said, "Mommy, get up."

"Come here, you precious thing," she said, reaching for him. She took him onto her chest and cradled him. "Will you be my gay son who worships his mother and never leaves home?"

"Jesus, Perri!" cried Mike.

"Why is Mom acting like that?" asked Aiden.

"She had too much Champagne," said Gus, getting up herself. "Anyway, I should probably be going myself. Fun lunch."

"Bye," Perri called after her. Her sisters were total freaks, she thought—but also kind of hilarious, if you were in the right mood for them.

21

THE RESULTS OF GUS's second personal foray into the world of DNA testing were waiting for her when she arrived home from work on Friday. While the envelope was nondescript, she immediately recognized the address in the top left corner. At the sight of it, Gus's first emotion was relief. Just getting both parties to cooperate had proven to be no easy feat. First, Gus had had to arrange to see Lola without Olympia hovering — a mission she'd accomplished by asking Olympia if she could babysit Lola one night while Olympia went out. Then Gus had had to convince Lola to open her mouth extra wide — ostensibly, so Gus could "see how many teeth" she had. At that point, she'd surreptitiously scraped the inside of the child's cheek with one of the so-called buccal swabs that had come in the Home DNA Kit she'd ordered online. Lola had, of course, screamed and cried, but Gus had subdued her afterward with a big bag of Gummi bears.

Convincing Patrick to contribute his sample had been equally trying. Gus had finally gotten her way by employing a combination of flattery, cajoling, and, well, threats. "I'd really rather not have to get the state of New York involved in this," she'd told him. "Maybe you're not aware that I'm a certified family court lawyer for the state of New York?" After that, he'd committed to the task, even as he'd been something short of pleasant about it.

As Gus's fingers tore hungrily into the paper, she wondered why she was so invested in the results. What was it to *her* who Lola's real father was? Was she trying to bring joy and clarity into the life of her lonely middle sister? Or were her motives more self-interested than that? Maybe the mission had more to do with proving that she was right and that she wasn't the clue-less little sister that her older ones still seemed to think she was. It had also crossed Gus's mind that, should she succeed in reuniting Olympia's family, Olympia would be permanently indebted to her.

Of course, Olympia might also be furious. What if she didn't actually want to know who Lola's biological father was? Or what if she already knew and had been lying to others and pos-sibly even to herself to protect her fragile heart? And what if learning who Lola's real father was only made Olympia lone-lier? What if Patrick still wasn't available? In truth, Gus had no idea of his relationship status. For some reason, these negative outcomes only occurred to Gus as she unfolded the paper and scanned the letter...

"Dear Ms. Hellinger," it began. "There is a 99.9% chance that Lola Rae Hellinger is the biological daughter of Patrick Arthur Barrett." It was a match! She'd been right all along! Gus was so excited by the letter—and so desperate to share it with the implicated parties—that she immediately folded it in fours, stuffed it into her back pocket, grabbed her keys and wallet off the countertop, and headed out. She dreaded the drive to Brooklyn. It took so fucking long at rush hour! But she didn't have the energy to take the subway. And she felt that news like this was probably best delivered in person.

22

OLYMPIA WAS SERVING Lola her usual dinner of pasta, turkey, and apple slices — despite her affection for Disney's only African American princess, Lola would only eat white food — when the buzzer rang. Which it almost never did. "Who is it?" she said.

"Pia?" came the response.

"Gus?" said Olympia, baffled. It was the third time in seven years that Gus had been over to Olympia's apartment. The previous time had been just last week, following a mysterious offer on Gus's part to babysit Lola. Her younger sister was so strange, Olympia thought. Maybe she was gearing up to have a kid herself and looking for practice?

"Can I come up?" Gus asked.

Then again, maybe someone had died, Olympia thought suddenly, her chest tightening as she buzzed her sister upstairs. "What's going on?" were the first words out of her mouth.

"It's nothing bad!" said Gus.

"Then what are you doing here?"

"You're my sister. I'm not allowed to visit?"

"Of course you're allowed. Though most people call first."

"Can I come in?"

"Fine, come in," said Olympia. "I'm just giving Lola dinner."

"Did you bring your doctor's set?" Lola asked Gus.

"What doctor's set?" Olympia squinted quizzically at her sister.

"Hi, sweetie!" said Gus, ignoring both questions as she leaned over to kiss Lola. Then she turned back to her sister. "I was sort of hoping to talk to you about a grown-up matter."

Olympia rolled her eyes. Couldn't Gus wait until later? Then again, Olympia was perpetually curious, always had been. Maybe that was her dirtiest secret of all—that it took all her willpower *not* to be a gossip, like Gus. At that moment, she had none left. "Lola, go watch TV in the bedroom," she said, suddenly beset with name regret. She should have called her daughter something primmer and more dignified, Olympia thought—like "Alice" or "Molly." There was no way around the fact that "Lola" sounded a tiny bit slutty.

"But I'm eating dinner!" Lola moaned.

"You can finish later. Take the apple slices with you." Olympia ushered her into the bedroom and flicked on the TV. "Look, it's *Yo Gabba Gabba!* You love that show."

"No, I don't," said Lola. "It's for babies."

"Well, pretend you're a baby. I'll be back in five minutes." Feeling guilty but not that guilty, she shut the door and returned to her sister. "So, what's going on?" she asked.

"There's something I need to tell you."

"Oh, no," said Olympia, laughing. "I don't know if I can handle another family revelation. We have a brother too?"

"Not quite," said Gus, rocking from one foot to the other.

"Are you going to sit down? You're making me nervous."

"I'd rather stand."

"Fine," said Olympia, sighing and about to reach the outer limits of her patience. Was her sister going to drag this out any longer? "Just tell me what this is about."

"It's sort of about you," said Gus, biting her lip.

"What about me?"

"Well, it's about Lola, really."

Olympia could feel her chest contract. Lola was the most precious thing in her life—maybe the *only* precious thing in her life—even if she sometimes had trouble showing that to Lola.

"So I was on my way out to our first Sisters' Summit, the weekend before last," Gus began, "when I thought I'd stop at Fairway for some groceries. I was in the fruit aisle, feeling up peaches—"

"What is this?" Olympia interrupted her. "Some kind of erotic story about fruit?"

"Let me finish!" said Gus. Olympia stifled another eye roll. It was her younger sister's favorite line—also the one that drove Olympia the most batty. It sounded so desperate and, at the same time, so aggressive.

"I ran into Patrick," Gus blurted out.

"You what?" Olympia felt her heart diving into a void.

"I recognized him."

"How is that possible?"

"You introduced me to him once at a party. Also he looked like—well—"

"Looked like—who?"

Gus took an audible breath. "He looked like Lola."

"What are you talking about?" Olympia shot back at her.

"You know what I'm talking about."

"If it's what I think you're talking about, I used a sperm bank, Gus."

"But Patrick is Lola's father. He agreed to take a DNA test. And it was a match with Lola." Gus pulled an envelope out of her back pocket and held it aloft. "I had them both tested."

Olympia felt as if she'd been shot out of the room in a rocket ship and was looking back at it from a good distance away — possibly from Mars. "You organized this by yourself?" was all she could think to say.

"Yes," said Gus.

Her hands trembling, Olympia took the letter out of her sister's hand and scanned it. But how was it possible? True, there had been that one night when the two of them had had "breakup sex." But Patrick had told Olympia that, at Camille's behest, he'd gotten a vasectomy, since it would have been dangerous for Camille to carry a baby to term. Had Olympia gotten the story wrong? Had the vasectomy not worked? Was the letter authentic, the lab reliable? Reality appeared as unstable as an old black-and-white TV set channeling static.

"The other thing," said Gus, interrupting the maelstrom in Olympia's head, "is that since a certain other person learned this news, there's someone he's anxious to meet." She smiled giddily, unable to control her excitement. "And —"

"Why don't you let me handle that," Olympia cut her off, suddenly aghast at the thought of her younger sister having contacted her ex-boyfriend behind her back. As if Olympia couldn't take care of her personal life by herself! (As if Gus were the older of the two.) "I appreciate all your help," she went on, as calmly as she could, even as her teeth began to chatter. "But I really need you to take a step back now."

"Okay," said Gus, sounding disappointed, "but he's actually on his way to the coffee shop on your corner. I promised I'd call to let him know if he could come up, or you could go over there and meet him."

"JESUS CHRIST!" cried Olympia, suddenly livid. "Are you done meddling in my life?! What does it help me to know that the father of my daughter is a married man?" Tears filled Olympia's eyes. Gus never stopped to think how her actions affected others, she thought. All she did was meddle and manipulate.

"I'm sorry," said Gus, seemingly on the verge of tears now herself.

But Olympia wasn't done with her. "Why don't you spend a little more time worrying about your own life and a little less time worrying about mine. For one thing, you might want to figure out if you're gay or straight." Olympia was aware that she was being cruel. But didn't Gus deserve the abuse?

The charge clearly wounded Gus. "I was just... trying to make you happy," she stammered, then bit her lower lip, her own eyes shimmering with tears now, as well. "And make up for what I did. And he's not married anymore—I don't think."

"You don't think?" Olympia shot back.

"He doesn't wear a wedding ring."

"Lots of men don't wear wedding rings." Olympia tsked and shook her head. "I can't believe I'm even having this conversation with you. Please leave me be. I need time to think."

"If that's what you want," muttered Gus, clearly dejected.

Lola wandered back into the living room. Embarrassed as ever by her own display of emotionality—and worried that she'd worry Lola—Olympia turned away. But Lola had already seen. "Why is Mommy crying?" she asked, as she always did.

"Because Aunt Gus was trying to make her happy but actually upset her," Gus said solemnly as she collected her belongings.

"I love you, Mommy," said Lola.

At those words, Olympia turned back around. "Come here, sweetie," she said, opening her arms. Lola rushed between them, and Olympia buried her nose in her daughter's warm scalp. "I love you, too," she said. Never before had she felt so thankful for the physical fact of Lola.

"You're the best mommy in the world," said Lola, clearly enjoying the attention.

"I should go," Gus mumbled on her way out, her head hanging. "I'm sorry again — for everything."

Olympia didn't answer. But at the sound of the door shutting behind her, she experienced a sharp pang of regret. Maybe she *did* want to see Patrick right now. And maybe she wanted Gus to summon him from the coffee shop, after all. Maybe it was the thing she wanted more than anything in the world. And if he really was Lola's father, they needed to talk about the future — a future she'd never allowed herself to imagine, except back in the early days of their affair when passion had momentarily blinded her to the reality of the situation.

Only, if Gus was to be believed, the situation was not what it had once seemed. Moreover, maybe Olympia was being too hard on her sister, who, for once, was only trying to do some good in the world. Dislodging Lola from her lap, Olympia ran to the door and poked her head out it. Gus was already halfway down the stairs. "You can tell him he can come up," she called to her.

Gus paused on the landing and looked up, her eyes searching Olympia's face. "Are you sure?" she asked.

"I'm sure."

"Okay."

"Oh, and would you mind taking Lola somewhere for a half hour?" asked Olympia. "I'd really appreciate that."

"No problem," said Gus, turning to climb back up the stairs.

"There's one last thing."

"What?"

"Thanks—for everything." For the first time in months, Olympia offered her sister a genuine smile.

"Any time." Gus smiled back...

"I thought you went home!" Lola declared at the sight of her aunt.

"I came back," said Gus. "Get your shoes on. We're going out for a candy bar."

"Yay!" said Lola, jumping up. "How come you always let me have candy and Mommy doesn't?"

"Because crazy lesbian aunts are more fun than boring old hetero mommies," said Gus.

"Gus—she's only three," said Olympia. (She was still her older sister.) "Does she really need to know about this stuff now?"

"Know about what?" said Lola.

"Never mind. Shoes—now!"

Three minutes after leaving with Lola, Gus texted Olympia to say that Patrick would be over in ten. Olympia frantically applied makeup and tidied the apartment. If she still cared too much about appearances, so what? She couldn't begin to imagine what would happen next; couldn't even say for sure what she wished would happen. All she knew was that she wanted Patrick to know what he'd been missing.

When the buzzer rang again, her stomach fell out of her body and rolled onto the floor. At least, that was how it felt.

She'd seen Patrick's face in her head so many hundreds of times over the past four-plus years — which was the length of time since they'd last seen each other — that the actual sight of him standing there was both completely familiar and utterly shocking. "Patrick," she said, gulping.

"Pia," he said. He kissed her hello on both cheeks. He smelled faintly of strawberry jam. He was wearing cargo pants and a blue T-shirt. On second glance, his face seemed more angular and drawn than Olympia remembered and, at the same time, exactly the same. And how had she never connected Lola's freckles to his? Never mind his reddish brown hair. Had that ninth-grade unit on Gregor Mendel been all for naught? "Do you want to come in?" she said.

"Thanks," he said, stepping past her and into her apartment. He looked from one end of the living room to the other. "It looks exactly like I remember it — except for the plastic toys." He laughed cautiously.

"No getting around them, I'm afraid," said Olympia with a quick smile. She took a seat on the sofa. And then, so did he. There was silence. "So!" said Olympia, trying to upend the awkwardness.

"So," Patrick repeated. "I can't believe—"

"I had no idea myself," said Olympia, lest he think this was some elaborate ploy.

"You didn't?"

"No, not until five minutes ago, when Gus told me. You told me you'd gotten a — vasectomy!"

Looking uncomfortable, Patrick stared into his lap. "I had it reversed."

"Reversed?! When? Why?"

"Around the time we broke things off. I guess I just didn't

like the idea of having others determine my future. Honestly, it wasn't that thought-through. I mean, I'm not even entirely sure myself why I did it. Obviously, my marriage wasn't in very good shape at that point."

"But why didn't you tell me?"

"We weren't really in regular touch anymore."

Olympia took a deep breath, feeling a sudden need to confess herself. "After we broke up, I felt so upset and alone—"

"I know, I'm sorry," said Patrick, closing his eyes and sighing. "I'm sorry for that whole period."

"It's okay, it's a long time ago now. I just want you to understand that when I got pregnant, the idea was to do it on my own. At least, that was the plan. To be honest, at that point, I'd had enough of men!" She laughed nervously, worried he'd judge her for what she was about to say. "Which is why I went to a—sperm bank. Maybe that sounds crazy."

"A little crazy but maybe not that crazy." Patrick smiled sheepishly back.

"So, until just now, I'd assumed that Lola's father was the donor I used. Now I want my money back!" Olympia laughed again.

"So, it must have happened that one time after we broke up—"

"I guess."

Patrick shook his head as if in disbelief. Then he moved closer, took Olympia's hand and laced his fingers through it. "Pia," he said, looking into her eyes. "I've thought about you so many times."

"I think about you every day," said Olympia, feeling herself melting in his gaze. But another impulse pulled her away. Until just then, she hadn't realized how angry she still was. "I also think about the incredible pain our relationship caused me," she told him. "You shouldn't have let me fall in love with you. It wasn't fair." Suddenly enraged—even if the whole thing had been fifty percent her fault—she yanked her hand out of his grip.

"You're right," he said. "It wasn't fair to anyone. I led myself on too."

"But I was the one who ended up alone."

"Not quite."

"What do you mean?"

Patrick let the silence gather between them before he spoke again: "I sent you an email this past winter. You never answered."

"I didn't answer because I was scared of getting sucked back in."

"Well, I wanted to tell you that Camille left me."

At this latest piece of shocking news, Olympia felt her heart quiver with guilt and glee entwined. "And why did she leave you?" she dared to ask.

"She told me she didn't love me anymore. Also, I wasn't exactly a model husband." Again, Patrick hung his head.

"Neither of us were model anything. To be honest, I hate myself for what I did," Olympia said forcefully.

"Well, you don't need to anymore," said Patrick. "She met a new guy—in physical therapy. Another paraplegic. His accident happened cliff diving in Hawaii. She said I didn't understand her anymore. But apparently this guy does."

"Did you tell her about"—Olympia could hardly get the word out—"us?"

"Not directly, but I think she knew."

"So the demise of your marriage is my—our—fault?" Her lower lip quivering, Olympia probed Patrick's face. It was her worst fear realized—that she'd ruined someone else's life.

"It was my fault, not yours," he said. "I tried to do the right thing. And I failed." Choking up, Patrick looked away.

"But you did try," said Olympia, taking momentary pity.

"Not as hard as I should have."

In that moment, it also seemed clear to Olympia that they'd all suffered enough. "Well, you can be good to us instead," she said, her voice splintering. "We need you, too. How's that?"

"That's fine," he said, turning back to her and nodding up and down. "In fact, that's great."

"So, you want to be my daughter's father?"

"Yes."

"And you want me to introduce you as her father?"

"Yes."

"I have to think about it," she told him, feeling suddenly proprietary of Lola.

"Why?" he said. "Did you already tell her that her father was someone else?"

"I told her she had no father. And to be honest, she was fine with that answer. She's a really happy kid—"

Just then Olympia heard the key turning in the lock, and Gus and Lola reappeared. By Olympia's calculations, it had *not* been twenty minutes. But whatever. Lola's face was smeared with chocolate. "I guess I'll be going now," said Gus, ducking out again.

"Thanks—bye," Olympia said distractedly. Then she turned to her daughter. "Lola, come meet Mommy's friend."

Lola approached the sofa, where she curled up next to Olympia, her thumb in her mouth, and stared at Patrick in the open-ended way that adults are permitted only in theaters.

Patrick took a deep breath. Then he said, "Hi, Lola."

"Who are you?" she asked, her thumb still in her mouth.

"I'm—Patrick," he answered. "Does that thumb taste good?"

Lola didn't answer, kept staring.

Figuring she'd find out eventually—so why not now?—Olympia announced, "This is your daddy, Lola."

"I thought I don't have a daddy," she said, scowling.

"Yes, you do," said Patrick. "I'm him."

Lola squinted at him. "Where do you live?" she asked.

"In Manhattan, in the city," he said. "But hopefully one day I'll get to live even closer to you."

Olympia's stomach convulsed. She still loved Patrick, she realized—always would. But even with this shocking development, they'd never be a normal family. Too much poison had already been released into the ecosystem. "Not all kids live with their daddies," Olympia told Lola gently.

"I was actually thinking of moving to Brooklyn," offered Patrick.

"And why is that?" asked Olympia.

"I might be leaving my job," he went on. "Or, rather, my job might be leaving me. Budget cuts. Unfortunately, in the new economy, youth centers are considered dispensable."

"I'm sorry," she said. "So, what neighborhood were you thinking of?" As if she were just asking, just curious.

Patrick paused, shrugged. "Well, I guess I was thinking of somewhere around here."

"Here?!" cried Olympia.

"Well, not right here—I mean, not to this actual apartment"—Patrick laughed quickly—"unless of course you wanted me here." He looked into her eyes, then straight through her, it seemed to Olympia. (She thought she'd pass out.)

"Where will he sleep?" said Lola, turning to Olympia.

"I'm not sure yet," said Olympia, wondering if, after all the terrible things she'd done, she even deserved this outcome.

"I don't mind crashing on the sofa for a night or two," offered Patrick. "That is, if I'm invited."

"I guess he could sleep on our sofa this weekend and see how it goes," said Olympia.

"That sounds like a great plan," said Patrick. "And maybe Lola"—he gave a quick stroke to her blankie, Dinky-Do—"would let me take her out for an ice cream or to the playground or something."

"Mommy, can I get an ice cream?" asked Lola.

"Of course," said Olympia.

"Let me get my coat again," said Lola, standing up.

"Sweetie! Wait!" Olympia laughed as she lightly pushed her daughter back down. "He means this coming weekend. It's bedtime now."

"I hate sleeping! It's boring."

"I know what you mean," said Patrick. "I hate sleeping, too. But the fun part about going to bed is that you get to dream about anything you want to dream about. Let's say you always wanted to be a lion tamer. Well, in your dream, you can be one."

"I want to be the tooth fairy."

"Well, you can be," said Patrick. "Do you want me to show you how?"

"Okay."

"You have to get in bed first."

How Patrick managed to coax her daughter to sleep at eight fifteen that night, Olympia never found out. But twenty minutes later, she and he were back on the sofa, talking about the past and the future—and Lola.

"I can't believe she's my daughter," said Patrick, beaming. "I only wish I'd known sooner. I feel like I've missed so much already."

"Well, you would have missed even more if it hadn't been for my sister Gus," said Olympia, beaming back.

"I'll say this—you have one scary lawyer sister." Patrick laughed. "And I guess I owe my refrigerator, as well, for breaking down. I might not have gone to the supermarket that afternoon." He paused, pressed his lips together, looked deep into Olympia's eyes. "I owe you, as well."

"You don't have to say that," said Olympia.

"She's so beautiful," he said. "Just like her mother."

"Well, she looks just like *you!*—not me," said Olympia, pretending she didn't still love the occasional compliment with regard to her looks. "I don't know how I never saw that until now."

"You *really* never considered the possibility that she was mine? Not even for a second?" Patrick asked, squinting.

"No," said Olympia. And she thought she was telling the truth. Though it was hard now to say for sure. Maybe there had been moments when she'd allowed herself to imagine that Lola was the product of passion, not science. But if and when those thoughts had popped into her head, she'd quickly banished them. Apparently, that action was no longer necessary.

It was only a few moments later that Olympia's and Patrick's lips found each other. Lips, of course, led elsewhere. Soon they were pulling each other's clothes off and pressing their bodies together. Nearly five years of frustration lifted in fifteen minutes. At least, that was how it felt to Olympia—like elation and exhaustion all rolled into one.

• • •

Olympia woke the next morning to find Patrick in the kitchen making pancakes and eggs. Lola was already at the table, making primitive conversation with this stranger who claimed to be her father. Except, to an about-to-be four-year-old, maybe that was no odder than the appearance of a full moon. Lola was still in her elephant pajamas, Patrick in his cargo pants with bare feet. It was the most beautiful picture that Olympia had ever seen — more beautiful than anything she'd ever seen at the Met, the Prado, or the Hermitage. Not to mention Kunsthaus New York. "Good morning, Daddy-o," she murmured to herself.

"What was that, Mommy?" he asked.

Olympia's heart jumped. "Oh, nothing…Hello, precious." She leaned over and kissed Lola on the cheek. (It was warm and rosy.) "How did you sleep?"

"I dreamed about being a lion tamer!" she exclaimed.

"Wow, really?!" she said.

"Would you like some pancakes?" asked Patrick.

"Thank you. I'd love some."

"Daddy Patrick is taking me to the playground."

"How nice. And will Daddy Patrick be spending the whole day in Brooklyn?"

"If you don't mind."

"I don't mind at all."

There were no happy endings in life, Olympia thought. But even if everything went to hell from here, she'd remember that morning with the buttery smells and a hazy sun peeking through the old wooden windows of her Brooklyn floor-through as the happiest in her entire life.

postscript

AN WE EVER truly forgive? Maybe not, but we can try—and keep trying until, over time, things get blurry enough that we're no longer even sure what it was that we were so worked up about.

After ten weeks of counseling, and countless hashing-outs that never seemed to lead anywhere, Perri had grown, if not bored, then at least weary of trying to figure out what exactly had happened in the kids' bathroom between her husband and her middle sister after she fled to Florida. Besides, her middle sister and her "baby daddy" were suddenly in love and engaged.

Perri suspected that Olympia had known all along that Patrick was Lola's father and had simply been trying to create additional drama. Apparently, he was no longer married to the paraplegic? In classic Olympia fashion, she was incredibly secretive about how their reunion had even come about. And if Gus knew anything, she was keeping quiet, determined as she now was to dispel her reputation as the family gossip. In any case, it began to seem petty to be dwelling on what, in the bigger picture, turned out to be a nonevent.

As for Mike, from what Perri could tell, he too had grown weary of trying to figure out what exactly had happened—in her South Beach hotel room with Rasta Roy. Also, the new job kept him crazy-busy—so busy that, just as Perri had foreseen, she actually began to miss the months during which he'd been lying around, failing to buy milk, and turning his kids into screen-time zombies.

Bob and Carol were a different story. Carol vowed never to forgive her husband for his postengagement (if premarital) sin of fathering a child with Shirley Yu. But she also had a singular talent for blocking out any kind of negative news. After her cast came off, she never mentioned the streetlamp accident again. As for the matter of her newly discovered stepdaughter, the tacit agreement was as follows: Bob wasn't allowed to publicly acknowledge that Jennifer Yu was his daughter. In return, Carol was happy to host Jennifer and her daughter at all family functions—so long as she could pretend the woman was an old family friend. It was ridiculous, of course. But somehow, it worked.

Debbie, on the other hand, had proven far less willing to absolve. After learning that Gus had had an affair with Mike's brother, she'd gone ballistic. Never mind that it had been Debbie who had left Gus for Maggie. Somehow, she didn't see the crimes as equivalent. To Debbie, sleeping with a man was a special kind of betrayal. From what Perri could tell, Debbie and Gus were arguing all the time now, just like they had been the previous year. Another breakup seemed imminent. However, Perri was working behind the scenes to try to prevent that outcome. It wasn't just the thought of Gus seeking Jeff out again that gave Perri conniptions. Over the past few months, Perri had grown strangely fond of Debbie, who she'd gotten to know over dinners at the apartment in Washington Heights. (As part of her campaign to win back the love and trust of her sisters, Gus had been taking cooking classes and hosting family dinner parties.) What's more, Debbie, despite being the far superior player, had agreed to become Perri's regular hitting partner. Twice a week now, Debbie trekked out to Larchmont to play tennis at Perri's country club.

In other news, much to Perri's horror, Olympia and Patrick were thinking of moving to Westchester. Somebody had given Patrick seed money to open a new center for at-risk youth in Mount Vernon, while Olympia had gotten a job in the education department of a small museum up the Hudson. (Viveka had apparently written her a glowing recommendation.) Moreover, to Perri's amazement (and Olympia's delight), one of her middle sister's bunny paintings had been included in a group show at a highly respectable nonprofit space in Chelsea. And since then, several private dealers had approached her about representation.

Even more amazingly, Olympia claimed to be trying to get pregnant again. Although she was coming up on forty herself, she was hoping her eggs were still viable. She desperately wanted Lola to have a sibling—preferably a sister, she'd said. If worse came to worst, Olympia had told Perri, she'd defrost one of the embryos she'd had frozen years earlier at her sperm bank. But she was really hoping to conceive naturally. Olympia had also told Perri that, in her quest to get pregnant, she and Patrick were having an "unbelievable amount of sex."

Well, lucky her, Perri thought. In truth, while things were better with Mike, that had been hard for Perri to hear.

acknowledgments

Special thanks to my brilliant readers and editors: Judy Clain, Maria Massie, Cressida Leyshon, and Ginia Bellafante; and also Sally Singer, Ann Shin, Nick Varchaver, Sarah Wadelton, Liberty Aldrich, Rosie Dastgir, Steven Cassidy, and Jan Dekker; and finally, my family — especially John, but also my daughters, Bebe and Tiki, my mother, Lucy, and my sister, Sophie — for their love and support.

about the author

Lucinda Rosenfeld is the author of four novels, including *What She Saw*... and *I'm So Happy for You*. Her writing has appeared in the *New York Times, The New Yorker, Slate,* and many other publications. She lives in Brooklyn, New York, with her husband and two daughters — and is the youngest of three sisters.

BACK BAY · READERS' PICK

Reading Group Guide

The Pretty One

a novel
about
sisters

by Lucinda Rosenfeld

A Conversation with
Lucinda Rosenfeld

Why did you decide to write about sisters, and are the dynamics in the Hellinger family at all similar to the relationships between you and your own sisters?

Well, to an enormous extent, my identity in life is a product of being the youngest of three sisters — and not just any sisters but, to my mind, singularly talented, accomplished, and glamorous ones! For the first half of my life, possibly more, I felt as if I were playing an impossible game of catch-up. So I've basically been obsessed with the topic my whole life and always wanted to write about it. But it was many years before I could figure out how to create fiction around it.

I don't write memoir, so, in answer to the question that I suspect everyone will ask me, the Hellinger sisters are not the Rosenfeld sisters. Are there emotions and dynamics in there — and even the occasional personality quirks — that are true to life? Absolutely. In some ways, *The Pretty One* is my most personal novel, though my first novel (*What She Saw…*) was more autobiographical. But I don't write memoir.

I actually feel that it's a far harder genre to pull off than fiction, insofar as (a) what really happened is usually unsatisfying

3

or uninteresting from a narrative perspective; and (b) there's no way to write about living people or even yourself without a certain degree of self-censorship. And I simply can't construct a sentence if I think others are looking over my shoulder. It's also why I don't write in the first person ("I"). As soon as I type the letter, I feel stymied.

Each sister in the book has been labeled by their mother: "the pretty one," "the political one," "the perfect one." Why did you decide to use The Pretty One *as the title? Do you see that sister, Olympia, as the main character in the novel?*

Well, I probably shouldn't admit this, but the title was actually suggested to me (okay, presented to me) by my publisher, Little Brown. That's never happened before, but no one was happy with the title I'd submitted with the manuscript, not even me. I won't say what it was, but it was long and wordy, and I remember someone saying it sounded like second-rate Cathleen Schine (i.e., *The Three Weissmanns of Westport*). So that's the short answer.

The longer answer is that Pia, the pretty sister, is at the heart of the book. She's obviously as flawed a character as Perri or Gus, but I do think that ultimately she's the most sympathetic one. (Tell me if I'm wrong!) It was also an interesting experiment for me, as the youngest sister, to try and put myself in the shoes of the middle one. I really do think that middle children have it the hardest in life. Though obviously Pia has many things going for her, including her beauty. My intention, however, was to show that even that perk has gotten in the way of her happiness in life, as she's fallen back on it too many times at the expense of developing other areas of confidence.

More generally, the labeling that goes on in families and its detrimental effects is also one of the major themes of the book. Some of it is unavoidable. People have natural attributes that elicit comment. I understand that. But I also think that parents should bend over backwards *not* to label their children as certain types. It fosters competition between siblings and can end up being a limiting force in one's life, I think. So the title is mocking, too.

Your last novel, I'm So Happy for You, *looks at female friendships. How do those friendships differ from sisterly relationships, in your opinion, or are there more similarities than differences?*

That's a good question. Well, I do think that, in nonfamilial female friendships, the code of niceness is in effect in ways it isn't between sisters. Women friends tend to save the cattiness for behind each other's backs. On the surface, self-deprecation and flattery are the norm. With sisters, on the other hand, the criticism is way more "in your face."

To give you a fairly benign example, my own sisters have never had any problem telling me that an outfit I'm wearing is unflattering. I just don't hear female friends doing that. Instead, it's always "You look so great!" "You're so thin!" Etc., etc. Also, I've noticed lately that the only people who call me anymore are family members. I don't think I've heard from one of my close friends in weeks! These days, all our communication is done in text or email messages, or, on the ever rarer occasion, in person.

In future novels, will you return to the character Phoebe Fine, the heroine of your first two novels, What She Saw ... *and* Why She Went Home? *Why or why not?*

I'd say it's highly unlikely that I will return to Phoebe Fine. Even though there's no reason she can't progress through the ages as I have (in the second book, she was thirty, not twenty-five), she belongs to a younger chapter of my life, where self-loathing and doubt were more the norm. I don't really have any interest in revisiting that psychic complex.

Also, I have certain regrets regarding the sequel (*Why She Went Home*), and there's simply no undoing that now. I feel the narrative went in an overly fantastical and unrealistic direction, whereas *What She Saw* . . . derived its punch from being brutally honest (about growing up a girl). Also, the language in the second book — as many readers pointed out — was somewhat convoluted. I fear I was trying to be fancy in some way, and it backfired! But enough of putting myself down. Besides, I just told you I don't want to revisit Phoebe Fine because she's too insecure.

What's next for you?

I'm not sure what's next. I'm working on some short essays for various publications. I might try to write a novel on gentrification. As I've watched the area of Brooklyn I live in change dramatically — and as I've become involved in the New York City public school system on behalf of my two young daughters and found that it's completely segregated and that separate does not mean equal — I've gotten more and more interested in race and racial politics. It's a hard subject for a "whitey" like me to take on, but at some point I'd like to try.

At another point in life, I'd also like to attempt a historical work based on my great-uncle Zeno Rosenfeld who ran away from home at sixteen, reputedly for the Panama Canal, never to be seen again. But I do worry that what Henry James said was right: it's impossible to capture the nuances of an era in which you haven't lived. So maybe it would be more of an experimental thing. We'll see.

Anything else we should know?

Just to set the record straight, growing up, I was definitely *not* the pretty one.

Great Novels About Sisters

by Lucinda Rosenfeld

Pride and Prejudice, Jane Austen

In addition to being one of the most beloved novels of all time, Austen's 1813 classic may also be the greatest novel ever written about sisters. Heroine Elizabeth Bennet is one of five. Sensible older sister Jane is her best friend, but flibbertigibbet younger sisters Lydia and Catherine are the cause of much eye rolling (and even more embarrassment). When Lydia disgraces herself, however, the sisters close ranks. It was Austen's genius to realize that, when it comes to sisters, love and exasperation go together.

Sense and Sensibility, Jane Austen

The trope of sisters as both caretakers and best friends is on even more robust display in Jane Austen's first published novel (from 1811). A dual love story about sisters Marianne and Elinor Dashwood, the book presents an almost idealized version of sister relations that might have irked me if it hadn't been written by Jane Austen (and been so damn good!). Financial and romantic troubles dominate the novel, as various misunderstandings leave both sisters estranged from the men they love. What is never in doubt, however, is the love the sisters have for each other.

Little Women, Louisa May Alcott

I must be one of a handful of female novelists in America who, as a child, didn't devour this American classic, first published in 1868, and identify with aspiring writer and tomboy Jo March. Reading it for the first time in my early forties, I admit that I found this tale of four impoverished sisters trying to "be good" in small-town Massachusetts to be hopelessly corny. But I did identify with the way that each of the four sisters was labeled in the family — with Jo as the impulsive one; Amy, the vain one; Beth, the selfless one; and Meg, the proper one.

Middlemarch, George Eliot

This masterpiece of nineteenth-century English literature isn't typically thought of as a "sisters novel," but the different paths taken by heroine Dorothea Brooke and her less idealistic, more practical sister, Celia (who marries the suitor who Dorothea rejects), are a reminder that sisters can be incredibly close — and incredibly different — all at the same time. The Brooke sisters are also a painful reminder of the way that women's choices were once so thoroughly prescribed by the men they married.

Housekeeping, Marilynne Robinson

I can't say I actually enjoyed reading this cult classic about orphaned sisters in the Pacific Northwest, published in 1980, but the book stayed with me and even haunted me long after I turned the last page. After their mother drives her car off a cliff, sisters Lucille and Ruth, who are left in the care of various unreliable relatives in a falling-down house, become soul mates—at least until teenage Lucille rebels and takes off. The book made me realize how close sisters can be and also how fragile the bonds that tie family together really are.

A Thousand Acres, Jane Smiley

Smiley's 1991 reimagining of *King Lear,* set on a family farm in Iowa, features all the grand motifs that Shakespeare brought to his 1606 tragedy—madness, betrayal, etc.—but also Smiley's no-nonsense prose, which makes the sensational revelations that emerge that much more dramatic. As told from the perspective of eldest sister Ginny, the novel paints a picture of siblings who, if far less evil than Goneril and Regan, have relationships with each other that are every bit as complicated. (And I love complicated.)

Also keep in mind:
The Transit of Venus, Shirley Hazzard
The Three Weissmanns of Westport, Cathleen Schine
The Believers, Zoë Heller
How the García Girls Lost Their Accents, Julia Alvarez
In Her Shoes, Jennifer Weiner
The Secret Life of Bees, Sue Monk Kidd

Questions and Topics for Discussion

1.   Olympia is supposed to be "the pretty one" in her family, as well as "the flaky one," "the chronically late one," and "the artistic one." To what extent do you think the labels are accurate? How do you think they've hindered or encouraged her progress in life? If you are a sister (or brother), what is your reputation in the family, and how do you think it has affected you as an adult?

2.   Characterize the dynamic among the three Hellinger sisters when we first encounter them together on New Year's Day. Do you think they treat one another fairly? Unfairly? Explain.

3.   What do you think of Olympia's having sought out information about her anonymous sperm donor? In her circumstances, would you have done the same thing?

4.   How does the Hellinger family dynamic seem to change after the sisters' mother, Carol, is struck by a falling streetlamp bulb? More generally, what do you think of the way Carol has raised her daughters?

5. Speaking of motherhood, what do you think of Perri's approach to raising kids? Do you think she's too uptight? What about Olympia's approach? In what ways are Perri and Olympia trying to do things differently from how Carol did them?

6. Do you think Perri is justified in walking out on Mike? How so?

7. How does the arrival of Jennifer Yu affect the Hellinger sisters? Do you think Olympia is right to forgive her father for what he did? Do you think Perri is right to be critical of Jennifer Yu for showing up at the house without an invitation?

8. Do you think Gus is meddling or acting out of love in going behind Olympia's back and trying to find out who Lola's father is?

Also by Lucinda Rosenfeld

I'm So Happy for You

A Novel About Best Friends

"Lucinda Rosenfeld has a written a funny, subversive, and altogether outstanding novel that will very likely seduce critics and many, many thousands of readers. I'm so happy for her."
—Joseph O'Neill, author of *Netherland*

"The book's confectionery veneer belies a heart of poison, as Rosenfeld tartly dispels the cherished chick-lit notion that female friendship conquers all. Equally ruthless is her send-up of overachieving New York women in feral pursuit of have-it-all motherhood without having first ascertained if they even like children."
—*The New Yorker*

"Capturing the surprisingly competitive world of Brooklyn brownstones and Bugaboo strollers, Lucinda Rosenfeld's *I'm So Happy for You* takes the comic measure of the unlikely friendship between two women."
—*Vogue*

"If you've ever gritted your teeth and offered a phony smile to that one friend who always seems to get everything she wants, Rosenfeld's frenemies tale will ring true.... A witty, scathing novel that's a breeze to read."
—*Entertainment Weekly*

Back Bay Books
Available wherever paperbacks are sold